BLOODLINES

SIN CITY OUTLAWS (BOOK #5)

M.N. FORGY

DEDICATION

*DNA cannot compromise the true bounds of trust and loyalty between
souls.*

Also, to my right-hand woman, Brie.
She's my ride or die when it comes to my career.
Oh, and Bishop is yours.
xoxo

PROLOGUE

Simone 8 Years Old

SITTING on my back porch just outside of my home, I grind the yellow chalk into the concrete patio. The sun paints my cheeks red, and the breeze blows the pieces of hair in my face around my ears. My baby blue dress is dusted with grains of muted colors.

Setting the yellow chalk down, a shiny black shoe slams on my hand out of nowhere. Pressure and a piercing sting slither up the bones in my fingers, curling around my palm.

"Ow!" I cry, trying to pull my palm out from under the foot. Using my free hand, I tug at my wrist until the prisoned fingers free. With heated eyes, I glare up at the person who purposely stepped on my hand.

IT'S a boy I've never seen before. The sun shines behind him casting a cold shadow amongst me and dulling the bright colors on the sidewalk. I suddenly feel cold, as if winter brushed upon the back of my neck in the midst of the summer. He's wearing a suit and has his hands on his hips as he looks down at me like a dirty bug crawling across the ground.

"Oops," he sneers, stepping from the sunlight. Without the rays blinding me, I can really see him now. He has dark unruly hair curling around his ears, tanned Indian skin, and the meanest eyes I've ever seen.

"Why did you do that?" I rub my sore fingers. "Who are you?"

"I'm Veer Walsh, and haven't you heard? You're to be my wife." He growls, his voice low as if he's starting to become a man.

I frown. "That's not true. I'm nobody's." I stand, angry. I don't know who this boy is, but he's about to get a piece of my mind.

He whips his hand out, clutching my wrist with a cold touch.

"Oh, it's true. You're going to be my first kiss, my first lover, and have my babies while I go and make all the money. Just like my daddy!"

I resist, trying to pull from his clutches. He's vile, and has a mouth made of sewage.

HE CHUCKLES before grasping me harshly by the cheeks with his free hand, causing my lips to pucker.

"HOW ABOUT I get a taste of the bride to be." His eyes close, and his lips come near. My stomach clenches into a tight knot, my heart slamming in my chest as his lips come closer and closer. I slam my knee into his balls just before he makes contact. He cries out, dropping to his knees on my bright colored sun I colored, and I run toward the house.

Jerking the sliding glass door open, I sprint inside the cool air-conditioned rooms.

"MOM! MOM!" My dress whirls around me as I search the mansion for my mother and father. Finally, I find them in the study along with two other adults. They all stand as I enter.

"THERE'S this boy out there, and he says I'm going to marry him. I don't want to marry him." My eyes water.

MOM LOOKS at the floor like she often does when she's not thrilled with what's going on around her. Dad chuckles, unbuttoning his jacket.

"YES, Simone. Veer and you are to marry when you come of age—"

"But I don't love him." I enjoy reading and watching TV, and everyone always marries when they are so deeply in love they feel sick. Veer makes me feel a different kind of sickness.

"YOU WILL LOVE HIM," the man standing across from my dad states. He must be Veer's father.

Dad strides to me and takes a knee. Clasping my sore hand in his while he looks me in the eyes.

"THE WALSH FAMILY has agreed to work with Daddy if our blood become one. You, my dear, are going to be the end of an era of spilled innocence," Dad explains, and my blood suddenly runs cold.

I SNATCH my hand from his, this joke not funny at all.

"STARTING tomorrow you will shadow me, so when the families become one, you'll know what to do as your place as a wife."

I shake my head, not okay with this in the slightest. I'm too young, this is too fast. I should be making friends, getting into trouble, not getting engaged and getting a job.

"NO!" I snap, my eyes stinging with the urge to cry. I want to say so much more, but the only word that seems to escape the clutch in my throat is, no.

"I THINK that's enough for one day." Mother steps in between me and father, her soft hand on my shoulder.

I LOOK UP TO HER, my eyes filling with unshed tears.

"I DON'T WANT to marry anyone." I whimper, begging my mom to interfere with what's happening.

"COME, child, let's get you cleaned up." Mother ushers me out of the room, and my eyes meet Veer's before leaving. He blows me a silent kiss, the devil dancing in his eyes. The way he looks at me, makes me feel, is dangerous and dark. I've never felt like this before. I want to stab him.

ONCE INSIDE MY ROOM, mother drawls me a bath while I stand at the window watching my dad escort our guests from the front door. The Walshs have been our sworn enemy since before I was born. My grandmother has told me many stories before she passed last year from cancer. Our battles go back decades, innocent blood spilled over land.

I know why Dad wants me to marry Veer, he'll have more business if he has more land to do business on. I don't know what Daddy does for a job, Grandma would never say, but I'm about to find out. But what about what I want? I can't see myself ever loving a person as evil as Veer.

MOTHER UNZIPS my dress as I watch Veer and his family leave in their limo. We don't say a word to each other as she helps me into the hot suds spilling over the rim of the bathtub, my body enveloping with warm water.

"SIMONE, sometimes the things you want to feel, come when you're not feeling it at all."

I glare at her, her pep talk not helping or making sense.

GRABBING A DOLLOP OF BUBBLES, I blow them across the bath, angry at everything.

"LOVE IS A MAGICAL THING. You never know, Veer may be your someone. Fall in love with his soul, before you even have the chance to make contact. That's when you know if he's truly the one," she winks playfully. Oh, I made contact all right, with my knee right in his crotch.

"I'LL NEVER MARRY that monster. I'd rather stick a fork in his head." I scoff.

"SIMONE RAY!" Mother scorns. But I don't apologize, and I don't feel guilty.

I don't feel guilty for wanting to be so violent to another kid. That thought scares me, it's unlike me. I want to be friends with everyone, I'm nice. At least I think I am.

Sighing, I sink into the warm water. My eyes closing and ears filling with water to wash out the lame words coming from my mother's lips.

I KNOW in my soul that Veer is not for me, and I will tear this house down brick by brick before I ever say 'I do' to that butthead. I'd like to think I'd marry someone shy but edgy. He'd be smart, but just as street-smart so I know he'd protect our family if he needed to.

THAT IS the man that is going to rescue me from stupid Veer. The little hope that burns in my belly tells me so.

Mac
Ten Years Old

SITTING IN MY ROOM, my butt on the stained carpet, charred pockets from cigarettes falling, I try and concentrate on what the YouTuber is telling me about firewalls, but my parents fighting in the other room is becoming distracting. Shutting the laptop that I stole from school I lean my head back on my bedframe and look up at the ceiling fan that holds just one dusty blade.

"IT WASN'T my fault she caught me for the rent!" my step-mom shouts. She's skinny, and always wearing flannel shirts with jeans way too big for her. I don't know what Dad sees in her.

"YOU SHOULD HAVE MADE up a fucking lie, how are we going to eat!" Dad responds before a loud crash vibrates the floor.

I don't flinch, or jerk from the sudden racket. I'm used to it, he's probably hitting her again.

CLOSING MY EYES, I stand up and flick the light switch off that is missing a faceplate. Being careful of the wires curling out from the wall because if I touch them, they will zap you.

CRAWLING ONTO MY THIN MATTRESS, I pull the blankets that are spilling cotton out from the many holes over my head and think about firewalls and binary code. How cool would it be to write messages to a friend that lived across the street from me? We could hold up codes, while the other tried to decipher it late at night. At lunchtime, we could speak in our own language nobody would understand. On the weekends we could binge watch Star Wars and play Mario until our eyes bled.

THAT WILL NEVER HAPPEN THOUGH, because no kid is like me. I live inside a computer and to be honest I feel like one. Living life on like it's on reply, day after day.

TURNING over on my side the shouting and banging of my parents lull me to sleep, the images of Princess Peach picking me up and driving me away from this shit hole.

———

THE NEXT DAY I hop off the school bus and pull my hood over my head. It was the same old crappy day at school. I sat alone and got made fun of because I drew a storm trooper on the back of my hoodie. My parents couldn't afford the one I wanted at the store, so I made do.

I HOLD my backpack strap close to my chest with my only prized passion inside my bag. The stolen laptop. I've always wanted one, and when I asked my dad, he laughed. So I got one the only way I knew how.

Stealing it. I've had it for several months, and nobody has found out yet.

PASSING TRAILER AFTER TRAILER, I get closer to my house. I notice yellow tape wrapped around the yard and a black shiny car parked out front with a woman standing beside it. Dark curly hair is shoved into a hair tie, and she's wearing a blue suit. She works for the division of family services. I've seen their kind at least five times. Now what did Dad do?

I PULL my hood down and frown at her as I close the gap between us.

"ARE YOU RHETT?" Her thick brows raise, paperwork in her hands.

"YEAH," I mutter under my breath. I wonder what house I'll be going to this time. The old lady with ten cats, or the man who drinks his breakfast from a fifth.

"I'M with the division of family services, there's been an accident—"

"WHAT KIND OF ACCIDENT?" I cut her off, my anger dissipating to worry. Taking a step to the left I look at the front door of my house, it's all busted up like someone kicked it in. My throat suddenly dries, and my heart beats faster.

THE LADY STEPS CLOSER, and I take a step back. She tenses, her cheekbones tensing with my reaction.

"Just tell me what happened!"

HER NICE SHOES scoff to a stop, and she sighs, irritated.

"YOUR FATHER MURDERED your mother and has been arrested until further notice." She interlocks her fingers and purses her lips. Her eyes showing no sign of emotion with the news she just vomited at my feet.

MY MOUTH PARTS but I snap it shut, I almost cared for a second. "She wasn't my mother," I respond. "My mother died giving birth to me."

"I'M SORRY TO HEAR THAT." She tilts her head to the side, there might even be a bit of sympathy in her eyes. Everyone seems to feel sorry for me when I tell them that. 'The boy that killed his mother'" It doesn't get more tragic than that, does it?

I LOOK at the damp ground from the recent rain, the smell of wet dirt heavy in the air. My father was an asshole, he never accepted me as his after my real father died. I didn't play football or bully the kids next door either, so I was a pussy.

He would drink until he couldn't stand, said it helped him sleep at night. He was right in a way, he'd slump into walls, yelling about shit that didn't make sense, slap me and my step-mother around, and then pass out on the couch almost every day.

Seems he started drinking early today, and my step-mother said the wrong thing.

Her eyes close for a moment before opening up and looking anywhere but at me.

"Look, kid, I got a decent family lined up for you—"

I turn around and start walking, cutting her off mid-sentence. I'm not going to a foster family. Not again. They don't care about anything but a check, and it would be my father all over again.

I'm better off by myself.

"Rhett!"

I ignore her and continue walking. I don't know where I'll go, or where I'll stay, but anything is better than here or there.

"Rhett, get back here!" I hear her heels click along the ground, and it makes my heart pick up its pace, urging me to sprint as fast as I can away from the lady and the blood riddled trailer.

Two weeks later

A HEAVY WIND blusters through the buildings, my face already chapped from the sun today, I can't take much more. I grab some cardboard soiled in something sour and wedge myself between to garbage cans behind a casino.

HOLDING my dead laptop close to my chest I squeeze my eyes shut for a quick rest. It can only be about midnight, here soon businesses will close up shop, throwing out food tourists didn't buy, and I can get something to eat for the first time today.

MY STOMACH CLUTCHES PAINFULLY, and I moan in pain from being so hungry.

MY HAIR FALLS in my face, sticking to the sweat beading on my forehead. Reminding me I haven't showered in a week, and my clothes are all torn up from hopping into dumpsters and trying to climb into buildings for coverage from the hot summer.

LIVING THE STREETS IS HARD, fighting other bums is the worst part. I'm younger than most, and not as strong so I get stuff taken from me a lot and chased off the good corners.

ARMS TIGHT AROUND MY COMPUTER, I close my eyes to sleep until the moon is on the other side of the sky. It's not just going to be a normal day tomorrow like it was when I lived with my dad and went to school, being homeless is unpredictable and an adventure every day.

———

THE ALUMINUM TRASH CANS RATTLE, and I stir awake, my eyes widening as big as saucers. Is it another homeless man? A store owner sick of bums tearing into his trash?

A TALL MAN with dark leather boots kicks one of the cans, the lights of Vegas splashing across my face.

"WHAT THE?" He bends down, dark black hair surrounding his face as his eyes meet mine.

I SWALLOW and recoil against the grimy wall. He's big and scary looking. Bending down to get a better look at me, he holds his hand out, his fingers tattooed and lined with shiny rings.

"COME HERE, BOY." His voice is so rough it sends shivers down my back. I don't move.

HE SEPARATES THE CANS, the cardboard that was hiding me blowing off into the wind. I'd run away if I thought I even had a chance at escaping this guy.

Slowly, I outstretch my hand, and he pulls me out from the bed I made of trash.

He brushes me off and looks down at me. Looking to the ground, I curl my toes in my torn sneakers.

"What's your name?" He's so tall he blocks the lights from the signs behind him. He also has on a sleeveless leather jacket with lots of patches on it, it's cool and scary at the same time. An engine has me jump where I stand, and I notice dozens of motorcycles sitting behind the tall man.

I don't answer him as I observe all the angry looking men around the bikes.

"You want to come into the club, get some food and sleep for the night?" he offers. "Has to be better than this," he waves to the trash. My cheeks burn from the caked-on dirt, and my stomach growls at the mention of food. I nod, not caring how mean looking he is, or that I might end up cut up in little pieces if I go in his club. I need shelter for the night and having a night of sleep without the worry of someone taking my laptop is all I can think about.

"You can call me Mr. Deluca." He grins wildly and places his hand on my back.

INSIDE THE CLUB, as he called it, there are men with tattoos and leather jackets standing all around. The smoke of cigarettes, and cigars rolls in a blanket of fog near the ceiling, and there are very pretty women who are barely wearing any clothes staring at me. I can't take my eyes off them, I've never seen side boob the size of one of the girl's.

"This is home to a lot of lost souls," Mr. Deluca says. Slowly taking my eyes off the girls, I look up to him. He's smiling down at me, nodding. I'm a lost soul, could this be home to me?

A WOMAN TAKES her top off and shoves a man with a big belly face first in her bare chest. My jeans strain at the sight of her creamy tits. One of her boobs is bigger than my head.

"THAT'S MILKS," Mr. Deluca whispers in the back of my ear. I clear my throat and look away from the very sexy lady.

"MILKS?" That's a weird name.

"YEAH, THINK ABOUT IT." Mr. Deluca presses his finger to his temple, and I look back to the older lady. Maybe she has milk in her titties?

A BOY my age crawls out from under a pool table in the middle of the smoky room, his dark hair matching Mr. Deluca's. He has on a Kiss shirt with the sleeves ripped up and dark black jeans. He's cool, he's the kind that would beat me up in school.

"HEY ZEEK, THIS IS, UH..." He looks down at me, and I nervously tighten my arms around my laptop a little harder. "Mac." Mr. Deluca and I look at each other as he nicknames me the brand of computer I'm holding. I don't disagree, I like it. New name, new place, new possibilities. "Will you get him set up in one of the rooms?"

"MAC, this is Zeek, one of my sons. He will help you get settled in." Mr. Deluca pats my head before strutting off in the direction of Milks.

Zeek looks me over, one eyebrow raised before he sighs and turns around.

"Follow me." He waves me on. Clutching my dead computer, I follow him down a narrow hallway to a room. There are naked women pictures torn from magazines taped all over the walls, a big bed, and a ripped chair in the corner.

"YOU CAN SHOWER IN THERE," he points to a door to the left. I glance at the door, and then back to him.

"YOUR NAME REALLY MAC?" he asks, his left brow raised.

I DON'T ANSWER HIM.

"DO you always carry that laptop around?"
Looking at the floor, I decide not to tell him. I don't know him and can't tell him where I got it.

"Do you know how to talk?" He bends at the knee trying to catch my eyesight, like I can't hear him or something.

"Look, my dad told me to be nice to special kids so—"
     "I'm not retarded!" I snap, my face turning red.
     Zeek holds his hands up and smirks.

"So, I see," he chuckles.

"I just... I don't like people, and they don't like me either," I shrug, not sure what to tell him about my staying silent.

Zeek nods with a toothy smile.
     "You're in the right place then. Nobody likes us either."

"I'm a geek, but why don't people like you?" Zeek looks cool, has naked women around him, and his dad is kick ass. Surely, he's with the popular crowd.

"Duh, we're the bad guys. Outlaws," he holds his hands out like I should know this. He's not just talking about himself, but everyone in the club. They look rough, but I wouldn't expect people to not like them unless they were some kind of gang or...

"Bikers?" I question.

"FUCK YEAH." He's proud.

ZEEK SITS ON THE BED. The blankets matching the images on the biker's leather jackets when I came in. A skull with dice in its eyes.

"You want to be a biker?" Zeek lowers his head, challenge in his voice.

I SCRUNCH my lips to the side. "I don't know anything about being a biker."

"It's easy. Let me see your muscles."

Setting my laptop down on the bed, I flex my left arm. Patches of dirt stick to my skin, revealing I haven't bathed in a while. Not to mention my lack of meals, I'm mostly bones and have no muscle.

Zeek's face frowns at my attempt at showing off. Pushing my sleeve down, I grab my laptop, feeling stupid.

"Yeah, we'll have to work on that." Zeek scratches the back of his head unimpressed. "What do you think about breaking the law?"

I laugh. "I do it every day trying to survive." Breaking and entering at least once a day, not to mention I really wanted a laptop and stole mine from school without feeling bad about it at all.

"NICE!" Zeek laughs. "Do you think you can beat me up?" Zeek stands from the bed. His face conveying, he wants to fight.

I tense, my teeth grinding against each other. I knew he'd be a bully, all boys that look like him want trouble.

"Don't," I warn, holding my hand up. I've gone through enough shit to have some boy try and boss me around. Bum

Hicky is two times bigger than Zeek, and I fought him over a bottle of water last week and won.

"Come on, do you think you can beat me up?" He shoves at my shoulder and my chest combusts with anger.

"I'M WARNING YOU!" Arrowing my finger at him, I try and hold my temper. I need a bath and food. I don't want to fuck this up, but this boy is pushing his luck.

"COME ON, PUSSY!" He pushes me again, and all I see is my dad calling me a pussy for not being man enough. Everything I've been holding inside races through my limbs until I yell in a fit of fury and I shove him so hard he falls into the dresser behind him, knocking the contents on the top to the floor. My fists curled I ready myself to pound into him.

"COME ON!" I scream.

HE BEGINS TO LAUGH, and I seethe with anger. Why is he laughing? I'm serious.

"WOW, the streets have made you tough, Mac!" Zeek smiles, pushing himself off the dresser. Dusting himself off, he gazes at me with smiling eyes holding his hand out to shake mine. As if he respects me now that I stood up to him.

UNCURLING MY FISTS, I look at his hand in confusion.

"I don't get it. I thought you wanted to fight?"

"I wanted to see if you had what it takes to be a biker. Never back down," he explains. "Of course, that will be up to my dad when we get older, but to hang out with me... you have to have the elements of an Outlaw at least." He clasps my hand, holding it tight.

NOT SURE WHAT the hell just happened, I shake his hand anyway. Did I just make a friend?

"GET A SHOWER, and I'll show ya around. Get you some food or something. You look like one of those kids on a starving commercial."

I'd argue, but he's probably right. I've lost a lot of weight.

Patting my back, he heads to the door.

"HEY, you any good on that thing?" He points to my laptop, now on the floor from when I attacked him. I look at it, missing the screen illuminating and getting lost in worlds far greater than the one I'm stuck in.

"It's dead, but when it's on, I can do just about anything. Why?" This is the most I've spoken in forever. Why do I trust this boy so much?

Zeek looks at me with dark eyes.

"Dad might be able to use your skills. I heard him talking about looking for a hacker to some of the guys. You a hacker, Mac?"

I don't reply, I just look at him with a lost expression. I'd never tell anyone what I can do with just a laptop, but I can do whatever I set my mind to, that's for sure.

Reading my mind, Zeek nods with a vile grin.

"Yeah, you can. Can't you?"

I don't reply, I won't tell anyone my secrets.

"Hey, why are you living on the streets. Where are your parents?" He crosses his arms, his hip resting against the doorframe.

LOOKING TO THE GROUND, I feel void of any sudden emotion I might have been feeling.

"THEY'RE DEAD," I mutter with more anger than sorrow.

"HUH," he replies with closed lips.

"My mother died giving birth to me, and my dad is just gone," I reveal, risking a look at his face, I look up through my lashes. He doesn't show sympathy, or sadness. Which is a first. "Hmm. That sucks, clean up and I'll see you around."

He turns and leaves without saying a word. No lines of sympathy or that look everyone gives you when you disclose you're an orphan.

I respect that. A lot.

ALONE IN THE ROOM, I look it over. I'm in a biker gang's clubhouse, and they want me to be one of them. I'm not scared, I'm excited for the first time in my life.

Maybe this will be my new home.

1

SIMONE FIFTEEN YEARS LATER

PART ONE

"Simone, come down here!"

Already halfway down the hall in the west wing, I step left and find my father at the bottom of the marble stairs. He's dressed to impress today, wearing his best Armani suit, and silk red tie. His dark hair is evenly combed back; not in its disheveled way as if he's been running his hands through it like normal. The flooring shines as if it was just waxed, the center table in the middle of the room holds fresh roses the handmaids just picked this morning.

"Yes?" I ask, my steps slow and deliberate as I descend toward him.

"It's time." My father holds his hand out, gesturing toward the front doors. Pausing my steps, I watch as a tall man walking through the doorway wearing an expensive, no doubt tailored suit. His hands tug on the lapels of his jacket as he looks left before right and walks into our home. His black hair is short and spiked, with more product than a man should have in his hair. His dark features consisting of black eyebrows, and tanned Native

American skin, but the lightness in his cheeks conveys he's not full Indian. He's a half-blood, as my father would call it. His eyes sweep across the foyer before stopping on me.

A COLD BREEZE crawls across the floor like a surly serpent, coiling around my body before stealing the very breath from my lungs. As if a harbor breaks, a familiar terrorized feeling creeps through my body. One I've only felt once in my entire life when I was a little girl.

I FORCE myself to take a deep breath and ignore the sudden chill in the air. My hand on the banister, I slowly take the last step down the grand stairs to shake the man's hand.

HE SMILES when I'm near, the smell of smoke and cologne dancing around me like a dark spell.

I PLAY the part my dad has taught me over the years. Smile, and keep the chat simple and to the point. My father is a business-man. Now, when I say the word business, I imagine a big office that overlooks the city, coffee in the morning as you look over your schedule for the day as your assistant rattles off the things you're behind on. That image is wrong. My dad is a businessman of many outlawed tastes, ones that are dangerous and lethal. His day consists of overlooking who owes us money, who would benefit us financially, and who dies tomorrow. I've been by his side since I was nine learning the ropes of how to be in charge one day. We finance gangs around the border, and charge interest as they get up and running. I've been working the books and helping my father decide where to invest since I can remember. Many think women are weak in such a powerful position, so I am constantly challenging myself to stay ahead of the game and prove them wrong. It excites me when people underestimate me. I've taken medical classes, learned foreign languages, and I'm always yearning to learn more.

When our clients turn their back on me because they see tits, I show my fangs and suck the life from them and their business. Leaving them lifeless, and at my mercy. I'm not a violent person, I leave that to my guards, but I will drain them financially and leave them on the side of the road on their asses.

I'M NOT ASHAMED. I'm taking life and making it mine.

"YOU DIDN'T TELL me how beautiful she's become." The man lifts his chin, his face serious as he devours me with black abyss irises. His voice is rough and husky. The undertones of his voice summoning me as if I was his territory. He's kind of attractive, but the way he is staring at me as if he owns me distracts me from how handsome he might be. He has a malicious energy about him.

I clear my throat, dropping my hand like a dead weight before he has the chance to make contact. His comment is clearly out of context, and not welcomed. Who is this man.

Just as I'm about to open my mouth to object to his statement, my father cuts in.

"I THOUGHT her educational background would be more of interest," my father pronounces with an irritated state of voice.

MY BROWS FURROW. Why isn't he berating him for speaking to me like that? Why were they discussing me so intently behind my back? Taking my stare from my father to the man, I get the sudden idea that this man is not a normal client of ours.

His dark eyes smile, and my head slowly tilts to the left. He looks familiar, but where have I seen him?

MY FATHER COUGHS, interrupting our staring contest. Blinking myself back to the situation at hand, I run my sweaty hands down my dress nervously.

"EXCUSE ME, but what is going on here?" The bitch in my voice painted on thickly.

"SIMONE." My father steeples his hands as if he doesn't know how to speak to me. This is a first, he and I always tell one another everything without hesitation. Little hairs on the back of my neck stand. Something isn't right.

"FATHER?" My words meek and unsteady. My cheeks flush with warmth as I become vulnerable for the first time since becoming a woman.

"DON'T YOU REMEMBER VEER?" Dad tilts his head to the side. His thick brows matching the frown on his lips.

My spine straightens, the breath in my throat catching as fear cuts through my chest like a hot knife in cold butter. I remember him, all right, I had nightmares about him for over a year.

AN INCREDULOUS LAUGH wracks my body. I'm terrified and entertained at the same time. I harbored every flint of terror I had for this man through many therapy sessions my mother set up as a child. The fear I felt when I saw this man walk through my front door today, was the same darkness I felt the day I met him.

THEY BOTH STAND SILENT, looking at me with blank looks as the reality of what is going on sets in.

"No, this is as real as it gets. You're a woman now, and it's time," Dad explains.

"THIS- THIS IS NOT the eighteen hundreds, you can't just sell me to our enemy!" The words push through my teeth as if I'd just touched a hot pan or a spider just bit me. Opening my eyes, I snap my head toward my father. My face flushed and sweaty from the betrayal circulating the room.

"I'M afraid our feud goes that far back, and nothing is off the table in love and war," Veer comments, his sentimental statement cutting my skin like a dull razor.

I SCOFF, and glare in Veer's direction. I am not a pawn, I'm not ready to marry anyone. Especially a stranger; an enemy. When I turned eighteen, I sat on pins and needles wondering if Veer would come for me, and when he never did... I let out a breath I had been holding since I was eight years old. I never asked my parents about it, and I never thought about it again. Almost as if it would bring the devil to my door if I mentioned his name. Delusional lullabies from books and movies gifted me hope that I was a free woman. Yet, here the villain stands... ready to collect me like a forgotten prize.

"I'M NOT MARRYING ANYONE," I declare matter of fact. I've been so invested in my family's business and what I'm doing with my life right now, that I've never explored my sexuality. I get up early, work until the morning hours, sometimes requiring travel which is from hotel to hotel. At the end of the day, all I can think about is a bath and wine.

How do I even know I want to marry a man?

"YOUR PLACE in our family is to settle a feud between the Walsh family and ours, Simone. They'll split territory into the United States with us if our bloodlines cross. Meaning you... marrying into the Walsh family and having a child. I'm getting too old to do this anymore. You need someone to take care of you and giving you to Veer ensures you a wealthy life, and security as well as us."

I gasp. This is about him retiring.

MY STOMACH CLENCHING with an unbearable cramp as if the thought of holding a Walsh child makes my uterus coil in detest. "It's what's best for our future," my dad says in a near whisper

"BEST FOR OUR FUTURE, or best for you?" My eyes squint pointedly at my father. He opens his mouth to defend himself, but he quickly closes it, and looks away.

I TURN AWAY from the two men, my hair falling in my face as I look to the floor for answers. An explanation as to why my dad would do this to me without my consent. Is there a way out of this arrangement?

"I KNOW THIS IS SCARY." Veer's voice cuts through my own thoughts and I close my eyes and reach for the banister for balance. How dare he speak to me. "But, I will make you happy. I will give you everything your heart desires."

A FAINT LAUGH breaks through my highly glossed lips, and I look over my shoulder with glossy eyes.

"Then die," I grit angrily. Who does he think he is coming in here thinking I would just agree to this. His dark eyes blaze with my disrespect and his hand darts out, catching mine by the wrist. His hand is cold and void of any human warmth as it curls around my own.

"THAT'S no way to talk to your fiancé, now is it?" he growls. He never even asked me to marry him. I don't have to look to see my father tense. Clearly, he didn't suspect this kind of behavior from Veer. I did.

I TEAR my arm from his and spit on his shoes, my disrespect clear to everyone.

"I'd rather die than be your wife," I snarl, my nose turned up.

His eyes fall to his shoes with my spit splattered across them, before slowly slipping up my body and catching my gaze like a hooked fish.

Dark ominous eyes dig in my chest and clutch my soul, catching my breath painfully. His shoulders lift as if he's trying to control his anger in front of everyone. I can see it in his body language. His taut biceps, and curled fists- He'd hit me if we were alone.

Dark eyes that reflect everything he's looking at telling me I'm right. He'd slap me if we were already married.

PULLING a handkerchief from his pocket he swipes my spit off his shoe and shoves it back in his pocket. His shoulders rolling in an attempt to calm himself.

"HOW OLD IS SHE AGAIN?" he questions, not taking his eyes off of mine.

"Twenty-five," my father states with a shaky voice. His forehead beading with sweat.

"She's feisty, are you sure she's still a virgin?" Veer looks over his shoulder at my father and my dad just looks at the floor with sad eyes. I can't contain my reaction as I gasp in horror. *Am I still a virgin? Who asks someone's father that?*

My mother steps in behind my father from the dining room. Her pink champagne dress trailing behind her as does her long thick braid down her back. Surely, she won't let this charade stand for another moment.

"Mother..." The word a mere cry for help to tell me this is just a test or a sick game at best.

"She is untouched... as far as we know," my mother adds, her hands clutched together in front of her. My mouth drops in dismay. She's conspiring with them.

Veer looks back at me with wolfish eyes. Ones that tell me he's going to do *very* dirty things to me, and I'm not going to like it one bit.

"Because I don't buy anything used, let alone my women," Veer adds with an arrogant tone.

"I'll never let you between my legs." My thighs squeeze together on their own accord.

"I will be the *only one* between those legs." His words a threat more than a statement.

I SHAKE MY HEAD, taking a step back to look over the people who see me as an object rather than a human being. My eyes sting with the urge to cry and it unnerves me. I don't cry. I am Simone fucking Ray!

TURNING, I grab the ends of my dress and run up the stairs to my room, the material of my train sweeping around my feet as I flee for solitude. I need away from everyone, a minute to gather my thoughts and find a solution to this.

Slamming the door behind me, I slump to the floor in a pool of silk material.

My giant sleigh bed with pink silk material made perfect, blur behind with my tear-filled eyes. The crystal chandelier hanging from the center of the room blinding me from the reflection of light and crystal.

"THINK SIMONE," I tell myself, my hand petting the thick strands of tan carpet on the floor. The confidence in my tone lacks for the first time since I can remember. I always have a solution to everything, that's what I've been learning from my father for years now.

The manicured finger of my left hand taps on my trembling chin as chaotic thoughts scramble through my head so fast I can't pinpoint one. I am Simone Ray. Born to lead, and ruler of my tribe.

I dictate my future, not my blood. My father showed me how to be confident, powerful, and above all else - silently lethal.

I say who I sleep with.

Who I love.

Who I marry!

It won't be with a Walsh either. The Walshs have fought my family for many years over land to turn gangs over. Starting with building homes to moving drugs. So much blood has been shed between our people, that there's no way I can turn a blind eye to the slayings of our heritage. Whether it's for money or settle a feud. I will not be the solution.

He thinks handing me over to the Walsh family will keep me and our future family safe. Maybe he's right, but I just... I can't bring myself to do it.

LOOKING THROUGH WARM UNSHED TEARS, I clench my teeth thinking about him only interested in my innocence. "*I don't buy anything used, let alone my women.*"

My eyes widen, the solution coming to light like the sun bleeding through a dark cloud on a gloomy day.

That's it. I have to void this contract on my own and lose my virginity. Tonight!

2

SIMONE

Flipping my head up right after blow drying it, dark brown curls fall to my breast with trundles framing my sharp face. "Rock Star" by Post Malone plays from the speakers inside the walls of my room. My pulse drumming to the beat as I stare at my reflection with a lost gaze. Fisting my lipstick, I drag the fire engine red across my lips, my eyes never leaving my reflection in the mirror. I pucker my lips and place the lid on the sinful lipstick. My black garter and thong the only thing on my body, I turn on the pads of my feet and leave my bathroom walking into my large closet. Trailing my fingers along the material of the expensive clothes hanging from hangers. Some still have tags on them even. I find a tight lacy black dress in the black section-yes, I organize my clothes by color-and pull it from the rack. I slip the material over my body, the dress hugging my figure like we're made for one another. My heart beats rapidly, my body clammy since I declared this night, *the* night. The one night that every girl over thinks about. Who will be the lucky one to take her virginity? Will it hurt? Should I be on top or bottom? Will I fall in love?

CLOSING MY EYES, I take a deep breath and tell myself this is no big deal. This is just like work, just another contract... only this is one I'm voiding and making sure it is burned beyond reconciling.

I'M FUCKING shit up tonight.

OPENING MY EYES, my heart beats a little slower, at least at a pace I can breathe normally. In my shoe closet, I grab my thigh high boots, I've only worn them once. I saw them in a shop in New York and thought they were so erotic looking I had to have them. I wore them in the hotel room, and that was it. I was saving them for a special guy one day.

I guess that day will have to be today.

Slipping my foot into one leather boot, I feel like Cinderella's twisted sister. Her mission of sex and sin on her mind rather than finding her one true love. I zip the last boot up, the sound of the zipper making my spine prickle with goosebumps.

NO MATTER what I tell myself, tonight is not going to be easy and I know that. The whole 'no strings attached, and it's just sex and nothing more' routine is for pros. I've seen enough movies to know it's not going to be easy for me to give my innocence to someone and just walk away with empty feelings.

GRABBING a blue jean jacket sitting on a bench in my closet, I toss it over my shoulder and inhale a shaky breath. One that is confident, and vexed.

I can do this. I *have* to do this.

Leaving my room, the click of my heels on the polished floor echo behind me as I make my way through the mansion. The sound resembling a ticking watch counting down the days I'm expected to walk down the aisle with Veer.

Passing the antique mirror in the hallway, the smell of my Gucci perfume leaving a trail of forbidden sin in my wake, I glance at it from the corner of my eye. I look like someone else and feel like someone else.

Down the stairs, the front door in sight, my mother walks out of the study with a perplexed look on her face. I don't stop to talk to her, I keep my feet moving.

"Simone?" my mother calls after me as I pass her. "Simone Ray!" Ignoring her, I toss my hair over my shoulder, ignore the guilt in my stomach and stay focused on the mission at hand.

"Where are you going? What are you wearing?"

"Don't wait up!" I say, but I can't hear myself say it. All I can think about is the blood pounding through my veins like a toxic drug. Drowning my pure blood and replacing it with something darker and foreign.

This is my one night out, and I'm going to fucking ruin everything Veer might see in a Ray.

I'm breaking all the rules of being a lady, tonight.

———

I drive two hours away just to make sure Dad's men won't find me. I'm sure they are trying to track me as we speak, freaking out about my sudden defiant behavior. I pulled the GPS hidden in the car air freshener attached to the vent and toss it out of the window halfway down the driveway.

Pulling my phone out I search for bars in the area, looking at ratings and reviews.

"POST TRIP?" I nibble on the tip of my nail, looking at the thumbnail picture of the bar. I guess it's okay as far as bars go.

SIGHING, I set the GPS on my phone to the location. My hands white-knuckling the steering wheel, my heart drumming in my chest like a circle of Indian's chanting their ultimate sacrifice.

PULLING into the gravel parking lot, my tires crunch into the little rocks until I park.

Ducking my head, looking through the windshield I size the place up.

POST TRIP IS a one-story brick building with a small patio on the left. It has the usual bar lights hanging in the windows displaying different beer brands, and there's people standing outside casually laughing to one another as they smoke.

TOSSING the keys into my purse, I climb out of my BMW and sashay toward the entry. I'm a little surprised there's nobody at the door to check my ID or anything so I just slip inside

This must be a very low-key place if nobody is here to say who can enter and not.

ONCE INSIDE OF the building the smell of beer, cologne, and a hint of peanuts fills the air. The lights are dimmed, and it's foggy and thick from everyone's hot breathing in such a small space. But more importantly, there's a lot of guys here tonight.

Pushing my nerves to the side, I smile, and head to the bar to order a drink. I need something to loosen me up a little. I'm as tense as a mannequin, and my stomach is in knots at the thought of what I'm doing tonight.

Slipping onto the hard-wooden stool, a woman with black leather shorts, tattoos up and down her legs, takes drink orders behind the bar. Her long jet-black hair frames her pale face, and a skull necklace hangs between her breasts which are barely covered with a red corset.

Sliding to my side of the bar, she lifts her chin at me.

"WHAT YA WANT, BABE?"

I look around curious what everyone else is drinking.

"Do you have wine?"

She raises a brow as if to say, "do they look like have wine?"

"Um, two shots of tequila?"

SMACKING HER GUM LOUDLY, she grabs two shot glasses from under the counter, places them on the granite, and pours cheap tequila into them, spilling more onto the counter than in the glass.

"FIFTEEN BUCKS." Her hand slaps the wet countertop.

Opening my purse, I hand her twenty.

"Keep the change." I smile.

She fists the twenty, looking at me as if she's waiting for me to change my mind. She must not get tipped much. Forcing a smile, I reach for my drinks and she finally steps to another customer. Downing one of the shot glasses, I clench my eyes as the burn slips down my throat.

Ugh, it's like swallowing broken glass. Opening my eyes, I smack my tongue around, eyeing the next shot glass. I bet it's just as bad. I toss it back, trying to hold my breath as I swallow the harsh liquid down. Coming up for air, I gasp and push the empty glasses back to the edge of the bar so they know I'm done with them.

CROSSING MY LEGS, I turn around on the stool to look around the place, curious who my mark may be. A tall blonde man with glasses dances on the dance floor. His sweater looks like something a golf enthusiast would wear, and those khakis are a major turn off. I scrunch my nose. No way.

MY EYES SLIP across the space falling to a man who is bobbing his head in the corner next to the fake dusty plant. The strong silent type perhaps? He has dark spiky hair and a choker on. His tight black shirt that looks like spandex is stretching across his chest way to tightly, and his black jeans are way too baggy for my taste.

BLOWING AIR THROUGH MY CHEEKS, I turn around and twist the empty glasses on the counter the bartender has yet to pick up. What is my type exactly? Do I even have one? Maybe I'm being too picky.

You know when you feel someone staring at you even though you're not looking, that sensation that almost burns? The hairs on the back of your neck might even stand?

I instantly have every one of those sensations, but the burning is so intense I think someone dubbed their cigarette out on the back of my neck, singeing the peach fuzz on the nape of my neck. Carefully, not too eager, I casually glance over my shoulder and my eyes instantly catch two men sitting in a u-shaped booth just behind me staring directly at me. Not just any men, but bikers. Hot as fuck bikers.

The one on the left has a young youthful soft face. Dark short hair, and various tattoos up his thick arms. The leather cut claiming his chest proudly makes me tuck my bottom lip between my teeth. His eyes dig into mine with hesitation before looking down at his beer and up at me again. It's as if he is drawn to me but doesn't want to be.

Lips parting, I draw in a deep breath and look to the other man in the booth. He's Indian for sure; like me. His glowing skin tan and beautiful, his thick black hair pulled into a sexy bun fitting his rugged look. Sharp cheeks with delicious dark stubble color my cheeks red, warmth spreading down my body and swirling in areas that has me sweating. They're so good-looking, too good-looking. Butterflies swim in my stomach, and I can't stop the nervous laugh bubbling through my lips. He smirks in my direction, and my heart skips a beat.

Tossing my hair off my hot neck, I turn back around trying to act unaffected. They're really cute, what do I do? Should I go over there? Wait and see if they come to me?

"WANT TWO MORE?" the bartender suddenly asks standing in front of me. Looking down at the cracked counter I nod, my teeth biting my bottom lip nervously. I feel like an angel tempting the devil's disciples. I should go over there. Wait, no, I'm already being easy tonight, I should at least make them come to me.

INSTANTLY SHE REFILLS MY GLASSES, and then clears her throat. I lose my smile and look up, finding her waiting. Oh right, I have to pay her.

I give her another twenty, and reach for my drinks, needing them more than ever right now.

I glance over my shoulder to see if they're still looking and notice the Indian one pointing at me as he talks, the younger biker staring at me with smoldering eyes.

I'M GOING OVER THERE.

NOT SURE IF my heated cheeks are from the alcohol or the men behind, I don't over think it and down the two shots of tequila. One after the other. My skin warms from the alcohol, and I feel brave. I decide I need to make a move. I need to get up and – and dance. Yeah, I'll let my body language do the talking to these two men, because the only other thing I have to start a conversation is corny pick-up lines.

Besides, my mother said if a man can dance, then he's good in bed and I'm about to put her words to the test tonight!

MOVING my head back and forth, my hips start to sway to "Devil" by Shinedown. My hands slide up and down my curves, my head bobbing to the music. I can't help but feel a little silly, I've never danced in front of anyone before. Hands in the air, I turn to face my two admirers curious if they're still looking at me, only to find them both headed my way side by side. Their heads lowered, arms at their side, and eyes hooded. As if in slow motion the lights flicker, their wolfish eyes only on me. The crowd splits as if they fear these two men, and I never take my eyes off either of them as they descend toward me like two hungry wolves.

CLOSER NOW, I can see their patches on their leather cuts, they're from different clubs. The Indian looking one is named Kane and is from a club called The Devil's Dust here in California. The shorter Burnette biker is from a club based out of Las Vegas called Sin City Outlaws, and his name is Gatz.

THESE ARE my kind of men. Bad boys. I work with men like these all the time, and I know how to handle them. Never show fear and keep your chin high with confidence.

KANE REACHES FOR ME FIRST, fisting me by the hips and pulling me flush with him in one swift move. His hard-warm body presses up against mine and my breathing shallows to near nothing.

"Hey sweetheart," Kane whispers into my ear, and it sends a shiver down my body. His voice is deep, so sexy I want him to keep talking to me. Using his free hand, he gently grabs my wrist and lifts it to his neck before slowly sliding his knuckles down the back of my arm.

EACH TOUCH AND CARESS, sends my toes curling into my boots in search of release.

WRAPPING my arms around his neck, I start feeling good from the tequila shots. Hair in my face, lips parted, I grind myself on Kane's knee to the beat of the rough music. My body's alive, my nipples ache with excitement, my body slick with sweat, and my thong is soaked with arousal.

GATZ INTERTWINES his fingers with the left hand of Kane's on one of my hips and rubs his erection in a circular motion along my backside. Glancing over my shoulder at him, he runs his nose over my shoulder before biting down on the bare flesh. My head falls back, it feels so fucking good.

I'm sandwiched between two large bikers, that are grinding and dancing on each side of me. Moving my ass along one, I rub my heavy chest on the other. Their hands slide up and down my curves, with their legs in between mine. I don't know where I begin and they end. It's as if it's just us three lost in a fog of lust and desire, the rest of the club faded and lost to the clouds of staring citizens. I feel beautiful, I feel wanted, and I never want it to end.

PRESSED between two of the hottest men in the bar we dance on top of each other to the song "Bad Girlfriend" by Theory of A Deadman. Our eyes locked on one another, our bodies grinding and pulling each other as close as we can get without completely dry humping on the dance floor.

KANE LEANS DOWN, his hot tongue flicking my earlobe. I moan at the wet contact, my nails digging into the skin of his neck. God, I want more. I need it, and now before I break my big toe from curling my toes in these boots for some kind of relief.

"YOU WANNA GET OUT OF HERE?" Kane whispers.

3

SIMONE

Pulling back, I look deep into his eyes to see if he's serious. He doesn't blink, his face void of any emotion. So, I nod. I'd go anywhere with him right now. He gives Gatz a look, and they both grab one of my hands and drag me away from the dance floor. Women stare at me with awe, men with angry expressions giving me a once over before their girls slap them in the chest for staring too long. I feel like the luckiest girl in this bar tonight.

ONCE OUTSIDE, my skin prickles from the night air brushing up against my sweaty skin.

Kane and Gatz don't stop once outside, they don't ask me my name, or care for chit-chat.

They drag me along like the hooker they picked up from the bar and nothing more, heading toward their bikes parked at the end of the lot.

PASSING MY CAR, I slow my steps.

"I um, I drove." I point toward my car.

Gatz glances over at me with a blank look.

"You've been drinking, you're not driving." His dominant tone forces my sex to throb achingly. Nobody tells me what I'm doing, but then again, these men don't know who I am. It's refreshing as it is infuriating.

Swallowing the sudden knot in my throat, I breathe through my nose and keep my mouth shut the rest of the walk to their motorcycles.

They're quiet, not saying a word, but the sexual tension is unmistakable. Just glancing at us you can see it glowing around us like a halo of temptation.

I came here with the idea of sleeping with one man, and I have two freaking bikers.

I should be scared, terrified they might take me somewhere and tie me up, but I'm so turned on, it's as if I can't filter in to that side of my brain right now. All I want is to be touched, to be free of any adult responsibilities for one night.

Two shiny motorcycles sit side by side with helmets on them. They're sexy as fuck, but I have no idea what kind they are. I've seen plenty of them, and have always wanted to go for a ride, but it would be unprofessional of me to ask a client for a joy ride. They'd want favors if I did that.

"I'VE NEVER RIDDEN BEFORE," I say more to myself than to them, my finger trailing along the dew beading on one of the fenders.

"A night of many firsts." Gatz smiles handsomely, handing me a helmet. My face goes stoic as my fingers accept the heavy helmet. What does he mean a night of many firsts? Does he know I'm a virgin, is it that obvious?

Tingling sweeps up the back of my neck and across my face, and I hide behind my hair. Turning away from them, I place the helmet over my head, the soft liner smashing my face into safety. Kane grins and fastens it for me.

"This is a night you won't forget." The soft words draw from his lips like a roofie. His eyes never leaving mine. He's cocky, arrogant even, and much different than Gatz.

"YOU'RE VERY SURE OF YOURSELF." I cock a smile, and he grunts in that man-way guys do before turning around.

Twisting a strand of my hair that escaped the helmet, I look back at my car. If I get on one of these motorcycles, there's no turning back.

"YOU GUYS AREN'T like serial killers or anything like that are you?" I half joke, but that part of my brain is starting to throw up some red flags. Like I said, I work with men like this and know what they're capable of.

"A SERIAL KILLER has to have three or more kills, right?" Kane asks Gatz, his tone of voice lacking emotion.

"Yeah, something like that," Gatz states, shrugging.

"Oh, then yeah, we're good." Kane's shit-eating grin is almost contagious. "We're way past three, so what's that called?" he asks me. My stomach drops. Does he mean he's killed way more than three people?

My mouth dries, my hand dropping from twisting a lock of hair.

"Ignore him." Gatz laughs and shakes his head. His hand grasps mine, squeezing it reassuringly. His touch is soft, even with the callus of his fingertips. "He's an asshole— "

"Yeah, but that's what you like about me," Kane interrupts him.

Gatz doesn't deny it as he looks down with a silent smile. Lifting his bright eyes to mine, he tilts his to the side. "We'll make him pay later." He winks, and it's the most charming thing I've ever seen. Are they a couple?

Gatz throws his leg over the seat of his bike and starts it, the rumble making my chest vibrate. My fucking heart is beating so fast I feel like it's going to explode. I feel... free!

Gatz pats the back of his bike, inviting me.

Sliding behind him, I place the heels of my boots on the pegs and wrap my hands around his waist. He's much smaller in the torso than Kane.

"Damn girl, you got some legs on you," Gatz admires, and all I can think about is having them wrapped around him later.

"Let's go play, kids," Kane states, revving up his bike and taking off.

Gatz follows, the jerk of the bike nearly making me squeal, and the people in the parking lot nearly throw themselves to get out of the way.

Diving in and out of traffic, we head to a destination I'm unaware of. Maybe I should have asked a lot more questions before jumping on the back of a handsome stranger's motorcycle.

Staring at him from behind, his short hair swipes against his ears from the wind rushing past, his leather jacket flapping into my knees. With this helmet on, I can barely feel anything but the drumming of my heartbeat. I want the wind on my face, and I want to experience the rush of having nothing between me and the road. Taking my hands off his waist, I clench my knees onto his thighs and unhook my helmet. Pulling it off my head, I set it in my lap and the cool wind hits me so hard it nearly takes my breath away. It's warm, but cold. Fresh and crisp.

I've never felt anything like this before. Adrenaline pushes through my veins like a new street drug, freedom wraps around me with fragile hands fueling my reckless behavior until I'm laughing so hard I don't even recognize myself.

Gatz peeks over his shoulder and smirks. Leaning his head back, his lips move as if he's saying something, but I can't hear him from the wind whispering in my ear.

I LEAN FORWARD, tucking my wild hair away from my face so I can lip read if I have to.

"What?" I yell so he can hear me over the motor and breeze

"You'll never want to ride in a car again!" he hollers louder, and he's right. You'd have to drive one-hundred miles an hour in a car to get the same rush you feel on a motorcycle going the normal speed limit.

"I love it!"

WE DESCEND around a corner on a back street, our speed slowing down to below the speed limit when a small hotel comes into sight. It's made up of yellow brick, and flowers and bushes are all around the property. It's got a country aura to it.

The New Inn reads in bright yellow lights above the main office.

How fitting the name, because after tonight, I will be a new woman.

Gatz pulls his motorcycle into the parking lot and sets his feet down on the ground walking it in backward into a parking spot; Kane parking right next to us.

After cutting the engines off, I climb off Gatz's bike with a smile on my face I can't seem to shake. I never would have guessed a simple ride on a motorcycle would be so enjoyable.

Kane's boots stomp onto the pavement, the scoff making me glance his way.

"YOU SHOULD HAVE KEPT your helmet on," Kane scolds, his finger pointing at me as if I'm a disobedient child. Is he always in this kind of a mood?

ARMS WRAP AROUND MY LEGS, and I'm lifted from the ground like a princess, forcing a squeal from my lungs. Wrapping my hands around Gatz's neck, a name brand cologne and something woodsy intoxicates my senses. His body is warm against my cool skin from the breeze of the ride, and his chest is hard against mine.

GATZ STARTS WALKING toward Room 7, and Kane follows behind us. His heavy boots thudding into the pavement, his dominating eyes looking around, his facial expression hard and unfriendly. It's sexy in a way.

TURNING BACK TOWARD THE HOTEL, it occurs to me that we don't even check in. Have they been staying here? Together? Do their clubs no they are seeing each other? Are they enemies?

So many questions rattle my mind.

"Do you stay here often?" I can't help but ask one question, but I just get a smirk from Gatz, and Kane doesn't even look at me, let alone answer.

KANE STEPS in front of us, pulls a key from his pocket and unlocks the door. Holding the spring-loaded door open for Gatz and I as we step inside. It smells of men's soap and sweat. My hormones going crazy from the testosterone fogging the air. My eyes immediately sweep across the room. A king-sized bed made up of red and white blankets and sheets with a wooden dresser and black mini fridge that buzzes on the opposite side. I notice a black duffle bag in the corner, explaining one of them must be staying here. Possibly Gatz because he's not from here?

GATZ SUDDENLY PLOPS me on the bed, my legs sprawling out to where you can see my thong. Pressing my knees together, Gatz's hands press into each side of the bed as he leans into my space. He's handsomely beautiful. Like a man you would see on a GQ cover. Reaching up, I palm his face, his beautiful eyes seeking mine. They're soft, but swimming with danger. Like the ocean, beautiful from the surface but within harbors dangerous things from the unknown.

NOT ABLE TO HELP MYSELF I lean forward and press my lips to his. They're soft and supple. He inhales deeply, his eyes squinting as if he's in pain from my touch. It causes my brows to furrow, not expecting that reaction. His lips slowly pucker, and he kisses me back.

AT FIRST, it's slow and formal. Then hunger strikes as his tongue flicks against my lips, and I nip at his bottom lip playfully, the kiss deepening and taking my breath away. He's such an amazing kisser.

PULLING AWAY, I inhale the breath he took, and he looks over his shoulder at Kane, who is laying lines of coke out on the dirty dresser.

Gatz rubs his hand through his dark hair, he looks sexy with messy hair. I run my nails through it, truly fucking it up and he chuckles, stepping away.

GATZ GRABS KANE's nape and kisses him. Kane tasting my spit off Gatz's tongue. Kane is rough when he kisses, demanding the lips of Gatz. Pushing my thighs together I watch the two men make-out before me, something I've never seen before but find incredibly hot. Gatz breaks away, their eyes silently speaking to each other before he bends down and sniffs up a small line of cocaine, Kane following after him.

This is getting real, this is all happening tonight. Wetting my lips, I stand, deciding I'm going to do the cocaine too. I need something a little stronger than a couple of shots to settle my nerves. I'm so uptight and nervous there's no way I'm going to enjoy tonight.

Walking quickly to erase the distance, I eye the drugs with confidence.

"You sure?" Gatz asks, gently touching the inside of my wrist with his soft touch. I look to Kane, and he lifts his head. Flicking his chin with his thumb, his eyes challenge me.

"YEAH, I'M SURE," I mutter under my breath. A wolfish smile pulls at his mouth, his hand wrapping around my long thick hair and gently pulling. Kane is mute. The silent type. His face rough and displaying hardships and need.

USING MY HAIR AS A HANDLE, he pushes my face toward the snowy lines.

Using my index finger, I close off one nostril and use my free nostril to sniff the white powdery substance. It burns, causing my eyes to instantly water. My throat tingles forcing me to cough, closing my eyes a warm fuzzy feeling lifts me off my feet.

Opening my eyes, the room is in high definition. Every color feeling as if it were alive and moving. I feel fucking amazing. Kane pulls his shirt over his head; his tanned muscled skin makes me grit my teeth with desire. He's strikingly good-looking. With Gatz right beside me, I grab the bottom of his shirt and lift it over his head. I need to see him naked, to feel his chest beneath my fingernails. When his shirt is off, I'm surprised to see him covered in tattoos and is almost just as muscular as Kane. He's in a biker gang, I don't know why I'm shocked to see him inked and strong. Maybe it's his caring demeanor?

Lips skim across the back of my neck, and hands pull at my dress as I walk back slowly until the back of my knees hit the mattress. The room dances in shadows and lights, and when I lay down, I feel like I'm floating onto the mattress like a drifting feather.

Blinking, my face lax with a dopy smile, Kane appears in my line of sight. He kisses me deeply, his callused hands gripping my chin as he demands my mouth harshly. His tongue tastes of beer and sin, and I want to douse myself in it and dance all night.

Gatz pushes himself in between my legs, his hands touching the sensitive skin between my thighs, my panties pool with wetness, and throbs with the rhythm of my heart.

Suddenly I feel a void, like falling into a rabbit hole. There's no hands or lips touching me. Lifting my heavy head up, Kane and

Gatz kiss one another, their hands pulling on each other's jeans and underwear frantically.

KANE'S COCK comes out of his gray boxers first, and I can't help but stare. It's dark and thick. Gatz spits on his hand and fists it and pumps it, Kane growls in reaction, just as he rips the white boxers from Gatz's legs. His white long cock coiled with veins wrapping around it springs free, bobbing into the air like an arrow. I got it all with these two boys, length and girth.

BOTH ON THEIR knees they both suddenly look at me, and I hold my breath. Their eyes dark and dancing with temptation, as if I'm their dessert tonight.

"HI!" I wave seductively, and completely high.

THEY BOTH DESCEND ON ME, hands and lips everywhere. My skin prickles and warms from every swipe of their fingers, roughness of the stubble on their faces, and nip of their teeth. I feel like I'm lost at sea. The waves and ocean doing what it wants to me, and I'm just along for the journey. My fingers dig into the bedsheets as Gatz spreads my legs open. My eyes in a haze, I watch him bring a condom wrapper to his mouth and tug it open with his sharp teeth, Kane pulling his condom open with his fingers. The sound of the condom wrappers ripping apart, makes my spine drip with sweat.

HERE WE GO.

GATZ JERKS my thong to the side and slowly enters me. His eyes never leaving mine as he pushes in. My lips part, my brows furrowing with unease as inch by inch of his length stretches into my tightness. I close my eyes and breathe through the pain. Fuck this hurt, I can't imagine doing this sober.

"OPEN YOUR EYES," Kane instructs, his hands on both sides of my face. I open my eyes and find him hovering above me the opposite to Gatz, his knees brushing the top of my head. I blow out a steady breath and focus on keeping my eyes open. His hair brushes along my cheeks, and it mesmerizes me. It's almost as long as mine.

GATZ PUSHES DEEPER, and I can't help the moan vibrating my chest. It feels good, but it doesn't at the same time.

"WAIT A MINUTE." Concern thick in Gatz's voice has everyone still. My eyes snap to his, and he looks to Kane with surprise. "She's a virgin, man."

KANE LOOKS BACK TO ME, with raised brows.

"WAS," I whisper. "I was a virgin." Leaning up I kiss him, and he kisses me back. My act of pursuing this whole thing fuels them to continue. I don't want to stop.

"Who cares, just... just keep going," Kane orders.

Gatz begins to thrust into me over and over again. His cock throbbing inside of me, the hardness and warmth feels so good I never want him to stop. He pulls out of me, and the bed dips. When I open my eyes, Gatz is hovering above me where Kane was moments ago. A spot on his bicep causes me to turn my head sideways as I focus on it. It's a birthmark in the shape of a horseshoe, it's unlike anything I've seen before, then again, I'm high. I reach out to touch it, just as he leans down and kisses me. Kane now in between my legs, he spreads my knees wider to accommodate his bigger size. When he pushes into me, my sex burns with pain worse than before, and I cry into Gatz's mouth. My nipples harden, and my teeth bite into his lip until I taste blood.

"Shhh." Gatz kisses my pain away, his lips now smeared with blood, and I fall back into ecstasy. I kiss him, and then I kiss Kane. My body becoming theirs, I am their property, their toy tonight. Kane nips at my nipples, and Gatz sucks on my neck. Kane swirls my clit, and Gatz spanks the side of my thigh all while taking turns fucking me into forgetting why I'm here in the first place.

Gatz in between my legs, then Kane. Colors swirl, my world spinning with pleasure and pain.

I'm lost in a blur of sex, heaven, and drugs. Tiptoeing a fine line of sin and innocence.

My body winds up with tingles, and pressure builds in my abdomen until I combust into a million little stars. I'm not sure who makes me orgasm for the first time, and I don't really care. I'm on a cloud of pleasure, and never want it to stop.

MY HEART IS BEATING SO FAST, and my eyes are heavy from the drugs and tequila that it takes everything I have to remain conscious. Turning my head, I notice Kane and Gatz have moved onto each other on the end of the bed. The way their hands roam along each other's arms and bare backs I can see love in every movement and every touch. These two love each other. I wonder if I will find love like that one day.

WATCHING them make love to each other, I can't help but fall into a deep sleep hoping one day someone will make love to me like that. Like I'm their last breath.

4

SIMONE

"**H**ousekeeping!"

The sound of knocking has me lifting my head from the firm pillow. Drool and makeup smeared across the white material guaranteeing I look how I feel. Like death.

"No thank you!" I try and holler but my voice cracks with every word. My breath is rancid, my face contorting in disgust.

"Check out was an hour ago," her voice muffled from the other side of the door. Shit. Groaning I slide my hand along my face, trying to wake up. My throat is dry as the desert, and I have a bad taste in my mouth.

Looking around, sleep still in my eyes, I notice I'm alone in the room. Gatz and Kane are gone, even the bag in the corner is missing. Placing my hand on the bed to help myself up, I crush a note into the mattress.

Blinking a few times to see it better, I straighten the paper out.

WE HAD *club shit to do. Your car is in the parking lot.*
Thanks for the birthday gift.
Xoxo

I FROWN. Birthday gift? They didn't say anything about anyone's birthday, I wonder whose it was. Keys jingle against my thigh, I fist them.

"They drove my car?" I sigh, slipping off the bed. How long have I been asleep?

"MISS?" Knocking continues and my head pounds with every boom.

"Just- just give me a few minutes please!" Bitch high in my voice. Persistent she is.

GRABBING my crumbled dress off the floor, I pull it over my head. The fabric is itchy and uncomfortable today. I feel like crap and want something comfortable to wear.

Groaning, I grab my boots not bothering to put them on. Opening the door, I hold it open with my bare foot. An old lady with curly graying hair looks at me pointedly with her arms crossed.

"It's all yours," I mutter stepping past her. I tiptoe across the pebbled parking lot to my car parked in the back.

Opening the door, I toss my shoes and purse into the passenger seat and start the car.

I run my hands back and forth over my face trying to wake up. My mouth is dry and my stomach is upset. My thighs are sore as if I did too many squats and when I wiggle in my seat, I can feel where two men have been.

I need to go home. I want my bed, a shower, maybe some food. My stomach coils at the mention of food, and I belch. Maybe we will wait on food.

Turning from the parking lot, I drive the long journey home, ready for my walk of shame.

Mac

Riding my motorcycle down the freeway, lights flash behind me. I'm not speeding, so what the fuck? Glancing in my rearview I spot a police car right behind me. My brows furrow. It's odd for me to get pulled over, I'm a Sin City Outlaw, and nobody pulls us over because everyone is in our club's pocket. Including the police department.

I pull over to the shoulder, curious what is going on. Turning my motorcycle off, I balance my bike with my feet, and pull a cigarette from the pack, placing it between my teeth. Black shiny shoes stomp onto the pavement as a big burly man heads my way. He tugs on his utility belt, his huge belly pushing it back down.

HIS EYES SCAN the back of my bike before slowly sizing me up. It's like a fucking staring contest.

"YOU MAC?" he finally asks, his double chin jiggling. I could totally make a run for it, he'd never catch me. Unless he has a canine... I glance at his car but can't tell if he's a canine unit or not.

I SCOWL AT THE PIG.

"YEAH, why'd you pull me over?" Tilting my head to the side, I raise my hand to block the sun from my eyes.

THE COP REACHES OVER, clutching me by the elbow tugging me from my bike.
"You're under arrest."
My cigarette falls to the ground as I jerk my hands, my foot kicking the kickstand down before my bike falls to the ground.
"What the fuck for!"
"Shut up!" He jerks me off the bike and slams me onto the hood of his car, the metal hot against my face.
"You're really going to fucking regret this," I grit as he slaps cuffs on my wrists. The metal biting into the skin of my wrist.
Grunting, he pulls me off the hood and shoves me toward the

back of his car. Opening the door, he throws me inside. I fall sideways into the back seat. Using my feet, I push myself onto my ass as the big man climbs behind the wheel.

"You going to tell me what the fuck I did?" With every harsh breath, my hair blows from my face.

He ignores me, quietly talking into his radio. Sirens on now, he pulls off the side of the road, and my heart skips a beat.

"I can't just leave my bike like that, someone's going to fucking steal it." Looking over my shoulder, we get farther and farther away from it. This asshole doesn't care if it gets stolen and will cover his tracks to hold no responsibility if it does.

"You stupid fuck!" I slam my head against the plexiglass, angry and unrestrained.

He glances in the rearview mirror, worry wrinkling his forehead for a brief second before he focuses back on the road.

"You better hope my boys don't catch you before we make it to the station." Warning growling in my voice.

We don't get pulled over, and when we do... whoever is doing the arresting won't be arresting anybody any time soon after we're done with them. We are the Outlaws of Vegas. We make the law and dish out the repercussions. It's always been like that, and it'll never change. This fucker is going to figure that out when I'm done.

The short ride to the station does nothing to ease my anger. As soon as the cop opens my door, I throw myself sideways and strike my boot right into his chest. He stumbles backward; the fat fuck.

I shuffle out of the car, ready to fight this pig handcuffed.

"You little son of a bitch." He reaches for his Taser and I tense, readying myself for the volts to race through my body.

"THAT'S ENOUGH, GRUNDY," a female voice commands from behind us. Turning my head, a tall woman in a dark blue pantsuit, dark hair spilling over her chest, stares at us with her hands on her hips. She's hot, but a fucking cop nonetheless.

"THIS MOTHERFUCKER ARRESTED me without reading me my rights!" I inform her. Her face bored, she saunters over to me and gently holds me by the cuffs.

"THIS WAY." The words fall from her mouth like silk, but if I know anything about her kind... it's poison.

MARCHING THROUGH THE STATION, she takes me right to her office. Clean and smelling of strong coffee. She points to a gray chair sitting in front of her pristine desk and shuts the door behind us.

I SIT, but with my hands cuffed behind me, it's not very comfortable. I'm more lopsided.

"YOU WANNA TELL me what's going on?" I raise a brow. She starts rolling down the blinds to each of her office windows, keeping wondering eyes from snooping in.

"Do you remember July 7th of this year?" she fishes. I bite my bottom lip, thinking back. That's the day we had to fetch money for the mafia, playing errand boys. Machete got carried away and beat the fuck out of a casino security guard. Taking orders from the mafia isn't our forte.

"I DON'T KNOW what you're talking about." I look at the floor, acting aloof. Like I'm going to tell her anything, she's fucking dumb for a lieutenant,

"OH, NO?" She grabs the remote off her desk, flipping on the TV sitting on the shelves behind her. There it is, all in black and white. The Sin City Outlaws shaking down the casino bosses at Fimingway, and Machete beating the daylights out of a man who thought he was going to save the day with a pistol. I knew steps had to be taken, so then you see me walking into the main office taking tapes from the recorders. Looks like I forgot one, though. Fuck!

I hang my head.

SHE CLICKS the TV off and sashays to the front of her desk. She slowly slips her pretty little ass on the lip of it, her heels resting right in between my legs on the chair.

SHE SLIPS a piece of paper off her desk and holds it up in front of me.

"DO YOU RECOGNIZE THIS TATTOO?" It's an eagle with fire wings.

It's the insignia of a new upcoming gang on the lower east side. Pests if anything, they won't last long.

"Why?" Taking my eyes from the image to her, I fish in return.

"You know who it belongs to don't you?" her perfect brows raise, her lips pursed.

I look away and scoff. "I'm not a rat, babe."

HER HEEL between my legs casually slides farther up, nudging my balls. I can't tell if it's a threat or seduction.

"I'LL TELL YOU WHAT, you tell me who this belongs to, and I will make this tape disappear."

I GLARE IN HER DIRECTION. "You're in our pockets, you should make it disappear anyways!" My voice raising. We have a deal with these fuckers, we leave them alone, they leave us alone.

"THIS FUCKER RAPED a little girl who is now in the hospital. I can't find this tattoo in our database, and nobody is speaking on the streets. Tell me who it is, and I will scratch your back further than you can imagine, Mac." Her voice becomes sultry, the tip of her heel caressing my jean-clad cock.

I SMIRK. She wants my dick. Normally I'd make her beg, but the vile piece of shit who likes to rape little girls needs off the streets, and I don't see helping Lieutenant Lopez in doing that as ratting. More of a good deed for my city, which I haven't done in a while. I'm overdue.

"IT'S THE STARLING GANG. They just started up down south of the state. That's all you get," I bite my bottom lip, my eyes wandering over her tight body. Curiosity beads at the tip of my dick. I wonder if her nipples are pierced, or if she has a tramp stamp beneath that superior act.

SHE SMILES. "SEE, EASY AS THAT." She tosses the photo over her shoulder and slides into my lap. Her hands on each side of my face she kisses me hard. Not just a kiss that you'd present any one-night stand, but one as if she's wanted to kiss me for far too long. It's desperate, reeking of attraction.

I'M curious what she fucks like, and what's beneath this act of hers... so I kiss her back, her mouth surprisingly tasting of whiskey.

"Drinking on the job? You're more twisted than I thought, Lieutenant."

"Shut up!" She slaps me across the face, my face contorting into shock. Pain blooms across my cheek, but my cock throbs with excitement. I did not see that coming... Her dark eyes stare at mine, and within seconds our mouths clash against each other again, our breaths labored and bodies anxious. The chair flips over, but she doesn't stop. She unbuttons my jeans and pulls my cock out like she's unwrapping a birthday gift.

HER EYES LIFT to mine when she spots the barbell. I jut my chin out, summoning her to either ride it or get the fuck off. I got shit to do. Fisting my cock, her hand is cold like a nurse's, but that doesn't affect me in the least.

SHE DROPS her pants to her ankles, kicking a leg free from the material, her silky hand pushes me inside of her. Wet heat surrounds me as her body weight falls onto my hips, and the damn cuffs cut into my wrists. Her head lolls back, her heat slick and somewhat tight. I need to remember to get checked after this, who knows where this bitch has been.

USING HER LEGS, she pumps herself up and down. Her shirt hiding any glimpse of her sex. I wonder if she's shaved, or as hairy as cousin IT. She takes pleasure from me as I'm restrained and stuck in a shitty chair that scoots across the floor with every thrust. She's a bad bitch, obviously used to getting what she wants. Some might find it sexy, I find it desperate. She's a dirty little shit.

MY BALLS STRAIN WITH PRESSURE, the sliding in and out of her pussy pushing me to climax. She bites down on her bottom lip, her body tensing as she comes on my cock, and I come seconds later. It's not strong, or eye roll worthy, but busting a load is busting a nut. Her eyes open, a devilish smile spreading across her face. She stands, pulling her pants back up.

OUT OF BREATH, she steps behind me, the cuffs shuffling on my wrists as she undoes them. As soon as they're released I sigh with relief. I pull my hands to where I can see them, and purple rings mar my skin, my fingers throbbing from the lack of blood flow.

Not wasting any time, I jerk my jeans up and button them, ready to get the fuck out of here.

She looks at the photo on her desk with pointed eyes, her brows furrowed.

"I'll be in touch Mac! Grundy, he's ready!" she calls to her little piggy.

I'm dumbfounded. This bitch has some nerve to fuck me like a toy and throw me out. I'm not sure if I find it sexy, or completely slutty. Then again, I am an Outlaw. This is as good as it gets for me. Dirty sex on in a stained chair with a bitch who probably fucked her way to the top.

Fat man Grundy walks in, placing his hand on my shoulder. I flinch, not liking to be touched.

"Get your greasy fucking hands off me." I point at him. "Let me catch you on the streets out of uniform," I threaten. Grundy swallows, looking to the lieutenant for back up, but she's too lost in the photo of the tattoo to say anything.

I run my hands through my hair and crack my neck. Not taking my eyes off him.

"LATER LIEUTENANT."

WALKING through the station every turn the other way, avoiding eye contact. Pressing my hand on the glass, leaving a smeared print behind, I step outside to find my brothers ready to rampage the place, and my bobber parked and waiting for me. I chuckle, my right hand rubbing the scruff on my cheeks.

MY PRESIDENT, Zeek, stands next to his bike, his hands in his black jeans that match his dark hair.

Felix, our vice president, straddling his bike while he puts his hair up, ready to fight.

Machete, the animal of the pack, picking his teeth with his Machete casually as he leans over the gas tank of his motorcycle.

THIS IS MY FAMILY. I'm in the station for less than twenty minutes and my men are here without me having to say a word. It was probably one of the cops deep in our pockets that called them, informed them I was brought in. Still, for them to have my back without knowing what the hell I might have done. That's fucking loyalty.

"I TOOK CARE OF IT BOYS," I inform stepping down the stairs of the station.

"YOU SURE?" My president Zeek give me a concerned look.

Straddling my bike, I smile in his direction.

"SHE WANTED THE STARLING GANG, and in exchange, I got some pussy, and a tape I forgot at the casino the night Machete went cowboy." I give Machete a sideways glance. He shrugs, and Felix laughs.

"How was the pussy?" Zeek smirks, climbing on his bike.

I GRAB a cigarette and place it between my teeth.

"I WOULDN'T BRING her home to Momma anytime soon, but you know me, I don't turn down pussy," I chuckle.

THE BOYS LAUGH, and we all start our motorcycles, following Zeek back to the club.

5
___

SIMONE

"Simone!" My mother gasps in horror as I walk through the front door. I tried to wipe up as much smeared makeup as I could in the car, but there wasn't much hope for the mess that I am this morning. "Where have you been?" she snaps, but I ignore her and head up the marble stairs to my bedroom. She follows, the click of her heels drilling into my head.

"Please tell me you didn't do what I think you did?" she whispers.

"Depends, what do you think I did? I did a lot last night," I laugh, and then wince. Everything hurts.

Walking into my room, I head straight to the bathroom. Pulling off the itchy dress I step out of it and turn the shower on. Resting my head on the tiled wall, I realize I forgot my lingerie at the hotel. Oh well, it's not like I'll be needing it anytime soon.

Mother flurries into my bathroom, her long braid swishing

between her shoulder blades, and her red gown flowing behind her.

SHE SHUTS the door behind her, worry wrinkling her face when she looks in my direction. My being naked not affecting her at all.

"CAN THIS PLEASE WAIT," I beg. I just need some sleep, Advil, and for her to go away.

Her eyes widen to saucers, her hand coming to her mouth to stifle a gasp.

GAZING into the mirror to see what has her in such a horror, I spot a hickey on my collarbone. It's very light, but definitely a hickey.

I turn away from her and rest my hand on my shoulder. My arm covering it.

"IF YOU," she hesitates. "If you gave yourself to another man last night thinking it would make this whole thing with Veer go away, you were very VERY wrong!" she snaps, her eyes filling with tears. My heart skips a beat, worry stabbing me in the chest.

"WHY?" I face her head-on, not caring what she sees.

"VEER HAS TOLD everyone in the last twenty-four hours he is to marry you. He has a wedding coordinator coming to organize everything you desire for the perfect wedding. Simone, if you make a fool of him... he will kill you and your father for setting him up for a false arrangement."

I LOOK AT THE FLOOR, not thinking about the fact Veer would retaliate in such a way. I figured I would take the virginity out of the cards and he would move on to a new woman. How naïve of me.

"OH GOD, you did, didn't you? You went out there and- and laid with another man—" She begins to cry, not helping my anxiety.

"MOM!" I snap at her, and she flinches. I slept with two men actually, but I don't tell her that. She'd likely have a heart attack. It's still taking me time to wrap my head around what the hell I did last night. "I'll figure something out. I always do, right?" My question is weak, and Mother and I know it. Her lips stretching into a fine line, and she nods to me. I have no idea how to fix this. I gave something away I cannot get back.

TURNING my back to her I step into the warm water cascading from the showerhead. She pulls the curtain closed and leans against the wall next to the shower.

"I'm sorry," she whispers. The sound of the water hitting the floor of the shower muffles her words. "I know Veer is not the man for you, but we are blessed with many things, Simone, and having an arranged marriage isn't the worst." The way she says the words, I can tell she doesn't mean it. It sounds like something my father would say.

I scoff at her attempt to lecture something she has no idea of.

"That's easy for you to say."

"Your father wasn't my first choice either, it was arranged," she informs. The warm water hitting my back suddenly feels cold at the news.

I pull the curtain open to look at her, this is the first I've heard of this.

"What?"

She smiles fondly. "I hated your father when I met him. He was so arrogant, and bossy. Telling me how we were going to get married, that I was moving in with him and leaving my family. It wasn't until I had you that I really fell in love with him. He was so nurturing and caring. Our stubborn walls broke down over time, and we saw each other for who we really were." Her face glows as she recalls her and Dad's past.

WET HAIR IN MY FACE, I look at my mother in a whole different way. I don't know if she's strong or brave for living with a man she hated.

Lifting her head, shoulders back, she shakes her head.

"Don't be a fool, Simone. You're very stubborn, and your worst enemy at times. I fear I can't save you this time, my dear." She shakes her head and walks out of the bathroom with streams of tears down her tanned cheeks.

STEPPING BACK INTO THE WATER, I close my eyes. My heart beating with fear that I may be killed by my future husband. That I took things into my hands and killed my own life in the process. It's a never-ending domino effect. I fucked everything up.

I SLAP AT THE TILE, screaming as I throw hair products across the shower.

6

4 WEEKS LATER

Sitting at my desk, I glance across all the bridal magazines that Veer had his wedding coordinator flash in my face the last few days. The women are so skinny and smiling it makes me angry. Don't any of these women have hips? Dresses range from white to red, fluffy and lacy to modern and sleek. So many choices it gives me an instant headache.

I should get black as I'm mourning my life away the day I marry this prick.

I RUB AT MY TEMPLES, not sure what to do about this whole thing. I feel like crap, I have been for over a week now and my head hurts, I'm bloated, and am so freaking tired I can't even think of a way out of this mess.

"So, did you look at the swatches?"

MY EYES slowly drift from the desk to Kel. His hair is blonde and short, his chin sharp and face flawless. It's like he walks around with a Snapchat filter on his face it's so smooth.

He's skinny, pulling off his black spandex shirt and skinny jeans better than a model. Kel was hired by Veer to help me plan everything for the wedding while he's away for work and I haven't been very cooperative because this wedding isn't happening if I ever figure out how to get out of it without hurting anyone.

KEL SASHAYS INTO THE ROOM, and tosses the swatches in my lap, once again.

I thought I threw those away.

"Kel, I told you I'd get to it," I huff, throwing them on the desk and out of my sight. Again.

"VEER WANTS COLORS, SIMONE. TODAY!" Kel crosses his arms and looks at me pointedly.

THE LITTLE VEIN in my neck begins to throb and the words of "there isn't going to be a wedding" hangs from the tip of my tongue. Not looking, I snatch the wad of colors and hand him one.

IT'S BLACK. How fitting that fate should pick the color I was just thinking of. If Veer does get his way and this wedding happens, it will be over my dead body. A wedding and funeral in the same day.

"YOU WANT THE COLOR BLACK? Don't you think that's a little, I don't know... morbid?" He frowns, his fingers pinching the swatch like a splash of color is hidden between the threads.

"No," I sigh, leaning back in my chair. "It's perfect."

I yawn, not bothering to cover my mouth. "God, why am I so exhausted," I exhale.

"What flowers do you want?" he looks at me with excited eyes. "Roses? Tulips?"

"What kind are sent to funerals?" I deadpan.

Kel purses his lips and snatches the swatches off the desk. "I will just pick everything for you," he huffs. I shrug. Apparently, this isn't his first wedding where one of the participants... doesn't want to participate in a wedding because Kel has been organizing everything. I could care less about it all.

"How is it going?" I sit upward at the sound of my mother's voice entering the room. My chair creaking from the sudden movement.

Kel growls dramatically in response and hustles out of the room.

Mom closes the door after Kel leaves and raises a curious brow. Standing at the other end of my desk, she eyes me quietly.

"What?" I finally ask. I hate it when she does that. She's done it since I was a child. She'd stand there with wide eyes waiting for me to fess up to what I was up to. It's like a superpower.

"WHAT'S WITH YOU, Simone? You seem tired all of the time, you're distracted—"

"IT DOESN'T HELP Dad stuck me in here." I wave my hands around the office. "I should be out there doing what I normally do. I mean, who is going to approve percentages, and make sure payouts are on time?" I shake my head. These gangs and outlaws are not going to pay what they owe if someone isn't on their ass.

"YOU NEED to focus on the wedding," she defends. "Working time is over, you've learned enough. Besides, wives don't work."

"THERE IS NOT GOING to be a wedding," I growl under my breath, shaking my head. I wish my mother would stop pushing and help me figure a way out of this.

I'm independent, on the top of my game. Being with Veer, I'll only live in his shadows.

MOM SLOWLY PACES in her blue and gold sequin pantsuit. She places her hands on the tip of my desk and looks at me sternly.

"You need to wrap your head around this one, sweetie, it's happening."

I JUST LOOK AT HER, my eyes conveying everything I've said a million times. I'm intelligent, I outsmart outlaws and thugs every day. So why can't I figure my way out of this one?

"ARE THOSE... SWEATPANTS?" Her eyes fall to my lap. Squirming in my gray comfy sweats, I slide myself a little more under the desk.

"I HAVEN'T BEEN FEELING WELL." I brush my hair from my face. "I'm hot, I feel sick, but I am hungry at the same time, and I just – I just want sleep." I groan like a teenager, my hands raised in the air and strained.

MOM'S FACE pales like she's seen a ghost. It scares me.

"WHAT?" I frown. Her throat bobs, and she shakes her head before silently leaving.
    "Mom?!"
    Angry with her aloofness, I shove myself away from the desk. I'm done sitting in this damn chair for the day. It's not like I'm working anyways.

I HEAD to my room and tuck myself into of my thick comforter before falling asleep.

———

THE DOOR SUDDENLY SWINGS OPEN, and I fling upwards. The room is blurry, my eyes squinting in the direction of the noise.

Mom is standing in the doorway with a doctor we've seen inside the house from time to time. He's more of an herbal healer than man-made medicine. His hair is long and down to his waist, his white shirt buttoned and tucked into his black slacks.

"Dr. Moore?"

He steps to me and doesn't say anything. Raising his hand, he holds a small clear cup.

"Pee," he clips.

I glance at my mother who is standing behind him, her face ashen.

"What the hell is this?"

"Do it, Simone. It's important." Her face serious, and body tense.

Sliding out of bed, I snatch the cup from him, and I head to my bathroom. Sitting down on the toilet, I angle the cup under me and pee in the cup half asleep. Placing the cup on the counter, I wipe and saunter back into my room.

"It's all yours," I state sarcastically.

Dr. Moore doesn't say anything, he struts inside the bathroom with his black bag thrown over his shoulder.

"You want to tell me what is going on?" I cross my arms and tilt my head to the side. My mother purses her lips and lifts her chin but stays silent.

"Do you think I'm on drugs or something?" I half laugh, my stomach falls when it occurs to me I did cocaine that one night. Would that show up?

MINUTES LATER DR. MOORE walks out of my bathroom and sighs.

"WHAT IS IT, DOCTOR," Mother begs, her hands pressed together.

LIFTING HIS HEAD, he blinks a few times before finally speaking.

"SIMONE, you're with child. I recommend—"
"That can't be right," I interrupt him. My stomach suddenly tightens, and my heart stammers for its rhythm in my chest.

"MY TESTS ARE NEVER WRONG," he corrects in an offended manner. I'm stunned, not sure what to say next.

MOTHER PULLS out a 9-millimeter from her waistband and pulls the trigger, drilling a bullet right into the skull of our doctor. He slumps to the floor lifeless, skull and brain matter painting the wall behind him.

I STAND FROM THE BED, my mouth gaping open with a scream

trapped in my throat. The room smells of flesh and blood, and I puke all over the floor.

"I CAN'T RISK him having him tell someone," Mother states with a strong tone.

Wiping my mouth with the back of my hand, my breathing labored I can't help but look at the man who has was been here to help me with the flu as a child. Nursed my mother back to health when she had a tumor removed. He's been here since I can remember, and now he's dead on my bedroom floor next to a pile of puke.

MOM TURNS ON A SHAKY FOOT, her eyes quivering as they fall to my belly. I look down with her, the very thought that I am pregnant not registering. They wore condoms, how can this be?

Turning away, I rest my hand on my forehead and try to remember that night, but it's all a fucking blur.

"WHO'S THE FATHER?"

"I- I don't know?" My voice strains.

"WHAT DO YOU MEAN, you don't know!"

"I WAS with two men that night, Mom! The baby could be either of theirs!"

HER FACE DOESN'T cast judgment, and it doesn't show anger either. It wrinkles with worry.

"RUN." My mother's words a mere whisper.

"WHAT?" Tears run down my face, the dominos of my actions continuing to fall.

"RUN SIMONE! Run to one of the men. If Veer finds out you are pregnant, he will kill you and that baby." Her tone of voice is grave and solemn, making me suddenly frightened.

"I CAN'T LEAVE YOU. If I do, Veer will just kill you and father. This is my fault, I have to stay." I explain, but I don't know any other way out of this. I have played and plotted every scenario on how to escape this marriage and I end up dead no matter what.

MOM ERASES the gap between us, placing a shaky hand on my flat stomach. To think a life resides inside of me is startling. "If you stay, your stubbornness will kill your baby. Your father and I will be fine, now go!"

"I don't know how this could have—" I lose my breath, shock overtaking my brain.

"IT'S what the Great Spirit wanted, or it wouldn't have happened, Simone." She resorts to her religion as an excuse as to why I'm pregnant. The Great Spirit is a deity that guides us in our everyday, and often intervenes in our everyday. Mother uses it as an excuse for everything. Father is a Christian and belies everything happens because it's God's plan.

AS FOR ME, I don't know what to believe in.

"Mother—" I begin to protest her belief. Both of her hands grasp each of my shoulders, her face inches from mine.

"Grab the keys to the Range Rover, it hasn't been bugged. Run, and never look back, baby."

One hand cups the side of my face, her soft warm skin parental and endearing.

"DO IT FOR THE BABY," she whispers, encouraging me to run.

"OKAY, MOMMA." I give in, because I don't want to marry Veer, and I don't want to die either. I have to run, even if it makes me feel like a coward.

SHE PULLS me close and kisses my forehead. Her lips press against my clammy skin for a second longer than normal. The power and silent love behind the action tearing me apart inside.

"SO WHEN LIFE FADES, as the fading sunset, my spirit may come to you without shame," she recites parts of the Great Spirit Prayer against my skin. "Go. Go!" She waves me off, and I rush out of the room, and down the stairs. My feet pitter patter past the family motto etched into the floor. "All that I am, I carry with me."

I IGNORE it and hurry into the garage to the new Range Rover. Climbing into the leather seat, I start the engine with a shaky hand, my heart beating so fast I don't hear the engine turn over.

PULLING OUT OF THE DRIVEWAY, I look in the rearview mirror at the mansion, leaving behind the only family I have. The only life I've ever known and may never see again.

SHIT, I can't remember the club Gatz was in. Pulling my phone out, I google Devil's Dust Club, the one Kane's was in. Praying something pops up.

IT SHOWS CHARITY DONATIONS, pictures of parties, and then there's a Facebook tag. I stop, clicking on the map. Looks like a groupie or something Facebooked about being at the club and tagged the location. Thank God.

CLEARING THE HISTORY, I toss the phone out the window and head in the direction of the Devil's Den.

7

SIMONE

That's it, that is the Devil's Dust clubhouse. It doesn't look seedy or Illicit in the least bit but you can feel the power from just sitting across the way. Inside those walls conceals some of the most wanted criminals in L.A.

I blow out a steady breath and look across the parking lot at different colored motorcycles lined up next to each other. I've recited what I'm going to say to Kane over and over, but now that I'm here, I can't remember a single word. I remember how brooding he was before, I can only imagine what his reaction will be when I tell him I'm pregnant.

Turning the Range Rover off, I climb out of the seat and walk across the yard. My arms crossed, and hair blowing in the California air. Just as I'm headed to the front door of the club, I catch a glimpse of Kane hunched down by a motorcycle, wrench in hand. I pause, looking his way. He's wearing just a leather cut with nothing underneath, and light washed blue jeans. The hot sun kisses his tanned arms, and beads sweat across his wide chest.

"KANE?" He looks my way, his hand twisting away at the bolts on the engine. When his eyes meet mine, they widen. He stands, dropping the tool to the ground. He's not happy to see me.

LOOKING over my shoulder I head his way. He's still as sexy as I remember. Tall, dark, and brooding.

"WHAT THE HELL are you doing here?" he snaps. His eyes trail up and down my body, my sweats and baggy shirt different than the first time we met.

"I- I need your help, Kane." I uncross my arms and look up to him. Who knew asking for help would taste so sour?

"You want money or something?" He throws his arms out, eager to give me anything to get off the club property.

"WHAT? No, I don't want money. I need protection." My voice rises, the fact he's asking me if I need money is insulting.

He shakes his head with a half chuckle. "No, this isn't a charity house. You were a one-night stand, nothing else, sweetheart." He turns around dismissing me, brushing his nose with the flick of his thumb. Anger and worry swirl in my chest like fire and wind. I want to lash out, but I need him to protect me and the baby.

"I'm pregnant!" I blurt loudly enough for him to hear. He stops, his boots scoffing against the ground.

"What'd you say?" Glancing over his shoulder his face wrinkles with panic.

I CLEAR my throat and lift my chin with confidence.
"I'm pregnant, and the baby and I need a place to stay."
"How the hell are you fucking pregnant?"
"Good question?" Sarcasm coils in my throat. I was hoping he'd confess his condom broke or something.

"FUCK," he whispers. Nibbling on his bottom lip deep in thought, he places both of his hands behind his neck.
"If you want me to go, I'll leave. I just need Gatz's address." Shaking my head, irritated I can't even look at Kane. I should have known he would be just as arrogant as the night I met him.
"No. Just- just wait here, while I give Gatz a call and figure this shit out."

HIS SUDDEN CHANGE of tone has me do a double take. I can't help but think he just doesn't want me to go to Gatz. Jealousy practically pours from his smug face.

I NOD and stand next to his bike. He steps off into the middle of the parking lot and pulls out his phone. He's talking to Gatz, but I can't tell what he's saying. Maybe I should just go. Kane obviously doesn't want me here.

STARTING TOWARD MY CAR, Kane suddenly grabs my wrist, stopping me.

"Wait." My eyes trail from his tight grip on my skin to his heated eyes. "Gatz and his club are in some shit, so you're going to stay with me temporarily. I will set you up in a hotel or something, but if anyone asks, you're my sister."

"Sister?" My nose wrinkles at the word.

"Family means more to my club than some chick knocked up."

I nod, understanding that. They probably have lots of girls popping up claiming they're pregnant. "You said you need protection, what kind of trouble are you in?" He crosses his arms, tilting his head sideways.

I explain everything the best I can. Veer, the arrangement, me getting pregnant, and the whole time Kane just stands there with his arms crossed, eyes focused on me.

He sighs, dropping his arms when I'm done telling my story. Silence between us deafening.

"So, you used me and Gatz to prove a point to your family?" His eyes squint in my direction.

"Yeah." I shrug, feeling like this is all my fault, I get defensive. "And you guys used me as a birthday gift and now I'm fucking pregnant." He glares at me in return. "Your act of superiority can drop any time now." Yelling, I point at him.

We stare each other down, trying to size the other up. The night we met seemed so long ago and happened so fast, we were nothing but strangers. But, if he thought I was just going to play pregnant bimbo, he was very wrong. We were all fucked up that night and were grown ass adults when we made the decisions to fuck around with each other.

HIS EYES NARROW in on my vehicle behind me.

"WE NEED to chop that Range Rover up. You will listen to me while with me, and if at any time you don't fucking listen. You're out," he points at me. Him talking down to me is getting old. Fast.

"YOU KNOW, this could be your baby inside of me," I inform matter of fact, hearing myself saying 'baby inside of me' sounds misplaced. This whole thing hasn't hit me fully.

HIS FACE PALES as if he didn't think about that, but just as it softens it hardens again.
    "Yeah, and I never asked you to keep it either."

MY EYES WIDEN, my teeth gritting. The option to have an abortion never crossed my mind.
    I look to the ground, playing in my head if that's something I want.
    This child wasn't planned, but it has my DNA in it. My family's blood. My mother is risking her life for me to save this baby, I can't let that go in vain.

SWALLOWING HARD, I look up. My nostrils flaring.

"And I'm not here asking you or your biker boyfriend to play daddy!"

IN ONE LARGE STEP, our feet are nearly touching, my face to his chest.

"Keep your fucking voice down." He hisses with a scared face, apparently his club doesn't know he likes to swing with women and men. I take a step back, not intimidated by him. I deal with his kind all the time. More often than not, their bark is bigger than their bite.

"THIS IS A BIG LIFE CHANGE, and it's scary. Believe me, I know." My voice wavers with so much emotion I choke. "But turning your back on us will be the scariest thing in *your* life because you'll regret it if we get hurt." I poke him in the chest, and he sighs heavily. His hard eyes fall to my stomach and soften for the first time since I stepped out of my car. I think we finally see eye to eye.

"GET IN MY TRUCK, I'll deal with your car later." He points to a red truck parked beside the club, and we both head that direction.

CLIMBING INSIDE, he starts it, his eyes narrowing in at my torso. Clearing my throat, I buckle my seatbelt and look out the window. I feel vulnerable, and I hate it. This baby is already changing so much, and I've only been aware of it for a day.

KANE DRIVES me to the same hotel Gatz and us stayed in that night. It still holds that country taste and is even nicer looking in the sunlight.

PULLING up to the main office, Kane parks causing us to rock to a hard stop.

"Stay in the truck while I check you in," he states. The truck rocks back and forth as he climbs out.

TUCKING HAIR BEHIND MY EAR, I look the place over, flashbacks of the night before whipping in and out of memory. I wish I could remember more than I do. Maybe then I would know whose child this is. Pressing my hand to my stomach, it's still flat and seems illogical to be carrying a child inside of me. Kane steps out of the front office, and I look up. He waves me on, a key in his hand.

GETTING OUT, I follow him to room 7. Once inside, the room smells clean, the bedsheets made, and towels in perfect place. It's as if nothing ever happened in this room weeks ago. There's no residue of coke on the dresser, the smell of sex in the air replaced with air freshener.

STIFLING A YAWN, I sit down on the bed, looking to Kane for what's next.

"YOU'LL STAY HERE while I'm out doing club shit. I'll bring back some food and crap when I can—"

"By myself?" The edge to his sudden laugh, answers that question. "So, I'm just supposed to stay here and do what?" My brows raise to my hairline.

"Watch TV, read, do whatever it is you do, just don't let anyone see you." Noticing I'm not happy with my accommodations her scoffs. "Do you want my protection or not?" His controlled tone of voice and shifting of his feet make me aware of my attitude. Taking a calming breath, I look away from him.

I'm not unappreciative, it's just not what I imagined when he agreed to protect me. I thought I'd be in the clubhouse with him, or at least tucked away in a nice safe house or something.

"How long am I staying in this room?" My fingers mindlessly fiddle with the loose string hanging from my pants, trying to distract myself from this piss poor situation.

"Until you can go to Gatz. Fuck!" he booms irritated, slamming the door behind him.

Jumping to my feet, my nostrils flaring I jerk the curtain to the side to watch him drive away.

"That asshole!" I kick the wall, my eyes threatening to spill warm tears.

I'm not staying here, fuck him!

A phone rings from the corner, and I turn around. My eyes narrow in on a black phone on the floor.

GLANCING at the window to see if Kane has noticed it missing, I rush to it and find Gatz's name across the screen.

"HELLO?"

"HELLO? SIMONE?" His light-hearted voice grounds me, telling me everything is going to be okay.

"THIS – THIS IS HER." I cross my arms, tucking my bottom lip in between my teeth.

"OH. WOW." He chuckles. I can hear the nervousness in his voice.

"HEY TO YOU TOO."

"SORRY, this is just—ya know... different," he exhales.
    "Tell me about it." Anxiety laces around every word.
    "Kane set you up okay?"

RAISING A BROW, I look around the hotel room.
    "I'm in a hotel room, but Kane isn't here," I explain, leaving out the part where Kane was a complete shit.

"STAY IN THAT ROOM, babe. From what Kane told me, it's safer this way."

A tear spills from my right eye, I don't want to be locked in a room and forgotten.

"HE SAID I'm coming to be with you soon?"

"YES, that's the plan. I want to get a place, maybe even a baby room set up." A smile creeps along my face, one that hasn't been in place for a long time. I can endure this shitty setup if I know there's light at the end of the tunnel.

THE DOOR to the room opens, and Kane stands in the doorway looking like the reaper. His shoulders wide, arms bowed out, and face hard. I freeze. Gatz is talking, but I can't hear anything from the fear pounding in my neck.

"THAT MY PHONE?" Kane lifts his chin.

"IT'S GATZ." I shrug, trying to act unaffected. Stomping toward me, he snatches the phone from my hand and clicks it off. Not even bothering to talk to Gatz.

He looks at me with a heated stare, and if I didn't know any better, I'd say he's almost jealous I was talking to Gatz.

"WHAT IS YOUR PROBLEM?" I snap.

"You," he deadpans. "Gatz and I were fine until you walked

into our lives," he mumbles. Blinking slowly, my mouth parts.

"I'M NOT—"

"JUST STAY in the fucking room. You don't like the rules, then fucking leave!" he bellows, the flower painted picture raddling on the wall from his harsh voice. I'm sure the entire motel is aware of mine and Kane's arrival.

"FUCK YOU, I'm out of here!" I shove him, and head toward the open door. As soon as my foot reaches the threshold, I'm jerked back into the room, and the door is slammed in front of my face.

I TURN around ready to give Kane everything I have, and he slams his fist against the door right behind my head. I jerk and hiccup a mousey whimper. Taking a step back, my back pressed against the door.

"LOOK, for some reason you mean something to Gatz." His eyes fall to my belly. "Or this baby does, and I'm not going to lose him because of you wanting to be a snobby little bitch."

MY NOSTRILS FLARE, and before I can correct myself, I slap him across the face.
     His head doesn't even budge. You wouldn't even know I hit him if it weren't for the slight pink staining his cheek.

He takes a deep breath, his eyes dilating. "Just... let's just try and get along, for Gatz's sake," he growls.

"Then stay away from me," I sneer.

"You weren't saying that when my dick was fucking you into forgetting your problems," his voice serious. My hand itches to smack him again, but instead, I cross my arms and roll my eyes.

I know this situation isn't ideal for either of us, but we both seem to care about Gatz, and that alone makes me want to make this work. Besides, I don't have much of a choice if I want to protect this baby. My baby. My chest warms at that thought. My baby. I'm a mom now, and I have to rein in my hormones for the both of us.

"Just bring me back some chocolate." Sidestepping him I make my way back to the bed, I'm exhausted.

"I can do that," he grunts, jerking the door open.

Plopping on the bed, I grab the remote for the TV and settle in for the journey that's going to have Kane and I clashing teeth and breathing fire.

8

6 MONTHS LATER

The creakiness of the wheels from the cleaner cart, have me bolt upright and look at the clock. It's nine in the morning. Shit, Kane is late leaving today. Kane steps out of the bathroom freshly showered and grabs his motorcycle keys off the counter.

"YOU KNOW THE RULES," he mutters, and I roll my eyes. Stay inside, and don't let anyone see me. Same shit, different day. I'm a damn hermit staying locked in this room as long as I have.

"It's been six months, when do I get to go to Gatz?" I huff, my big belly making it hard for me to sit up all the way.

Kane shoots me a look; his eyes fall to my stomach as he steps out the door. The way he looks at my belly makes me uncomfortable. He doesn't want anything to do with the baby and leaves anytime I talk about feeling the baby move, or what sex it might be. I went on a run with him and his club shortly after I got here, only because he had no choice but to bring me along. He called me his sister, and I was hidden in another hotel. As soon as we got back here, I was shoved back in this hotel, never to be seen again. I haven't even seen a doctor about the pregnancy. I haven't told Gatz that last part yet. I know as soon as he picks me up, I will be in good hands. Whenever that will be.

GATZ IS like Narnia or Santa. I believe and hope I'm going to be sent to him, but the reality of it being true is starting to be questioned. If it wasn't for the one time he actually came here and I got to see him briefly, I'd call Kane a liar all together and leave.

SITTING ON THE BED, the door opens, the sound of deep voices echoing through the room. I sit up, curious if Kane brought one of his club members to the hotel. I could use some interaction with actual people. I'm so lonely it's pathetic.

Kane struts in, his face lit up more than I've seen in months.

"I found a stray," Kane said nicely, and then Gatz walked in behind him. His dark hair perfectly in place, his white shirt tight and snug under his cut. My eyes lit up. He's here for me, finally!

"Gatz!" I jumped up off the bed and hurried to his side. I couldn't help myself, I swung my arms around his neck and pulled him close. He was hard but smaller than Kane. The smell of his cologne, grounding me. He's just like I remember, soft and hard where it counts.

"Am I coming with you?" I pulled away from him, and his deep eyes darkened.

"Not yet." His eyes fell to my belly, and before I could register my sadness that I'm not going with him, I became elated that he was acknowledging the baby. "Can I?" He held his hand out, and I nodded. Kane never asked to feel my stomach.

He kneeled in front of me and very gently placed his hand on the round of my growing four-month belly. I look down at my now six-month-old belly. It grew fast.

"Can you feel it yet?" he asked. "Yeah, but it feels like butterflies," I replied with a huge smile.

"IT'S UNBELIEVABLE," *he whispered in astonishment before glancing up at Kane. Kane was hard in the face, his eyes dark and shoulders tense. He wasn't happy anymore.*

Gatz removed his caring palm and stood up, clearing his throat.

"The boys are probably wondering where I am, I better get," Gatz changed the subject, and my joy burst into flames.

"But you just got here," I protest, he's the friendliest face I've seen in months. He can't leave yet.

"Club duty," he shrugs.

"I'll ride you back to where they're staying," Kane mumbles, walking past us both like a pissed off girlfriend.

Gatz sighs, placing his hands in his pockets. Awkwardness swirls around us like confetti, we haven't seen each other since that night. He glances around the room and suddenly frowns.

"You don't have any baby stuff?"

I shake my head, my eyes gazing across the area. "I haven't really left the room since I got here, I have cabin fever like crazy." You can't miss the edge to my giggle. I'm happy for what Kane has given me, I'm just lonely.

"Well, I kind of got something—"

"You what?" My heart skips a beat, and Gatz reaches behind his back and pulls out a purple stuffed dragon. The creature is masculine, but the color of this particular one gives it a feminine touch. The wings are dainty, and it's face and eyes soft. It could be for a boy or girl.

Tears fill my eyes, and I lose my breath. It's the first thing I've gotten for the baby. It makes everything feel that more real.

"It's not much, but..."

"I love it." I grab it, running my finger over the stitched horns on the head.

The sound of the wheels on the cleaning cart, bring me back from the memory, and my eyes fall to the dragon sitting on the dresser across from me. I don't love Gatz like a lover, but I feel like we're family. I miss him.

STANDING UP, I waddle to the window and watch Kane drive away. He'd be pissed if he knew I came outside when he left. Opening the door, I spot the housekeeper, Miss Suzy.

SHE HAS a clipboard in her hand, and a pen in her black curly hair. Her white and blue uniform is wrinkled, and there's a run in her pantyhose today. When she places the clipboard on top of the cart, she spots me and lights up. She's the only other person I can socialize with, without having to worry about someone finding out I'm here.

"DID YOU FIND ANY NEW BOOKS?" I ask with excitement.

"ROOM 3 LEFT ONE, you're in luck." She bends down, grabbing a yellow book from a shelf and waves it in the air.

"OOOH!" I step out and waddle to her as fast as I can. The fresh air is amazing, so I don't go too fast.

GRASPING THE BOOK FROM HER, I run my hand over the cover.

"THE GOLD FINCH," I read the title aloud, flipping through the pages.

"YOU EVER READ THAT ONE?" she asks, grabbing her smokes sitting next to the hard bar of soaps. I shake my head. I have four books that Suzy has found left behind in rooms over the last six months. One by John Grisham, Fifty Shades of Gray, The Little Prince, and now this one.

"WELL, let me know if it's any good, yeah?" She grabs her clipboard and lighter and unlocks room 5 before going in to clean it.

"SURE THING, SUZY!" I say without taking my eyes off the book. This is what my life has become. Sitting in a hotel room reading leftover books. I take bubble baths a lot, and watch TV when I can, but the signal sucks. Once I snuck out to the pool but a man wearing black was sitting across from me in a lawn chair and I became paranoid. I mean, who goes to the pool wearing all of their clothes?

AT LEAST IN THIS ROOM, I'm safe. Shutting the door behind me, I slide to the floor and stretch my legs out in front of me. One hand on my belly, I feel the baby move and kick as I open the cover to the book, ready for it to take me from this hotel room and into a place far away.

I'M HALFWAY through the book, on the edge of my seat for the next chapter when Kane walks in the room. He's here early, so I glance up from my book. Untucking my legs from under me, I stretch out.

"You're back early," I yawn.

His eyes are watery, and his face is lax and defeat from his usual hard mask. Little hairs on the back of my neck stand on end. Something is wrong.

I drop my book and stand.
 "Are you okay? What happened?"

"Gatz, he's dead." Raising his head, teeth gritted tears spring from his eyes.

"Wh-what?"

Kane turns and sits on the bed, his head hanging in his hands as he cries. A man as brutal and infuriating as Kane crying makes the world freeze in time.

The baby kicks so hard I kneel over the bed, my fingers clawing at the unmade sheets. My clenched eyes fill with tears as I think about what Kane just said.
 "Are you sure, Kane?" I whimper. "How do you know?"

SNIFFING, he stands. His eyes fall on my stomach, and anger turns his face red.

His moment of vulnerability gone.

"GET YOUR SHIT, we're going to the Sin City Outlaws in Vegas."

HE DOESN'T GIVE me any answers, he doesn't hug me and tell me anything. He just starts grabbing my things and shoving them in a bag. If I didn't know any better, it's as if now that Gatz is gone Kane is getting rid of me too.

9
_____

SIMONE

tanding in a floor to ceiling window of a suite of the
Outlaw Casino, I look down upon the streets filled with
motorcycles. Everyone is here for Gatz- to show their
respect, some here not to show their support. Now that I'm here
word has gotten out about Gatz possibly being gay, or bi-sexual
and some members of affiliated clubs are outraged.

THE AUTHORITIES BLOCKED off the entire strip of Vegas, urging
tourists to explore other attractions of the Fabulous Las Vegas for
the day as things are predicted to become violent.

EARLIER TODAY A FIGHT broke out in front of the club sending
three men to the hospital, none from the Outlaws' club though.

IT'S SAD, why does someone's sexual preference make them any
less of a human than the person standing next to them. Gatz is

gone, we should be focusing on a loss rather than people being offended.

THE FUNERAL WAS BEAUTIFUL, but I felt detached to everything around me as the child in me kicked and moved around. What if Gatz is the father, did my child just lose its father? What about Kane, he doesn't even want to acknowledge the unborn baby inside of me.

I was distracted, wondering what would happen to us now. The plan was to live with Gatz, have a baby room and be the crazy idea of a family. Eyes fell on me from everyone. The Outlaws stared at my growing stomach, and I felt targeted. Kane did nothing as he stood next to me like a cold statue. I didn't feel protected or that Kane even cared about the baby, to be honest, if Veer showed up right then I'd probably be in the grave next to Gatz.

THAT WAS the last I saw Kane today, well, actually he took me up here and told me to stay before marching right back out. I didn't even get a word in edgewise.

SIGHING, my eyes searching the bikers down below, a familiar truck heads the opposite way of all the motorcycles down on the strip, Kane's truck. Drawing in a deep breath, my hand palms the tinted glass as he drives away.

MY GUT KNOTS as the idea he's leaving me sinks in the pit of my stomach. Deep down I knew he was getting rid of me. Gatz is gone, and Kane's obligation to him is gone too.

I was nothing to Kane, and never will be.

Doesn't he care that this might be his kid? Hand on my stomach, I cry. I cry for my unborn child and Gatz. I cry for everyone but myself because this isn't about me.

THE DOOR to the room suddenly open, but I don't turn around to see who it is. Their presence is just confirming what I'm thinking. That Kane is gone, and I'm alone.

"SIMONE?" It's a female voice. I hang my head, waiting for her to disclose the information I know she's about to spill. "Look, there's no easy way to tell you this—"

"He's not coming back," I help her, and I hear a deep sigh. I turn, finding a beautiful blonde wearing a sheriff's uniform.

I FROWN, the uniform throwing me off.

She looks down and realizes what has me concerned.

"I'M THE PRESIDENT'S OL' lady, weird, I know."

I don't say anything, it's fucked up on so many levels. Here I thought me having two possible baby daddies was unconventional, this lady takes the whole fucking cake.

SHE TAKES A STEP INSIDE, her hands fidgeting with one another. "The men sent me because they thought me having a vagina would make this easier," she scoffs, a meek smile brightening her round face. "But yeah, Kane is gone. He said the only reason he kept you was because of Gatz, and now that he's gone... he doesn't see any reason to have you around."

"That, or maybe he's too chicken shit to admit he was gay with Gatz, and I'm living proof of it," I snarl. It doesn't much matter why he's gone, it doesn't change anything.

I clear my throat, the sting slicing through my heart. I didn't love Kane, in fact, we pretty much hated each other but for him to turn his back on me during losing Gatz, is something I'll never forgive him for.

"What now?" I croak. Are they going to throw me out on the street?

"You're ours, and under our protection for now."

"You mean until the baby is born, and you guys find out if it's Gatz's or not?" The bitch in my voice can't be stopped, I'm abandoned, losing two men in my life in one day, and just plain tired.

She closes the gap between us instantly, her face perplexed.

"No, I wouldn't let them do that."

Her doe eyes take me aback, she doesn't know me, doesn't owe me anything. Why would she stand up to her president boyfriend for me? Maybe she doesn't know the whole story? Maybe she's just telling me what I want to hear?

I hiccup, the sob I've been stifling making its way up my throat. I'm exhausted and mentally drained.

"I think I'm going to go lay down," I whisper, the urge to vomit making my mouth water.

"Of course, if you need anything, my name is Jillian. Just... just stay up here so you and the baby are safe, Simone."

GLANCING over my shoulder at her, I don't say a word. Hiding in a dark room seems to be the only thing I'm good at anymore. "I know this is not ideal, but if Kane can just turn his back on you that easily, he's in no position to be in your or that baby's life." Her attempt at comforting me warms me, I needed to hear that.

"THANK YOU," I cry, the baby kicking me inside making me want to cry harder.

JILLIAN SMILES but doesn't say another word before leaving and shutting the door.

Warm tears stream down my face, the baby moving with my hysteria as I make my way to one of the adjoining bedrooms. It's decorated in purple and golds, modern-day furniture placed perfectly around the small space. I crawl onto the fluffy comforter, my fingers strangling the material as I cry harder than I've ever cried.

I DON'T CRY for Kane, or Gatz, or myself. I cry for my child because look what I've got us into.

The dominos just keep fucking falling.

Mac

THE CHICK with purple hair bobs and slurps on my dick. I can't remember her name, who cares. Lowering my head back, I close my eyes and take a drag of my blunt. My fingers are sticky from the electrical tape on them as I was working on a project for the club and cut it. I was putting GPS on all our bikes. Couldn't find a Band-Aid so I fixed it the best way I knew how. That's what I do, I'm the tech guy.

MY PHONE CHIMES, I ignore it trying to focus on the warm mouth wrapped around my cock. The suction pulling at my taut skin. It's been a rough fucking day, and I need the distraction.

My phone vibrates and begins to ring.

"Fuck," I hiss, grabbing it off the side table. It's Lieutenant Lopez. Bitch is driving me crazy. I swear she thinks we're a thing or something. I saw her two days ago, and I knew better than to. Stage five fucking clinger, man.

YOU OKAY BABY? *Just checking in and seeing if you needed someone to talk to. – Lopez*

Great, now she wants to talk about our feelings. Whatever the hell we were doing, it's done now.

A KNOCK at the door has me dropping my phone on the table.

MACHETE ENTERS, his red hair everywhere and his crazy fucking eyes landing on the bitch bobbing up and down on my dick. The way he's staring makes me a little uncomfortable, and I fidget.

"WHAT THE FUCK, MAN?" I finally say something.

"ZEEK WANTS YOU," he informs, his damn eyes finally looking at the floor. The woman lifts her head to glance at Machete, and I gently press on the back of her head, putting my cock back into her mouth. She's not done yet.

"I'LL BE THERE IN A SECOND," I tell him, watching the bitch slob on my knob.

SUDDENLY THE GIRL scrapes her teeth on my tip, and I wince. Irritated, and tired, I push her off me.

"YOU'RE DONE. FUCK!"

"SORRY, I'm not used to sucking on a pierced dick," she informs with a ditzy tone, wiping off her mouth with her hand. Shifting onto her hands, her small tits come into view.

GETTING OFF THE BED, I pull my pants up, I need to get to church before Zeek comes after me. Last time he made me sit in church naked for being late.

"YOU WANT TO FUCK THOUGH?" she nearly begs, I chuckle in reply. Thirsty chicks - same shit different day.

"GOT BUSINESS, BABE," I smile, grab my phone off the end table, and head to the chapel. I grab my dick; a slight sting still present from her nipping it.

THE CLUB SMELLS decent as it was just rebuilt, the smell of pussy and beer gone. We will have to work on that. A dark shadow looms over the main room, a piece of plywood covering a recent broken window.

"WHAT THE FUCK HAPPENED?"

"SOMEONE THREW A BRICK THROUGH IT," Felix, our vice president, says solemnly. He points to the bar, and a dusty brick with the word 'fag' spray pray painted on it.

CLOSING MY EYES, I harbor my anger and rein myself in. People are fucking ass backward.

HEADING into the chapel with Felix, all eyes are on me as I enter.

"WHAT?"

Zeek smiles. "Have a seat," he gestures toward my seat at the end of the table.

Slowly I make my way to my seat, not liking the tension in the room. It's been a rough fucking day, so the shit-eating grin on Zeek's face has me on edge.

"What?" I ask again.

"Simone is staying with us."

"Simone was the one Gatz and Kane knocked up, I know who she is."

"You are to watch her, keep her safe," Zeek continues. Opening my mouth to protest, I close it. Surely, I'm fucking high and heard them wrong.

"Take her shopping for diapers, rub her swollen feet," Felix adds before laughing, and the rest of the men follow.

"You're fucking kidding!" I bark, standing where I sit. How am I going to fuck bitches and do drugs with a pregnant chick around? She'll talk my damn ear off the whole time and I'll never get any work done.

"I'm not. That may be Gatz's child and we are going to make sure she has everything she needs. Pack your bags, buddy." Zeek laughs, slamming the gavel down.

COLLAPSING BACK INTO MY CHAIR, I rub my hand over the stubble on my chin. I can't fucking believe this.

A biker and a pregnant chick. This should be fucking interesting.

10

SIMONE

PART TWO

Commotion in the other room wakes me. My eyes are crusty from crying and swollen. Using my hands, I push myself up onto my elbows and try and look through the bedroom door, but I can't see anyone.

"Hello?"
Nothing.

Scooting to the side of the bed, I grab an ashtray off the night-stand and waddle to the doorway. There are condiments out of the fridge sitting on the counter, but I still don't see anyone. Well, if they're making something to eat they obviously aren't here to hurt me.

I take a step out, my eyes bouncing all over the room for who might be in here with me. Maybe it's Jillian again.

"You want one?"

I scream, swinging the ashtray behind me. It thumping as I make contact with the intruder.

"Fucking hell!" A man bends over, grabbing his forehead where I hit him. Gasping, I take a few steps back and drop the ashtray to the floor.

Hissing, he stands up. His blondish colored hair falls in his eyes, intricate tattoos swirl along his arms, and that jaw of his could cut glass.

"You crazy ass bitch!" My eyebrows draw inward at his tone of voice. Our eyes lock for a few seconds before slowly trailing up and down one another. His eyes are the lightest brown I've ever seen with a hint of green mixed within. Like a sturdy tree standing in an emerald forest.

He's taller than me, skin tanned, and holds a softness to his face, but there's a sharp edge there too. It's as if Kane and Gatz were mixed into one and made this man.

He glares, pulling his hand away from the bump forming on his forehead.

"Are you insane? My water could have broken sneaking up on

me like that!" Instinctively, I place my palm on my belly. "Who are you? What are you doing in here?"

IGNORING MY QUESTIONS, he walks back to the counter where the lettuce and bread were left out.

"MY NAME IS MAC, and I'm the fucking babysitter." His eyes slowly rise to mine, a chiseled smile crossing his smug face as he lifts his chin with more confidence than I can handle looking directly at.

"I don't need a babysitter," I sass.

"I'm here for that, not you." He points to my pregnant belly, his silver chain-looking bracelet sliding around his wrist. I shift on my back foot, and sigh. Over the past few months, death has not scared me but losing my child has. For Gatz's club to be here and help protect a fetus that might not even be their own. That stands for something.

"MY NAME IS SIMONE—"

"I KNOW WHO YOU ARE. The chick that got pregnant by two men, from two different clubs." The coldness in his voice drips like ice. "Are you a biker hopper?" His tone casual as if we're discussing a movie we just saw.

"A WHAT?" I snap, not familiar with the terminology.

"You know, like a mattress hopper, only you're jumping from biker dick to biker dick." He waves around a mayonnaise covered butter knife.

My jaw drops. "That's not who I am—"

"Are you a prostitute or something then?" His tone serious. My face burns with anger, and the urge to hit him in the head with the ashtray again flares.

"You're a fucking asshole, you know that?"

He smirks, and I can tell I'm in deep shit with this guy. This is not just any brooding biker, this is a man who plays with women's heads before leaving you shredded and confused. The lipstick on his shirt a hint that he's also a player.

He steps around the counter, his breath smelling of beer and weed. He towers over me a good foot, making me have to glare up at him.

"Easy, Pocahontas, I'll treat you like a princess for a few minutes after I let you ride my cock. I won't even judge you for liking it." He waggles his brows, and I shove him.

"I'm not a biker hopper!" I purse my lips.

His eyes blaze of burnt green irises, and his shoulders rise. Skimming me up and down, a wolfish smile fits his smug face. He's playing with me and enjoying the rise he's getting.

"Cut the shit, I know what your kind is and I'm not a toy."

"My kind?" His head tilts to the side with curiosity.

"Biker." My lips curl with the word. "I've grown up working the field of outlaws, and I've seen how you guys live. If you think for one second you can play me like one of your club bitches... you're wrong."

Lifting his hand, he rubs his chin.

"Maybe I was wrong about you," he says, his voice grave. I give a curt nod, proud of myself for taking charge of the situation. Seems I haven't lost my touch after all. "You're fucking stupid if you think for one second that I care about you, you're wrong. I'll cut that child from your fucking womb, and hand you over to the very people you're running from, Pocahontas."

My eyes widen, a lump forming in the back of my throat. I've never had anyone talk to me like this before.

"BUT YOU ALREADY KNEW THAT, right? Knowing my *kind* and all?"

TAKING A STEP BACK, we stare into each other's eyes, the room silent as we challenge one another.

AN ARROGANT LAUGH vibrates his body, his back turned toward me, he heads to his room which is on the other side of the suite.

HE SHUTS THE DOOR, and I pull at my hair in frustration.

FUCKING POCAHONTAS, screw him.

Mac

LYING IN BED, I pull my cigarettes out of my pocket and light one up. Blowing smoke into the room, I think about Simone. She's feisty for being pregnant and at our mercy.

I take another drag.

I thought I'd come in here to an annoying chick down for some kink, I mean, she did fuck two guys and get knocked up.

She insulted *my kind*. What bullshit.

Sure, she wasn't wrong. Bikers have been known to be ruthless and a little horny, but there's another side to us too. Just very few get to see that.

I GLANCE AT THE DOOR, she may not see that side of anyone if she continues to keep her walls to her bitch fort up. Nobody has seen mine, and I intend on keeping it that way.

GRABBING my iPod from my bag, I shove the earbuds in my ears and listen to "Hail to The King" By Avenged Sevenfold. Closing my eyes, I fall asleep. It's been a long fucking day.

———

WEIGHT on my chest and a piercing sting to my neck wakes me from a deep sleep. My eyes snap open with Simone straddling my body, her swollen belly sitting on my chest, with a knife pressed to my neck

"WHO IS the stupid one now, sleeping with your back turned?" she criticizes, fire and pain dancing in her eyes. Fisting her hips, I throw her onto her back, my arm whipping out from under my pillow, I press my gun to her head.

"I STAND BY MY STATEMENT, only a *stupid* bitch would come in here thinking I wouldn't expect it."

SHE DOESN'T RESPOND, her chest rising and falling. Opening her mouth, she closes it thinking better not to speak. Smart considering there's a gun to her head.

"SAY IT," I press on, wanting to hear what she has to say.

"I am not a whore. I was a virgin before I got pregnant!" Her voice cracks with emotion, her sad eyes tugging at the armor I wear from day to day.

Using the barrel of my gun, I push the hair from her round face wanting to see all of her sadness. She's so beautiful. Her misplaced strength breathtaking, and the weight of her sins sewn into her shoulders like a pair of dark wings.

"You don't have to fight anymore," I whisper, my softness taking me aback. Her throat bobs as she swallows my words. Why I feel the need to say that, I don't know. I can just tell this woman has been fighting fear with fear for far too long. Lifting my fist away from the mattress, allowing her to get up, I place the gun in my waistband.

Shifting off the bed, she stands. She's wearing a t-shirt that tickles the tops of her thighs, her dark green panties contrasting amongst her dark skin. Even with a pregnant belly, she's a fucking looker. The pressing of my dick in my pants agreeing.

Her eyes glance over her shoulder at me, and I see confusion and courage battling on what to think of me. She doesn't know whether to like me or hate me.

"Simone." I overstepped my boundaries telling her she was safe. "Simone!" She keeps walking, ignoring me. Jumping from the bed, I grab her by the shoulder, but she shakes me off.

"Goddamn it, stop for a second!" I demand. I need to clear the air, be mean to her or something.

"Why? We're not friends, you made that clear. So... don't be nice to me." Her voice cracks with emotion, and I feel like an ass. I can't force myself to be a dick to her. Why? Because she's pregnant?

Giving me a once-over, she walks across the suite back to her room, slamming the door.

"BITCH!" I growl under my breath, slamming my own door. This is why I'd rather talk to computers than a woman. They're fucking complicated!

11

SIMONE

A week goes by, and Mac and I haven't said so much as a word to each other. Just silent stares, and glares from across the room. We take turns coming into the main room, and then retreating back to our bedrooms. I'm seven months pregnant today, I wish I knew if it was a boy or girl. On the dresser I tap the horns of the dragon Gatz gave me. I'm so ready to give it to the baby.

HEADING INTO THE MAIN ROOM, I sit on the couch and turn the TV on. There's an ER program on, and someone pregnant is in distress. She's crying and weeping for the baby's care, and I can't help but tear up. Fucking hormones.

THE OTHER DAY a woman dropped an egg on a cooking show and I cried for her. She would have won that competition if she didn't drop that egg.

MAC'S BEDROOM DOOR OPENS, and he struts out wearing a low-slung pair of jeans, and nothing else. His strong chest displays the slightest bit of hair, and hard nipples. Stopping, he scratches his chest, eyeballing the TV.

"What the hell are you watching?" he asks with a cigarette hanging out of his mouth.

"IT'S THE MIRACLE OF LIFE." Gesturing my hand toward the TV, just as the woman's water breaks all over her and two nurses.

MAC SITS DOWN on the edge of the couch, smoke swirling around me.

He glances at the TV, and then me.

"ARE YOU CRYING?"

I WIPE MY CHEEKS, they're wet. Fuck, I swear my crying has no bounds. "No," I snap, snatching the cigarette from his lips and plopping it in an empty beer bottle on the coffee table.

HIS BROWS FURROW INWARD, his jaw ticking.

"SECOND-HAND SMOKE?" I point to my belly. "It's very dangerous for the baby."

"JESUS," he mutters under his breath. Collapsing fully into the couch, he throws his arm on the back of it and looks at the TV focusing on the woman giving birth.

THE WOMAN SCREAMS, and they show a vaginal shot. I can't help but wince, that's just scary.

"THAT'S FUCKING TERRIFYING! How does a chick come back from that?" He leans forward clutching the remote and turning the channel to Mad Max. I've seen it before, and like it but I was in the middle of that show!

"HEY!" I try and grab the remote, but he shoves it down his pants like a child.

"COME AND GET IT, POCAHONTAS." His hand slung across the back of the couch, a smug smile on his handsome face I don't know whether to take him seriously or hit him in the head with the ashtray again. Games. It's all games.

"OH, don't get all pissy with me, Pocahontas," he laughs. Standing, I'm pissed he keeps calling me a fucking princess.

GRABBING the beer bottle from the coffee table, I tilt it slowly and spill it on his crotch. The smell of ash and stale beer filling the air. He jumps up, droplets of liquid staining the floor.

"Fucking hell!" He quickly brushes the stale beer off his jeans before furiously glaring at me.

I turn, trying my hardest to waddle to my room, but of course he's faster than me. He grabs me by the wrist and halts me in my attempt to escape.

"If you wanted me to take my jeans off, you could have just asked, not fucking douse them in piss warm beer."

"Would you prefer cold beer? Not that your dick could get any smaller." I look down at the outline of his cock. It's not lacking in size, but I'm not about to feed his ego.

He shakes his head, a smile hidden under his grimace. I almost think he likes to hate me.

"You're playing a dangerous game, Simone."

"This is the only game I know how to play." A sinister smile crosses my face. Leaning in, invading my space, I suck in a tight breath. I haven't had a man this close to me in months.

"Then let's play. I play John Smith, and you're my Pocahontas." His teeth nip my ear, and I feel it all the way to my toes. "Where I fuck the respect into you and the defiant little bitch out."

"You have no idea how much bitch I have inside of me," I fire back, my tone of voice huskier than I want to let on.

"Is that right?" Amusement thick in his voice.

"Let's just say, I have your name on my list in bright red marker," I threaten. He quiets, taking a step back. He flicks his chin with his thumb, his forest eyes burning with intrigued interest rather than anger.

"You know, I'd almost believe you were a bad ass if you didn't have such sadness swimming in your eyes, Princess." I swallow hard, his words hitting home.

"I'm- I'm not sad." I shrug. *Am I?*

"You don't sound so sure." His hair falls into his face when he tilts his head to the side.

Opening my mouth to defend myself, nothing comes out. My empty chest feels cold and I suddenly feel sad. As if I've been suppressing how I really feel for a long time.

Looking at the floor, my hand twirls a piece of hair next to my face. I've been sad, I've mourned but I've never really moved forward from being forlorn.

He did it, Mac broke my exterior shell and I suddenly feel exposed. I roll my eyes, and turn my back, sauntering back to my room. This conversation is over.

12

SIMONE

Two days pass, and we say nothing to one another again. Back to silent glances and avoiding one another as I sit on the floor. I pull my toes up trying to paint them dark blue, but my belly is in the way.

I KICK my leg sideways trying to reach and I knock the bottle over onto the rug.

"FUCK!" I grab the bottle, but it's too late, polish soaks into the carpet. "Fuck," I whisper under my breath.

"YOU SAY FUCK A LOT." Mac startles me from the kitchen. His eyes judgmental, as if me being pregnant I can't say the f-word.

I SCOWL IN HIS DIRECTION. "I'm a drop the f-bomb kind of mom."

HE LAUGHS and sits next to me on the floor. Crossing his legs, he grabs the fingernail polish.

"What are you doing?"

HE GRABS MY FOOT, and the soft contact causes tingles to shoot up my legs. His hands are warm, and my feet are ticklish to the touch. His greedy stare drinks me in, and a shiver bumps its way up my spine.

"I CAN DO THAT," I insist, his touch unraveling me.

"NO, YOU CAN'T," he rebuttals calmly, focusing on my toe.

HE SWIPES the paintbrush across my toenail perfectly before going to the next toe. Leaning back on my hands, I watch him paint every nail on my left foot. Cradling my foot, he blows gently across my toes, and goosebumps pepper along my skin. His hooded eyes set on mine, dark eyelashes framing his forest eyes. He's so handsome and ruggedly good-looking at the same time. Every nerve ending I have is alive and thirsty for his touch.

"Is this your favorite color or something?" he questions.

"NO, I love dark green. Like forest green." His eyes meet mine and I hold my breath. Dark green like the flecks in his eyes, but I don't say that.

"WHAT'S YOUR FAVORITE COLOR?" I ask.

He ignores me, he does that a lot. Especially if I'm asking a question.

"YOU HAVE TO LIKE A CERTAIN COLOR," I press.

"BLACK," his tone dry. I like the color black for clothes, but that's about it. It's dark and bleak of any emotion. Then again, Mac is hard at showing what he's feeling exactly too. So, it's rather perfect I suppose.

MOVING his hand to the next foot he caresses my ankle, and I melt into his hold. I don't know if I want to be pissed at this man or ravish him. Damn hormones.

HE PAINTS each toenail and blows across them again. I've never understood people with foot fetishes, but Mac holding my foot, and blowing hot breaths across my sensitive skin... I'm starting to understand it now.

HE KNOWINGLY SMIRKS as he screws the lid on the nail polish. I look away, wetting my lips.

STANDING UP, he chuckles. He knows what he's doing to me. "Better clean that mess up, Pocahontas."

I'M NOT sure if he's talking about the polish... or me.

———

EATING A BOWL OF SOUP, I watch Mac do push-ups in the living room. His arms bulge, his back is sweaty, and his hair sways in his face. We've been cordial with each other for the last few days, which is a step in a better direction.

"ENJOYING YOUR SOUP?" he asks between push-ups.

"Mmhmm." I can't take my eyes off him. If I look hard enough, I swear I can see his pack sweep across the floor when he thrusts upwards.

A knock on the hotel door catches my attention. Waddling across my room, I open the door and find a man with black shaggy hair standing in the doorway of the suite.

"HEY SIMONE!" he nods with his chin. He's the president of the club, I saw him briefly before Kane swept me up here. He's tall and makes me shrink where I stand. Him standing so close to me, I swear I can hear the cries of his victims crying in my ear. He's dangerous. I've heard of this man from many clubs in the area but never had the pleasure to meet the Reaper himself.

"MAC, YOU GOT A SECOND?" Stepping past me, one hand in his pocket, he heads to Mac.

M AC JUMPS TO HIS FEET, his chest puffed out and falling and rising with each breath. Man, he makes me feel like a woman.

Z EEK TALKS to Mac in a hushed voice. Mac finally glances my way, his face ashen. I suck in a tight breath knowing what he's going to tell me... I'm not going to like.

Z EEK SIGHS and runs his hand on the back of his neck, before turning my way. Every passing second they hold their tongues, I deprive myself of air.

"S IMONE, I was just informed Kane was found dead this morning. His motel room was blown up."

My knees grow weak, and I have to grab onto the counter to keep myself up.

"W-what?"

My head lowers as my heart beat drums out my hearing. The hotel room was blown up? He's dead. Just like Gatz. Both blown up. My head snaps up, both Mac and Zeek looking at me with concerned eyes.

"Does both of them being killed the same way sound like coincidence to you?" My voice wavers. "Does it?" I ask louder, my heart needing some fucking answers for once. I won't turn around and be ignored on this.

Mac and Zeek look at each other before Zeek crosses his arms.

"We used to think a rival enemy killed Gatz but seeing how

Kane was just killed the same way, I'm rethinking our target," Zeek confides, telling me what I was afraid of.

"It's Veer. It has to be." Pressing my hand to my head, I try and fight back the tears threatening to fall. This is all my fault, the never-ending domino effect continues to curse me and anyone I know.

"I should go home before anyone else gets hurt," I murmur to myself.

Zeek sucks in a breath, catching my attention.

"What?" I side-eye him.

"I had a close contact check on your family, and your father was murdered some time ago, but your mother got away; nobody has seen her." Mac and Zeek's face etch with sympathy, but I can't accept it, I can't fucking do a thing but crumble piece by piece.

MY WORLD SPINS, my stomach threatening to upchuck the soup I just had. This is too much.

LOOKING AT THE FLOOR, a single warm tear slides down my cheek. If it weren't for this child, I would just hand my heart and soul over to Veer. He's taking everything away from me, soon enough it will just be me and the baby standing in the wake of corpses and ash.

"THAT'S ENOUGH FOR TODAY, MAN." Mac steps in front of Zeek. His protective act would be heartwarming if my heart wasn't splintered all over the floor.

THE THUD of Zeek's boots sound as he whispers to Mac before

leaving the suite. The sound of the door shutting and locking causing a choke to rip up my throat.

"SIMONE?" Mac's voice is lathered in sympathy, and I hate it. I need him to be a dick to me, make me clam up and not feel. Hand over my mouth, I rush to my room, but before I can shut my door, concealing myself from the world, Mac shoves his foot in the door jamb.

"Go AWAY, MAC!" I try and shut the door, but he keeps pressing against it. He's strong.

Reaching through the door he grasps my wrist, his hand warm and caring, forces me to stop my fighting. Glossy eyes feast on his dilated pupils. His thumb drawing circles on my wrist.

"YOU'RE SAFE," he whispers, but it's not me I'm worried about. It's everyone around me.

"PLEASE, JUST LET ME GO," I plead, my vulnerability making me want to hide. He exhales a ragged breath and reluctantly, lets go. I shut my door, my head leaning against it. Needing to process what's going on in my head; in my heart.

Why didn't Gatz and Kane tell me about my dad?

Where is my mother?

Where is Veer?

13

MAC

Staring at the door, I chew on the pad of my thumb. She's been in there for almost a day. She hasn't eaten, showered or gotten out of bed as far as I know. This can't be healthy, not that I'm the man to judge anyone.

I run my hands through my hair and blow out a breath, not sure what to do. Do I try and talk to her? Why is it bothering me so much that she's not out here annoying me?

This is fucking frustrating.

GRABBING MY PHONE, I hit up Jillian. She'll know how to deal with this.

"MAC?" Jillian answers.

"HEY, so Simone has been in her room for over a day, and I don't know what to fucking do." Concern is heavier in my voice than I'd like.

"Did Zeek tell her the news about her dad and Kane?"

"Yeah. I don't know what to do... or why I fucking care." I throw my hand in the air, this entire situation out of my bounds and making me uncomfortable. I'd rather fight and argue with her than this shit.

"Maybe I should come over there?" Jillian offers.

"No!" I answer a little too quickly. Zeek doesn't ask much of me, and this is my responsibility. Plus, if I'm being completely honest, I want Simone to trust me. I don't dig into that thought too deeply, it's scary.

"Well then, be nice for one," she scolds.

"I'm always nice," I defend, and she scoffs. "You're an outlaw, you're all assholes." Eh, she has a point. "Maybe make her something to eat and offer it to her. She probably feels alone, everyone around her is dying."

"Feed her? What the fuck am I, a housekeeper now?" Be nice, feed her? Does she know who the fuck she's talking to?

"Do you want help or not?" Sass high in her voice.

I growl into the phone, not liking this one bit.

"THANKS," I say and hang up. Looking at the door, I tap my foot anxiously. Maybe I should have Jillian come here and fix this for me.

"FUCK!" Jerking myself around, I head into the kitchen. I can do this. It's a woman, how complicated can it get?

I OPEN the fridge and I find shit to make sandwiches, some cut fruit, soup, and beverages. I scratch my chin. Someone should make a grocery run.

PULLING MY PHONE BACK OUT, I dial Jillian.

"YES?" she laughs into the phone.

"WHAT WOULD you want to eat if you were Simone?"

"THE GIRLS and I will be there in fifteen." The phone goes dead, and I hang my head.

SITTING ON THE COUCH, grabbing the remote, I flip through the channels. Nothing looks good. Turning the TV off, I fetch my laptop to catch up on some business. Just as I'm about to finish a project, a delicate knock pounds at the door.

RIGHT ON TIME, Raven, Alessandra, and Jillian show up stowing grocery bags.

"HEY, MAC DADDY!" Alessandra winks, placing shit on the counter. Her dark hair pulled into a yellow bandanna. I see what Felix likes in her, she's sexy and sassy.

"She in that room?" Raven, Machete's little demon points to Simone's door.

"YEAH," I nod, looking into the bags.

"WAIT, ladies, I think Mac wants to swoon her over, so let's just go in there and say our condolences, and let him take over," Jillian takes charge, the ladies nodding in agreement.

"What, no I don't. You're just making shit up now." I point at her. I do want to be the one to help her feel better, but I'm not the right person for the job.

ALESSANDRA SMILES, and they all head into Simone's room, noticing the door not closed all the way. They sit on the bed, Alessandra rubbing Simone's back as Raven stands and Jillian sits on the edge.

"HEY GIRL, rough times isn't it?" Jillian asks. Simone starts crying harder, and the girls all hug her. I look down, feeling like a creep for watching but I don't know what she needs. Looks like she just needs someone to be there for her. I suck at being there for anyone, caring is out of my league. I never had anyone for me besides a tough ol' biker, Zeek's father.

Closing the door, I unpack what the girls brought letting them do their thing. Waffles, ice cream, chips, pickles, and just a bunch of junk food.

Women are really fucking complicated, come to think of it, my brothers are nuts for settling down.

I grab what I know from the groceries... Sandwiches and ice cream.

Minutes later the women sashay out of the room, stopping at the counter.

"Just... be you," Jillian advises. Glancing at her, I don't respond. What the hell does that mean?

"No, then he'd be nose deep in his laptop he wouldn't even know she's in the room." Alessandra laughs at my expense.

I draw in a breath, trying to calm myself.

"You done?" Narrowing a brow at Alessandra, she smiles, proud of herself.

"Let's go ladies. Mac, call me if you need anything else- k?"

SILENTLY I NOD.

"GO GET 'ER, TIGER," Raven raises her hand her black nails acting out like she's going to claw me to shreds before walking away, the rest of the girls following.

"JESUS," I mutter under my breath. Fucking chicks, man.

I MAKE SIMONE A TURKEY SANDWICH, and even cut it in little fucking triangles for her. Grab the whole container of cookies and cream ice cream, with a spoon and head to her room.

"SIMONE, I got some food. Ya want some?"

SHE DOESN'T ANSWER. What the hell, she'll talk to the women but not me? I have to work harder for her attention, what kind of shit is that?

"COME ON, you gotta eat... Think of the baby." My brows furrow in as I try and listen for any sign of life in the other room. "I'm going to come in and shove this food down your throat if you don't eat now!" My patience gone.

"I'M NOT HUNGRY!" she snaps, and relief floods my shoulders she's finally talking to me. She's alive and still fucking mouthy.

"Then fucking starve!" I wince at my sudden outburst, I'm being too much myself.

SIGHING, I push the door open a little. "How is little man going to fight off the chicks if you're starving him?" I try one last time, my tone softer than before.

"I DON'T KNOW THE GENDER." Her voice louder than before.

"WHAT DO YOU MEAN?"

"I HAVEN'T HAD AN ULTRASOUND."

WAIT A SECOND, she hasn't had one at all or recently?

"AREN'T you supposed to get a few of those to make sure the alien baby is growing right and all?"

FUCK, why did Zeek make me do this? I know fuck all about pregnant women. When I fuck, I make sure to wrap my cock up extra tight to avoid this kind of shit.

SHE DOESN'T ANSWER, and my nerves have about had it. It's apparent Simone and I don't know what the fuck we're doing here.

"Do you even have any baby shit, or a... birth itinerary?" I heard the woman on that show talking about it is the only reason I know anything about it.

"You mean birth plan?" The sadness in her voice lifts a little at my lack of maternal knowledge.

"Sure." What the fuck ever. "Why don't you get up and we can talk or eat? Face to face."

She shifts in the blankets but doesn't get up.

"I just... I need some time, Mac." Her voice sad again. It crosses my mind to go inside and curl up behind her, hold her but it doesn't quite feel right either. Instead, I set the food on the end table next to her. My feet not wanting to move, encouraging me to climb up next to her. Her hand dangles off the bed, the only thing exposed from the blankets smothering her.

Running the tips of my fingers over her wrist she clasps my hand, holding it tight.

"Hey, Mac?"

"What?" I growl.

"What is your real name?"

MY SHOULDERS TENSE, my chest clenching with the question. It seems like a legit question for anyone to ask, but it's not for me. My real name is personal, and something only a few people know. Mac is strong and takes no shit, Rhett was someone who got bullied as a kid and hated his family. The mere mention of my real name makes me feel uncomfortable and like a fucking pussy. I'd like to see one of those asswipe kids from the playground now, I'd make them piss their fucking pants and fuck their mother. Swirling my finger on her soft skin, I break the contact.

I'M NOT ready to go down this road with Pocahontas. Let's keep the focus on her and off me. I'll talk to Zeek about getting a doc up here with a fucking ultrasound machine and get her some answers on the baby.

AND we also need to figure out what the fuck the plan is when this child decides to grace us with its presence because Simone looks like she's about to pop and I don't know shit about what the hell we're doing.

———

I LEFT a prospect at the door of the suite with strict instructions not to go inside unless he calls me first for permission. Any man inside the hotel room without me, alone with Simone doesn't sit well with me for some reason. Sitting at the bar of the club, beer in my hand, I wait for Zeek's response to my request.

"So, you want to get an ultrasound?" His brows furrow, his Adam's apple bobbing when he swallows his whiskey.

"Don't you think it's a good idea? I mean, what if there's a problem with the baby or something?" I shrug, not knowing what the hell I'm talking about, but I can't help but wonder if my mom had enough ultrasounds, if they would have seen something wrong before she had me and she'd still be alive.

Zeek runs his hands over his face. "I'm assuming they never got her much medical care because of the fear of records and shit. It would lead Veer right to her." Tinker, one of the club chicks hands Zeek a beer and winks at him before swinging her hips back behind the bar.

Scooting closer to Zeek so nobody can hear me. "Right, so I was thinking we could bring someone to the room. Someone we could trust."

Zeek squints his eyes at me, his lips curling around the top of the beer.

"You ain't fucking that, are you?" *That* referring to Simone.

I scoff. A little too quickly.

"Fuck no. That's Gatz's lady, that'd be weird." I scowl, but the idea of Simone being upset has me fucking pulling my hair out. I can't stand it. I'd do anything to have her out of that room and mouthing me again. She's sexy when she's mad.

"NEVER WOULD HAVE STOPPED YOU BEFORE." Zeek makes a point, one I ignore. "I'll make some calls, few threats, and see what I can come up with. Maybe it will make her cooperate with your more if we please her." He takes another swig of his beer. "What about your brother's club?" I suggest. Zeek has a brother in The Devil's Dust in California, the one Simone was staying at. They have a female doctor that is dating one of their boys, I bet we could trust her, hell, she might have seen Simone already.

"Yeah, maybe. Let me see what I can do." Zeek looks to the counter. His brother and him had some beef awhile back, but they've since sorted it out. "We have a club meeting tomorrow." Zeek changes the subject.

"I'LL BE THERE. I can get prospect Rooster to watch Simone."

Zeek laughs, the road name we gave the prospect amusing to him. He was a hangaround for the longest time, but one night when we were all shit faced we told him if he did four lines of coke and still managed to pick up a tourist chick from the Strip, we'd patch him in. With the way he was coked out of his mind, head bobbing like a fucking rooster we didn't think he'd pull it off.

BUT HIS GOOD LOOKS, and desperation for a woman at her friend's bachelor party won out.

I stand from the bar, finishing my beer.

"YOU KNOW that lieutenant keeps coming around here asking for you." Zeek peeks at me from the rim of his beer.

"Shiiiit." I can't shake this chick.

"She's a real bitch too," Tinker informs dryly from behind the bar.

"What'd you tell her?" I ask Zeek.

"You were on club business, you ain't meeting her up in the suite, are you?" Zeek lifts an eye.

"Fuck no." My brows furrow.

"Just don't want your dick making mistakes."

"Just push her in the direction of another dick," I don't do clingers.

Tinker rolls her eyes, turning to put ice in the bin.

14

SIMONE

Sitting on the couch with a cup of tea cradled in my hands, I stare out the window at tourists walking below. Wondering if any of them are pregnant, and what their lives are like. Do they have a significant other, a baby room?

Looking at the ice bobbing in my tea, I reflect on what the ladies said to me in my room. I reached my lowest and just needed time to process everything that was happening to my life. Raven was kind and understanding, Alessandra encouraged me things would get better if I let them, and Jillian told me to forget Kane and tug my big girl panties up.

It was kind of like a bad cop, free spirit, good villain kind of chat. Either way, I can't believe they came up here for me, it feels nice.

The door to the suite opens, and Mac walks in. Setting the cup down, I turn to talk to him. I feel like an idiot the way I broke down yesterday, but I just needed some time to process what was going on. The jaws of life devoured my soul and every time I think I might have escaped, something or someone around me has become a victim. Kane was an asshole to me and might have dumped me off like an unwanted step-child... but I could still be carrying his child.

Mac struggles through the front door, two bags in each hand.

I stand, hand on my belly.

"What's that?"

"You're out of your room," he says with an exhausted voice, but lightened eyes. I look to the wall, a guilty feeling surfacing. He really tried to help me yesterday. I know it doesn't seem like much to him, but his effort means so much to me. Nobody would have tried like he did.

He tosses the bags on the couch, grasps the back of the couch with both hands, and takes a deep breath.

"What's all this?" Peeling a bag open, I casually glance inside.

"They're for you," he points.

I frown, surely, I didn't hear him right.

"For me?"

Pulling the plastic open wide, my lips part. Books?

Reaching in, I grab them, pulling them out.

What to Expect When You're Expecting.

Baby Names Today.

The Perfect Baby Room.

My glossy eyes dart to his, my hormones about to open the floodgates.

"You got these for me?" Disbelief painting my voice.

"I don't know if you already know the shit, or already read the books but I didn't see you come here with much of anything, so I thought maybe it'd give you something to do while you were stuck up here. Keep you out of my fucking hair." He shrugs, reaching for the other bag.

I can tell he's trying to not care, but he does. He fucking cares. Gatz, Kane, nobody has gone to this length for me and the baby.

He pulls out a pack of baby bottles, and a baby blanket with black glasses printed on it, and even some maternity shorts.

"Are those..." I point at the shorts in surprise.

"Shorts, yeah. I held my hands up to tell the lady about the size of your waist, so I'm not sure if they'll fit, but it's better than you walking around in your underwear or the same ol' sweatpants all the time."

Taking the shorts from him, I rub my fingers on the material of the shorts, it's soft and elastic.

Shifting my eyes to him, I find myself becoming more and more attracted to him each day we're stuck in this place together. My cheeks blush, my thighs clench as a racing thought to flirt with him crosses my mind. Testing the waters to see if he finds me attractive.

"You don't like me in my panties?" I tilt my head to the side.

Hooded eyes fall on my ass, and my nipples perk from the sudden attention. "You keep walking around in those panties and I have a feeling we'll be crossing a bunch of lines we won't come back from, Pocahontas."

I laugh. "In your dreams." I don't want to come off too interested, then I'd be just like one of the girls from his club. But Mac is a catch, and as horny as my hormones have had me... I'd be lying if I said the thought of us blowing off some steam together hasn't crossed my mind a couple of times. When he's near, I'm suddenly aware of the feral attraction clawing to get out of me. There's a need inside of me that sees everything in Mac, and I'm terrified he sees me just as another chick.

The baby kicks, causing me to jerk forward. The movements are getting so strong I swear I'm going to pee myself sometimes.

"You okay?" Mac eyes me warily.

Grabbing Mac's hand, I press it to my belly. The baby rolls under his touch, my stomach visually moving. Mac's eyes search mine in confusion before lighting up. "Do you feel that?"

He nods silently, his face in awe and confusion. Like he's realizing for the first time there's an actual life inside of me. Taking my hand off his, he leaves his palm on my belly. The dark look in his eyes, the pinch of his eyebrows... I wish I knew what he was thinking at this exact moment.

Swinging dilated pupils my way, we sit there in silence as the baby and Mac get acquainted through my skin. The firm press of his palm and the heartbeat skipping in my chest is all I can focus on through the passing seconds.

Mac clears his throat, breaking the moment. He pulls his hand from my stomach, and a shiver bumps its way up my back. Leaning over the couch, he hands two blankets to me.

"Check out this baby blanket, it's muslin, or some kind of soft shit, I don't know."

It's as if getting too close scared him, making my assumption that Mac has a hard time feeling, accurate.

"Yeah, they're soft," I agree. One has little green and purple long neck dinosaurs on it, and the other pink and peach feathers.

"I figured you'd like the feathers, being Indian and all." He rubs his chin looking his purchases over. Silently laughing, I run my fingers across the feathers, the stories my grandmother used to tell me about our descendent tribes. It seemed so much easier back then.

"I also got you this." Pulling from his back pocket is a pretty pink iPhone. Taking it from him, I'm in awe of its slick screen and matte pink backing.

"It's under my name and all, so nobody can trace... but me," he winks, bragging about his tech skills.

Placing everything back in the bag, I realize Mac got a lot of things, the phone had to have cost him.

"How much did you spend on all this?" I can't help but ask.

"Doesn't matter. Oh"—he reaches in the bag and tosses a thing of pills at me—"fucking take those, they're important. All right?" I look the label over. Prenatal vitamins.

Closing my eyes, I control my breathing and reopen them. This man is breaking through my lust for him and lacing it with something so much more.

"You didn't have to do this, Mac." I try my best to hold the emotion back in my voice, but I can't help it. I'm overwhelmed, nobody has done anything like this for me and the baby. He may not know how to interact with people, but he does when it counts.

He shrugs. "It's no big deal. If it makes you stop sulking around the place, it's fucking worth it."

Dropping the pills on the couch, I wrap my arms around him and hug him hard. He tenses as if he's not used to someone hugging him. I'd do anything to hear this man's story one day.

"Thank you," I whisper into the soft skin lining his neck. He smells minty, and his body is so hard and warm against my skin I feel safe. It's so fucking good to touch another human being, that I don't want to let go.

The soft inhale behind my ear doesn't go unnoticed, his hand palming the dip in my lower back. I'm suddenly aware of every nerve ending in my body from the simple contact and have to pull myself away before I do something we both aren't ready for.

Letting go, my face is flushed, and my breasts feel heavy with want. I turn away from him not wanting him to see lust stinging my face.

"I love reading," I mutter, grabbing one of the books. Sitting on the couch, I run my thumb through the pages of hidden knowledge of having a baby.

He grunts in response.

"I've read the hotel pamphlet about a million times since I've been here and memorized the room service menu." I laugh awkwardly. The unmistakable tension fills the gap between us, something happened between us and neither of us know what to do with it.

"Well, I gotta do some work, so you just sit there and... I don't know." He runs his hands over the back of his neck, seeming out of character. Maybe I shouldn't have hugged him, I came on too strong. Wait, did he say work?

"Work?"

"Yeah, I hack shit on the side when I'm not doing club business," he mumbles.

"Or when you're not strutting around pregnancy stores." I smile, trying to ease the tension between us. Our eyes lock, and his bee-stung lips smirk in the cutest way.

"Shut up." He flips me the bird, marching to his room.

"Is that why they call you Mac, because you're the geeky computer guy?" I can't help but ask, he's full of mystery and sin I can't help but drown in curiosity. His steps slow, but he doesn't stop all the way before he picks up his pace again and heads into his room.

I bite my bottom lip, my finger tapping on the cover of the book he got me.

I'm going to learn Mac's story, even if it kills him to let me in. There's a lot more to Mac than the brooding biker, and he proved that today.

MAC

Sitting on the couch, my laptop straddling my knees, I hack and transfer funds for one of my clients. My focus on the firewall, and the music Simone has playing in her room.

Something from Selena Gomez, "Marshmallow Wolves" or some girly shit. I've tried to keep my distance since yesterday, something happened. Something I don't fucking understand. Yeah, I got baby shit for her, she needed it obviously but when I felt the baby kick. Something instinctive burned deep inside of me. I suddenly wanted to be more than an asshole, but the idea of it scares the shit out of me. My story isn't beautiful, and sad to say it's made me into the person I am today. What if I let her and this baby in and she decides she can do better?

Tapping my finger on the mouse anguish crashes in my chest like a hostile storm.

"What do you think?"

My eyes slip up my screen to Simone suddenly standing in front of me. She's wearing a tight black tank top, her breasts nearly spilling from the top, and the new maternal shorts I bought her. With her round ass faces me, you can't even see her belly bump.

Her thick hair spills down her back, her hooded eyes fluttering with black as night lashes peeking over her shoulder. Drinking her in inch by inch, my shaft tightens into a hard rod.

I suddenly don't care about boundaries or pasts. All I want is to touch her, and now.

Setting my laptop to the side, I saunter to her. My head lowered, eyes only on her. The way her hair is a sexy mess, I think about it splayed across my pillow. Her brown glossy eyes dilated with lust, I wonder if they'd roll into the back of her head when I sunk into her to the hilt. I wonder a lot of fucking things that've never crossed my mind before.

Stepping up behind her, my fingertips trace her bare shoulder. Her glowing tanned skin practically begging me to do despicable things to her. Brushing her hair to one side, I run my nose up the nape of her neck, the smell of her coconut skin forcing me to inhale deeper.

She's so clean and pure but fucked up in the head all at the same time.

"These shorts look hideous on you," I whisper into the back of her ear. Her breath hitches, her shoulders rising. I offended her.

Clutching the waistband, I jerk them down her legs and they slowly descend down to her ankles. Grasping her jaw, her lips parts, her head turning just slightly to where our eyes catch.

"Only a complete moron would tell you to put more clothes on, I never should have bought them," I admit. She leans into me, and I clench my jaw to keep from throwing her on my bed and diving my tongue deep into her mouth.

"Are you coming onto me, Mac?" Her voice laced with a husky sultry tone.

Dropping my hand from her shoulder, my fingertips teasingly caress the round of her ass cheeks poking out of her dark red panties. She has the thickest, sexiest ass I've ever seen.

"You're the one dropping your pants, baby." My finger slips beneath the lace of her panties and her chest rises from her weak attempt at controlling herself.

Clearing her throat, she eyes me with clearer eyes.

"I believe you did that."

"If I did it, I'd be pulling these off too." I fist her panties, the material rising up her ass crack giving me a full view of her round backside. Fuck, I could lose my dick in between those butt-cheeks all fucking night. I wonder if this is her normal ass, or from the pregnancy. Either way, I hope she keeps it.

She sighs, her body shivering from my touch. I want her, I want her so fucking bad I can close my eyes and taste it. So why haven't I had her?

"I- I think we should slow down," she whispers, but I don't think she means it. Not by the way her head lolls to the side for me to scrape my teeth against. My cock twitches from the rejection, and I suddenly wonder what the fuck I'm doing with this woman.

"Simone, I've been trying to slow myself down with you since I met you," I confess, and my chest burns realizing I've been holding back. I never hold back, every woman wants me.

She turns, her eyes wide and lips swollen.

I can't help it, I push for more and press my lips to hers. It's not sweet, or gentle. In fact, it's downright rude and commanding. I take her taste and fill my mouth with it. Her hands come up, hesitating against my chest and I swirl my tongue inside her mouth. Her supple breaths brush against my face as I take what I fucking want. Grasping her ass cheeks, I pull her onto me, grinding the wet spot on her panties against the bulge in my jeans.

She moans, her eyes popping open, and her hands make contact with my chest. Shoving me back. Rejection like a fucking atomic bomb lands right in my lap.

Flicking my lips, the taste of her still drenching my tongue, I shift my raging hard-on to one side trying to calm the throbbing some.

"I'm sorry, I just..." The back of her hand rests on her mouth as she stares at me with earnest eyes.

"Tell me you want me," I demand. I need to know it and now.

"I do, I just—"

"Got it," I cut her off. She's not like a club chick ready to drop to her knees and suck my cock. She's a woman who takes her time, gives a man blue balls until she gets to know them.

If I want to fully taste Simone, I'm going to have to hammer my walls down and let her in.

Guilt that I'm trying to fuck my deceased brother's girl tries to surface and has me suddenly feeling like a prick. These fucking feelings are giving me a headache. My eyes flick to her, feelings of guilt, but the wanting to pursue her conflicting with each other. It's all so new to me. I care too much what she thinks, and it makes me anxious.

Sitting on my bed, I grab my laptop, deciding it's night of porn and lotion.

I want Simone, but she comes with so much of the unknown I need a fucking map to decipher any of this shit going through my head.

Bending down, she pulls her shorts up, humiliation staining her face as she leaves the room.

Collapsing onto the pillows behind me, I exhale.

"Fucking Pocahontas is doing my head in."

15

ONE WEEK LATER

SIMONE

S itting on the floor with my legs crossed I look down at the street with my baby book in my lap, one hand on my belly. There are a ton of bikers down there today, more than usual.

THE SMELL of mint overtakes the room and I look over my shoulder to a freshly showered Mac. His wet blondish hair is swept back, and he's wearing an old looking Levi shirt with blue washed jeans.

HIS EYES slowly meet mine and I have to keep from smiling, a knot forming in the pit of my stomach. He has a look of torment dancing in his eyes, masking what beauty really lies within his soul. His bee-stung lips curve into a smirk when he catches me staring. We've been doing a lot of that, smiling and blushing around each other. I think we're both scared to make a dominant move. I'm terrified. I'm not just a one-night stand, I'm not that girl regardless of what my belly might convey at this moment. I want something more for me and the baby.

"CLUB IS HAVING A PARTY TONIGHT," he informs, digging his wallet out of a pair of dirty jeans. I look back to the motorcycles on the Strip, the idea of fresh air and being around other people appealing. I'm up for some conversation, loud music, and things that I'll never unsee.

"CAN I GO?"

He scoffs, and I narrow my eyes at him. "I'm serious, I'm so sick of being prisoned to a room. I'll blend in, just five minutes and you can take me back up here," I practically beg. I'm not a prisoner, I'm being protected and if I'm in his club I'll be protected from everyone, right?

HIS EYES FALL to my belly, a smile on his face. "You blending in at this point is pretty much impossible, babe."

My mouth parts, he called me babe. "Besides, it's not safe. The clubhouse has been blown up once already with your crazy ex looking for you—"

"He's not my ex!" I snap before he even has a chance to finish the sentence. Using all my strength, I pull myself up off the floor. My stomach is in the way of everything these days.

"I'm not done with this conversation."

"Zeek would have my head if I took you to the club." He shakes his head, grabbing his phone off the side table.

I place my hands on my hips, my lips pursed.

"I'm going, Mac!" I demand.

HE FREEZES, his cold eyes piercing through me.

"I'm not staying in this room for another fucking minute. I want to smell the pizza from across the street, hear the bikers chuckle over a few beers, and watch girls make a fool of themselves. I need... I need people." I shrug, hoping he understands I am human and need to socialize.

HE HUFFS, rubbing his left hand over his chin.

"PLEASE." I bat my lashes in the cutest, sexiest way I know how. Mac notices, his tongue sweeping across his bottom lip.

"FINE, you got five minutes and I'm bringing you back up even if I have to drag you. Understand?" He points at me like a child, and I can't help but smile. I don't even argue.

"Got it!"

WHITE TANK TOP that barely hides my swollen stomach, the shorts that Mac got me, and some flip-flops on my swollen feet, I follow him to the Sin City Outlaws' clubhouse.

I'm so excited to be out of the room I stare at everything we pass. People gambling in the casino, two men fighting and spilling beers over the blackjack table.

GETTING CLOSER, the smell of pizza makes my stomach growl and the baby kick. I've been staring at that damn pizza place for what seems like forever now. My taste buds salivate actually smelling it, being steps within its gooey cheese. I'll have to get Mac to take me by there on our way back.

TIGHTLY TUCKED behind the casino and hotel sits a newly refurbished clubhouse. I stop and look at it. Realization that Gatz died here pounding my excitement into grief. I place my hand on my belly, looking the place over. Mac stops, his hand reaching for mine.

"Stay close," he warns, not seeming to notice my unease. I wonder how he does it, being in the club and moving forward knowing his brother died inside of it?

ENTERING THE OUTLAWS' club, it's crowded with lots of people wearing leather. The smell of pizza replaced with cheap perfume, weed, and beer. The floor creaks beneath my flip-flops, and I notice it's clean. New even. I look around the place and notice it's all new. It was rebuilt after it exploded with Gatz inside. The baby kicks, and a sadness knots in my chest. Maybe coming inside wasn't the best idea. Everyone disappears, the brand-new interior turning gray and charred as ash and flames fall around me like confetti. It's as if I'm re-seeing the explosion the day it happened. Clenching my eyes shut, I will it all to turn back to normal. To hear the music, and smell the easy women, and see the men wrestling around.

OPENING MY EYES, breathing heavily everything is as it was, as if there never was an explosion here.

TRYING to take my mind off the loss of Gatz tugging the strings of my heart, I stifle a whimper and look around.

MAC COULD GET LAID HERE with a snap of his fingers, makes me wonder if he's holding out for me or just coming down here. I don't want to think about it actually.

EVERYWHERE MY EYES look there's something to make them widen with disbelief. I've worked with outlaws of every kind, but I've never gotten a peek behind the mask of their lifestyles before. Even when I lived with Kane, what I got to see was limited and strict. This though... is unreal. It's exciting, and I never want to return back to my room. I could stand here all night and watch everything. Like a wallflower at prom night.

SEX IS EVERYWHERE. A girl taking turns on two men with their bare cocks out sitting on the pool table, two women are making out on the bar, and there's a man in ass-less chaps walking around without a care in the world. It's a whole other world in here, and nobody seems to care of the carefree atmosphere.

A YOUNG MAN sitting behind the bar stares intently into a textbook. He looks out of place. His wavy blondish hair and sharp face lined with light stubble makes him appear ruggedly good looking. His shirt is missing the sleeves and is hanging off his shoulders to where you can see his hard chest.

"YOU MUST BE SIMONE!" A man with red hair steps in front of me.

He's tall, and lumberjack looking. My eyes catch his name on his leather cut. Machete. That's not scary at all. I feign a smile and hold my hand out to shake his. His eyes seem glued to my belly though, and I shift uncomfortably.

"HEY, keep an eye on her? I'm going to go grab a beer," Mac demands rather than asks the tall man. I swallow, my hand reaching out for Mac but missing by inches. Lips tight with a smile I look back up at the man.

"I'M MACHETE, I was close with Gatz, not Kane," he bluntly puts it. Gatz never mentioned him, but I sadly didn't get to do much pillow talk with Gatz.

"NICE TO MEET YOU," I holler over the music. He grins and turns to a man trying to talk to him over the loud music.

"THAT'S BISHOP," Machete points to the man I was staring at.
"He seems young to be in here," I shrug. God, I'm already starting to sound like a mother.

"HE'S SEVENTEEN, don't let that sun-kissed baby face fucking fool you. We all thought he was just a kid too, but he's about to be eighteen." I nod, seeing it now that I look a little harder at him. The muscle in his arms, the wrinkles on his forehead. He fondly smiles at the blonde behind the bar, chewing on the end of a pencil. "Trust me, he's better here than where he was."

My brows furrow, curious what that means. Where was he before that being in a motorcycle gang is better for him?

"Holy shit you're pregnant!" The wisecrack over my shoulder, has me glancing behind me at a man without a club cut on. He's got really blonde curly hair, and a neck tattoo of a spider crawling through his throat. I give him a look, one conveying how idiotic he is.

"You giving barebacks?" He chuckles, a man behind him giggling like a school girl. Glancing back at the lumberjack, he's gone, and I tense, not liking that Mac isn't here.

The man with the spider tattoo reaches for my belly, and I take a step back not wanting the contact.

He glares at me with heated eyes. Fear beads down my spine, my jaw clenching.

"What's your problem, bitch?" He reaches for my stomach again and before I can raise my hand to smack him away, Mac is standing in front of me slamming his knuckles into the guy's face.

They fall to the ground and the crowd surrounds us. I'm nearly knocked over, but a firm grip grabs me by the elbow. I follow the hand, finding Machete trying to pull me from the crowd.

THE MUSIC CUTS and a loud whistle has everyone looking to the left. Zeek stands on the bar, his face red with anger.

MAC STANDS from the ground his lip bleeding, but the other guy isn't getting up.

"You two, outside." Zeek points to me and Mac. My hand on my chest my eyes widen. What'd I do?

I follow Mac through the crowd until we reach outside. The fresh crisp air makes me hiccup, it was stuffier in there than I realized.

"WHAT THE FUCK is she doing down here?" Zeek wastes no time getting to the point.

"She wanted some fresh air, man?" Mac throws his arms out, his bloody lip making me feel bad.

"Get her back to the tower, and now!" Zeek raises a brow and turns to return back to his club. The way he's talking to Mac has me pissed, this was my idea, not his.

"I'm not fucking Rapunzel!" I clip. Zeek stops, his hand rubbing the scruff lining his cheek.

"No, you're a pain in my ass and until your little crush stops killing fellow brothers, your ass is to be hidden and not seen!" He lowers his head, his Adam's apple bobbing in his throat. "Got it?"

Dark beady eyes make me suck in my strength. If I didn't need his protection, I'd tell him to go fuck himself. So instead, I glare in a different direction.

"COME ON." Mac taps the soft skin under my arm, urging me to follow him.

Walking back to the hotel, that melty cheese smell has the baby kick and I stop in front of the pizza stand.

"Can we—"

"Keep fucking walking!" Mac barks.

"Oh, come on!" I argue, wanting it so badly I could cry. It'd take us just a few minutes to stop. Face pinched in rage, he jerks me forward by the arm.

"What the hell is your problem!" I tug in his grip, trying to free myself. I've never seen him so angry at me before.

He doesn't say a word the whole way up to our suite, which pisses me off. It's as if we went three steps back in our ... whatever we are.

Once inside the suite, he slams the door and pushes me up

against the wall; my head thudding off it. His hand punches the wall beside my head, making me flinch.

"Having you come to my club with me, was not an invitation for you to let just any fucking hangaround fondle you like street pussy!"

Rearing my hand back, I slap him across the face. He makes it sound like I wanted to be touched, and that is not even close to the truth. Little beads of rage form on my neck, my chest heaving with rage.

"Maybe if you didn't leave me, I wouldn't have had some cruddy biker putting his greasy hands on me!" I defend, not backing down. Our eyes lock, neither of us saying a word, but the silence between us is doing all the talking. It's sexual, jealous, and possessive.

"Do you fuck girls down there?"

His eyes narrow in on me in confusion.

"Since I've been here, have you fucked anyone?" I clarify.

He takes a step back, his hand on his jaw like he can't believe I'm asking him that. Maybe I have no right to ask him, we're not anything.

"Do you think I have?" he finally asks, his face devoid of any emotion.

"I don't know." Thinking about the man that Mac is, the glimpses I have seen of him, I don't think he'd get so jealous of me if I wasn't anything to him.

"Well, I haven't."

My head snaps up, our eyes meeting. Maybe my hormones are reading into it a little more than I should, but a biker who is being turned down by one woman and is refusing sexual favors from willing women says a lot to me.

"Really?" I can't hold the smile back that rips through my lips.

He doesn't reply, just smirks.

Raising my hand, I swipe at the blood crusting around his split, lip.

"You got punched for me," I whisper. Before I can pull my thumb away, he nips at it with his teeth, sucking it into his mouth. Warm wetness surrounds my thumbnail, and my clit twitches with arousal.

"While you're stuck in this tower with me, you and that baby are only to be touched by me, understand?" His throaty voice hitting me in every way.

I nod. Why do I nod? I'd never comply with being made an object.

Mac

In my room, I saunter to the floor to ceiling windows and press my forehead against the tinted glass. My chest is barreled tight with unfamiliar emotion. Seeing that guy touch Simone like that, it unlocked something feral and uncontrollable. The way that fucker's eyes seared into her pregnant belly like it was a fuel to getting his rocks off. I became... protective. I mean, Zeek ordered me to protect her, but what I felt, what I feel. It's more than just a job. A task.

Simone is more.

Her and that baby have become more.

I cannot deny it, and I will kill every motherfucker that tries to tell me different.

Maybe my mother dying being pregnant with me has torn the soft spot in my armor just enough for her and this baby to slip in, but either way... I can't turn away from them. I just keep pulling them in deeper, even if I know deep down Simone can do way better than me.

Winds blows against the glass, the city becoming foggy as a storm blankets over the streets. Heaven and hell are fighting tonight, and the gods know it.

I shove myself away from the glass and call it a night.

16

SIMONE

Wind bellows against the windows of my room. Howling and screeching waking me from my sleep. Scooting to the side of the bed, I push myself up and look out the window. I can't see a thing, there's nothing but sand. I stand, and the weight of my belly causes my lower back to instantly hurt. I don't know how much more weight I can take.

WOBBLING TO THE GLASS, I look out. Lightning strikes across the sky, and wind pummels against the glass. Little grains of desert making the scariest of sounds. Living outside of Vegas I've never really seen the full effect of a storm in the city. I frown, curious if the building is strong enough to withstand such hard wind gusts. The lamp I left on next to the bed flickers, and my heart skips a beat. A loud bellow outside the window snapping my attention from the bulb to the sudden crash. A bright lit up sign snaps in two, skidding down the street into complete darkness.

HAND ON MY BELLY, I open my bedroom door and look for Mac. Surely, he's seen something like this before and will know if we need to take some precautions or seek shelter.

THE MAIN ROOM is quiet and eerily dark, so I head to his room where the door is firmly shut. I stare at the handle, my bottom lip tucked in between my teeth. Should I open it? What if he's jerking off? Naked even.

A GUST of wind howls at the windows and I swear I feel the wind swish around my feet. Palming the chrome door handle I crack it open and find Mac splayed among the bed, his blanket tangled around his legs. I step inside, trying to be quiet. His chest is bare with just enough chest hair to show his rugged side.

HIS HAIR IS in his face and curled around his ears from turning his head back and forth in the plush pillows. He looks boyish, and vulnerable.

AGAINST MY BETTER JUDGMENT, my eyes trail down his abs to his dark blue briefs. His cock is hard, and there's no mistaking the barbell sticking through the tip of it. My eyes widen. That had to hurt, but the way it makes my toes curl into the floor with admiration, I can see why he got it.

It's sexy.

SOMETHING CRASHES OUTSIDE, and the baby kicks when fear

riddles through my limbs. Quickly I climb onto the bed and throw what blankets I can pull from Mac, over me. I close my eyes, hoping it's just a storm they normally get in this area.

"WHAT ARE you doing in my bed, Pocahontas?" The husky growl of his voice causes my nipples to bud against my top. I both want him to pursue me and wait like a gentleman.

I ROLL over to face him, his sleepy eyes looking right at me.

"I'M SCARED OF STORMS. This one seems pretty bad, are they normally like this?" I rest my head in my hands. The lightning outside casts a ghostly splash across Mac's face, his irises smoldering beneath the light.

HIS EYES FLICK to the window before landing back on me.

"They can get pretty destructive." He yawns before focusing on my hard-erect nipples. His lips curve into a smirk, before dark lustful eyes sink into me. "So you snuck into my room with"—he lifts the blankets, and I run my toe up my leg sexily—"just a small top and panties on?"

"WE WERE SCARED," I clarify, I push the blankets down. His eyes bolt to mine, his face softening.

REACHING UNDER THE BLANKETS, he rests his hand on my belly. "Is the baby awake?"

Just then the baby rolls against his hand, and Mac smirks. "I'd say so."

HE BRUSHES my shirt up and rubs his callused hand along my bare belly. Oh my God it feels so good on my stretched skin, I can't help but close my eyes and breathe into it. My toes curling into the mattress for more. My skin has been stretching so bad lately it never stops itching.

HE RUBS FARTHER UP, and a deep sigh catches in my throat. Inhaling a deep breath, I will his fingers to go just a little higher. As if he read my body language, Fingers swipe amongst the bottom of my breast and my knees arch on their own. My panties soak with arousal, I claw at the sheets, and my head presses into the pillow.

"FUCK POCAHONTAS, you're driving me wild with those little sighs."

"JUST DON'T STOP TOUCHING ME." Flexing my hips, I urge him on.

HE LEANS IN CLOSER, his breath hot and sticky against the crook of my neck. With his body tucked up to my side he's warm to the touch, with muscles bulging from holding his own weight. I cock my head to the side and stare into his hooded eyes. They're a heavy brown and focused directly on me. His erect cock presses into my thigh, and I widen my knees. Wanting him.

HE LOOKS DOWN, acknowledging my invitation.

"You have no idea what you're doing." His voice throaty.

His hand slowly slides down my belly and I can't help but tremble under his touch. His fingers tickling the inside of my thigh until a shiver laces around my neck making it hard to breathe. God just touch me already. My clit is practically throbbing with the need for his attention.

HIS FINGERTIP TUGS at the fabric of my panties, and a supple mewl spills from my mouth. Using the pad of his finger he swipes through my wetness, and I buck against his hand for more. I want to be filled and stretched by him so badly I physically ache with need.

"THIS FOR ME, POCAHONTAS?" He plays with my wetness between his fingers.

Lips tucked between my teeth to keep my composure, I nod.

The elastic of my underwear slaps against my sensitive skin, and my entire lower half blooms with warmth.

THE BED SHIFTS, and a cold draft slip over me. I open my eyes finding him biting his bottom lip and looking at me with an unfamiliar look. His eyes not as lustful as before. Sucking in a tight breath, I pull my shirt down to cover my bare stomach.

"WE SHOULD GET SOME SLEEP," he suggests, but the crack in his voice suggests he's struggling with this suggestion. Grasping the blanket, he throws it over us, and lays behind me, protectively placing his hand on my belly. The baby kicks it as if it knows it's him.

STARING AT THE CEILING, my body is so wound up if I move my thighs just right, I'm sure I'd come all over myself. I close my eyes, trying to focus on the wind blowing against the windows and not the sexy man behind me.

IT'S NO USE, I can't. What just happened? Why doesn't he want me? Turning my head, I look at him. He has his eyes closed. His nostrils flaring with hard breathing.

"WHAT WAS THAT?" I have to ask. His eyes open, but he looks past me.

"I CAN'T SLEEP with you, Simone." His voice dry. Rejection stabs me in the chest.
    "Why? Did Zeek say something?" I push. "Is it because I said I wanted to take it slow before?" God why did I fucking say that?

HE HUFFS, his face looking conflicted.
    "I just – I just can't, okay?"

"IS IT BECAUSE OF GATZ?"

HE FREEZES, and I know I hit the issue on the head. Sitting up, the blankets pulled to my neck, I wait for him to explain.

"HE-HE WAS MY BROTHER. We have a code not to fuck with another man's woman and you were his. Him not being here—"

HOLDING MY HAND UP, I stop him right there.

"I WAS NOT HIS. It was a one-night stand that led to this," I point to my stomach. "He loved Kane, Kane loved him. Neither of them loved me." The last few words a mere whisper. "I'm nobody's."

MAC'S FACE pales as if he's seeing me for the first time as a single woman. Opening his mouth, he begins to say something and shuts it. Brows furrowed, he tucks his arm around my belly, gripping my hip and pulling me close.

HORMONES WANT ME TO CRY. I want to yell and be mad, but I just scoot under the blankets, and tuck my head onto his shoulder. The smell of mint soothing me and the baby into a comforting ease.

"YOU'RE SOMEBODY'S," he mutters, his words vibrating his chest.
    Placing my arm on his hard chest, I close my eyes and wonder if he means I'm the club's, or his.

I DON'T KNOW what just happened, but I can't take much more of his soft touches, and hard comes on only to be left with wet panties, and unsatisfied.

17

SIMONE

Standing in the living room, I stare outside. The storm did a number on the city. There's dust all over the streets and signs down everywhere. The sun is high in the sky; it looks hot outside. My skin chills from the air conditioner and I shiver. I want to be outside where it's warm. I want to feel the sun on my cheeks. I sigh and turn to find Mac sitting on the couch, drinking a beer with his computer propped up on his ripped jeaned legs.

"CAN WE GO TO THE POOL?"

He scoffs but doesn't reply.

"I'm serious."

HIS EYES LIFT over the screen of his computer, clearly annoyed at my persistence.

"Yeah, because last time we left this room, it went so well."

He has a point, but that was all him, and the way his eyes dart back to his computer I can tell he's remembering him going all protective-boyfriend on that creepy guy.

"What are you doing on there that's so important anyway?" I lift my chin to his spaceship looking laptop.

HE TAKES a large gulp of his beer.

"STUFF," he clips.

Lifting my foot, I nudge his boot off the coffee table.

"Tell me, or I'll just keep asking."

HE GROANS, setting his beer down.

"Studying algorithms."

I raise a brow. "Why?"

"IF I TOLD YOU, I'd have to kill you." His line so cliché I can't help but roll my eyes.

"OK, JAMES BOND."

HE CHUCKLES, running his hand through the hair that's fallen in his eyes. The way his face lights up is contagious, so I grin.

"LET'S just say I'm trying to find a futile future for the club's customer network."

MY EYES RISE WITH APPRECIATION. Mac really is a smart guy, he could be on Wall Street or something if he wanted to.

"HOW'D you end up in a biker gang? You could do anything you want with those kinds of skills," I blurt my curiosity.

MAC BITES HIS CHEEKS, his eyes looking to something in the distance.

"BECAUSE NO NINE to five desk job would ever be home to me. Not like the Sin City Outlaws. Plus, I'm pretty sure they'd frown when I stole money from them because I was unhappy with their shitty pay. Besides, what fun would it be to play by the rules of a company when I can break so many and get away with it on my own."

HE LIFTS his brows at me, and I have nothing in reply. See, smart guy.

"Why don't you do real estate or some shit instead of giving the country the fuel it needs to flare up illegal gangs around the states?"

My mouth parts, him knowing what I did before... before this, it's surprising.

"What, you didn't think I did my research on you, Princess?" He tilts his head to the side, his face smug. "The Ray family is practically the Native American mafia."

I lift my chin, proud of what my family and I have accomplished.

"What fun would it be to sell a house unless it was a grow

house. I couldn't make the kind of money I did following Uncle Sam's rules."

"Exactly." He points the barrel of his beer bottle at me.

I tilt my head to the side, curious about this man more than I've ever been curious about anything.

"How long have you been with the club?" I press.

"Long time," his tone dry. He's done divulging any further information.

His hands go back to click-clacking on the keyboard, and my boredom returns.

Hand on my belly I rub it in a circular motion. "Either you take me to the pool, or I'm going on my own," I state, not done with my conversation. "Everyone will see you trying to tug a pregnant woman in distress back to your hotel room," I continue.

He slams his laptop down and rolls his eyes. "Damn it, woman, why do you have to be such a pain in my ass." The sentence draws out, really indicating how much I'm irritating him.

He stands, pulling his phone from his jeans.

It takes everything I have not to giggle. Being annoying to him really does entertain me.

"I guess I could use some fresh air too." His brows scrunched together, he turns, hushing demands into his phone.

Biting my nail, I wait for him to finish his call.

Sighing, he tucks his phone back into his jeans pocket.

"FIND SOMETHING TO WEAR, you got ten minutes at the pool and then it's back in here and you stop annoying me." He points at me, his face serious.

I SQUEAL with excitement and waddle off to my room. I don't have a swimsuit. Not anything even close to one, so I head over to Mac's room and open his drawer. He has a wife-beater shirt and a pair of drawstring shorts. I snatch them and put them on in his room. The shirt stretches over my belly bump just barely, and I have to double tie the shorts to make them fit, but they work.

GRABBING A TOWEL FROM HIS BATHROOM, which is much bigger than mine. He even has a damn tub. I head back to the living room.

"I'M READY!"

HE STALLS, his eyes widening. I look down to see what he's staring at.

"SHIT." I cross my arms. My nipples are hard, dark, and showing through the thin material like tractor beams. I forget how big my tits have gotten being pregnant.

"You are not going out there like that."

I scowl at him. "No shit." I shake my head and go to my room to find a bra.

Finally, after shoving my tits into a sports bra, we head out into the hall and go down to the fifth floor. When the elevator doors open, the entire hallway seems empty. *Where is everyone?* Mac opens a glass door, and we step inside, the smell of the pool close by.

We pass lockers and an empty desk with towels sitting on the counter before going outside to empty loungers, lifeguard chairs abandoned, and the pool crystal clear. The only sign of life is the vibrations from the speakers playing "Love Gun" by Kiss.

"Where is everyone?" I ask. I was hoping to watch some kids splash around, or some drunk people make a fool of themselves.

"You're not to be seen, remember? Zeek made that abundantly clear, so"—he shrugs—"I just informed everyone it was time for maintenance and now you got thirty minutes." He juts his chin toward the pool. "Go wild."

My heart flutters at the thought he went to such great lengths to appease me wanting a little fresh air by the pool.

"You did all this for me?" I mutter. He doesn't reply, just struts by me and sits on the concrete next to the crisp looking water. He tugs his boots and socks off and rolls his jeans to his calves. Watching him, he dips his bare feet into the water and swishes them around.

Fuck, why is Mac with rolled up jeans, in the sun, so sexy.

"You going to stare or join me?" he asks without looking at me. I clear my throat and saunter over to him.

Placing my hand down, I try and carefully sit down, but it's a process that is embarrassing and just plain fucking tiring. I can't get any bigger, I swear.

Finally, after sitting my ass down, I take a deep breath and plop my feet into the crisp water. Coldness wraps around my legs and soothes my cabin fever, and the warm sun kisses my dark braided hair. I close my eyes. This is nice.

"Better, Princess?"

"Mmm," I hum. "I've never been much of a pool person," I confide.
    "Just today, when we're trying to keep you from a psychopath?" Sarcasm drips from his voice.
    "Yep," I sass.

He kicks water at me, and I squeal as cold droplets soak my shirt. My mouth drops in dismay and the baby kicks at my sudden excitement.

"You asshole!" I splash water back at him, and his eyes widen that I retaliated.

JUST WHEN WE begin to have a full out splash war like a bunch of little kids, the doors to the hotel open, the sound of stomping boots grabbing our attention. Mac stands, pulling his gun from the waistband of his jeans.

MY HEART SKIPS A BEAT, seeing him go from normal to lethal in a matter of seconds. I didn't even know he had that on him.

"YOU WANT to explain to me why you cleared the entire pool deck for alleged maintenance?" The familiar sound of Zeek has me suck in a tight breath. Shit, we've been caught.

"FUCK MAN, you scared the shit out of me." Mac lowers his gun. The sight of him in his rolled-up jeans, wet bare feet, and sunburnt shoulders does things to a hormonal pregnant woman. Zeek marches farther out onto the concrete patio where I can fully see him. His large shoulders barely containing his leather cut and ripped up shirt. His dark eyes narrow in on me, and I raise a brow in response.

"NEEDED SOME AIR, thought if I took the risk of someone seeing us away, it'd be fine," Mac continues.

ZEEK NODS, running his hands through his hair. His eyes closing as if he's trying to be understanding.

"DOC from the Devil's Dust is here to see Simone, check out the baby and shit," Zeek explains with a husky voice. I didn't see Doc for the pregnancy at The Devil's Dust. Kane was very protective and didn't let me around the club much. Especially when I started showing.

"OKAY," I nod, pulling my legs from the water.

MAC IS BY MY SIDE, his hands on my hips helping me up. Zeek's eyes flash with an unknown look as he watches Mac helping me up.

MAC AND ZEEK stare at each other, unspoken words that I don't understand being spewed at each other. I can only imagine what Zeek thinks of me. Probably a club hopper, or whatever Mac called me when we met.

"SHE'S WAITING, LET'S GO." Zeek turns, stomping off toward the entry doors.

MAC PLACES his hand on the small of my back, and my entire

belly fills with butterflies. The baby kicks, noticing the emotion this man is stirring inside of me.

I palm my belly, silently telling little one not to get attached to Mac Daddy. Not yet.

Simone

BEING HIDDEN from any wandering eyes, I feel like the President of the United States as I'm escorted back to the top of the casino. The elevator takes us to our room, the cliché music doing nothing for the tension in the small space.

ZEEK GLARES AT MAC, and Mac sneers in response.

ZEEK LEADS the way to the suite, and we follow quietly. Not that Mac has to say anything, his tense shoulders are raised, his chest puffed, and jaw flexed.

INSIDE OUR SUITE, Doc is setting up a tall looking machine in the living room; a black duffle bag on the coffee table. I haven't seen her in what seems like forever, but she still looks as I remember. Blonde hair up in a ponytail, dark blue shirt fitting her curvy-self perfectly, and a pair of dark jeans to match. Even out of scrubs she looks like a doctor though.

SHE TURNS to our entering and smiles brightly.

"Hey guys, I just finished setting up. Simone, why don't you lay down?" she suggests, her hand waving above the purple couch.

Giving Mac a look, I clear my throat and head toward her nervously. This is the first ultrasound, one to tell me if I've been doing my job as a mother right. Sitting down on the plush fabric, I can't help the anxiety building inside of me as I lay down.

"There won't be any records or anything of this happening, right?" That was the whole reason Kane wouldn't let me have much intervention as far as being seen by doctors. He was protecting me and the baby.

"No, this is all portable, and won't sync to anything. I will delete all images and information after this visit. One hundred percent confidential." She nods confidently, looking to Zeek and Mac to assure them.

"Why'd you have her come all this way when we have our own doctors?" Mac asks dryly.

"My brother Lip from The Devil's Dust assured me it—"

"After I heard what kind of chaos Simone was in, I wanted to help. I told Lip to call Zeek and offer my services," Doc informs, not taking her eyes off her setting everything up. It takes me aback.

"THANK YOU," I whisper, grateful she's here. I feel like I can trust her, I've heard and seen her work on members of the club. She's loyal.

HER EYES MEET mine and I swallow the lump in my throat, she gives a tightlipped smile and sits next to me, grabbing my hand firmly.

"I knew you were pregnant, but I assumed you were getting care elsewhere." She sighs heavily, and I nibble my bottom lip nervously. "I really wish Kane would have come to me about this. If he would have just told us what was going on, we could have made sure you had the best care. Plus, if there's anything I've learned from being with The Devil's Dust, it's covering things up is a piece of cake." She grins, and I can't help but laugh. Who knew she was as dirty as the bikers. "Now, let's see that baby, hm?"

SIGHING WITH SOME RELIEF, I get comfortable and adjust my head to where I can see Doc. She squats next to me, pulling the pole that has a screen and wand attached to it.

"WHERE'S YOUR BETTER HALF?" I make light conversation. I remember a guy named Bobby being with her at the Devil's Dust. Surely, he didn't let her travel alone.

"DOWNSTAIRS PLAYING THE SLOTS. He'll lose," she arches her brow, and I smile in return.

SHE LIFTS MY SHIRT, my tan stretched out belly on display for everyone. She squirts blue looking jelly on my skin, it's coldness forcing goosebumps to rise against my skin.

"SORRY, they usually have a warmer for these things at the hospital."

"It's okay." I arch my neck to look at the screen, not concerned with the temperature of the gel. Black and white splotches blur across the screen, and she begins pressing buttons on the machine. Everyone's quiet as they watch and observe; it unnerves me. What is she seeing? Is there anything wrong?

"SO, from what I can tell, baby looks like it's growing perfectly," she mutters pushing and pulling the wand across my belly. "Now what I'm telling you isn't one-hundred percent because I don't have all the tools I would have if we were to do this at a hospital." she informs.

"IS IT HEALTHY?" Mac asks. Looking over, Mac stands behind the couch watching, one hand on his chin as he rests his elbow on his arm across his chest.

"SO FAR SO GOOD. Five fingers, five toes." She zooms in and I see little fingers. I gasp, my hand covering my mouth. Those are real fingers and toes. Oh my God! Doc smiles at me.

"Amazing, isn't it?" she whispers.

"Is it a boy or girl?" Mac asks, hovering over me. Doc looks at me, her eyes shining.

"Do you want to know?"

I glance at Mac, why do I look to him for confirmation? The thought takes me aback but only for a second because we both smile like fools.

"Yes, I want to know."

She slides the wand upward and two legs pop up on the screen. It's so unreal to finally see the baby as a human.

"Looks, like a... It's a girl!" She beams.

"A girl," I whisper, my eyes watering. Thoughts of dresses and hair bows fill my head. Will she look like me or her daddy? My skin prickles with excitement, ready to have my little girl already.

"A little girl," Mac mutters with awe.

"Do you have a name picked out?" Doc asks, looking at the screen.

I shake my head. "No, not yet."

"It'll come to you," she offers her wisdom.

Putting the wand up, she tucks a strand of blonde hair behind her ear and looks at the men.

"WHY DON'T you guys leave the room for this next part?"

"Why?" Mac snaps, his face of bliss disappearing fast.

"I need to check her cervix, see if she's dilating and—"

"I'll be in the kitchen," Mac waves her off, not needing to hear any more.

"PULL YOUR SHORTS DOWN, babe, I'll try to be as gentle as I can." She grabs gloves from a box attached to the pole on the machine.

TAKING A DEEP BREATH, I reach to each hip and shimmy my shorts and panties to my ankles.

Doc spreads my legs and inserts two lubricated fingers. I look to the ceiling, this is humiliating.

"ANY CRAZY CRAVINGS YET?" she tries small talk during this intrusive moment.

"Um, pizza."

"Pizza?" She chuckles as if that's not that odd.

"Yeah, there's a pizza place across the street I've been eyeing since I've been here," I explain, my stomach growling thinking about it.

I NOTICE her eyebrows pinch together as I swear she's digging for gold with her fingers. My toes curl, and my teeth grit as it begins to hurt.

"YOU SAID YOU'RE WHAT, seven and half months along?"

"Yeah?" I reply nervously. "Almost eight."

She pulls her fingers from me and nods at my shorts conveying I can pull them back up.

"What's wrong?" Mac is back in the room before I can even get my shorts up.

"She's dilated two centimeters and is forty percent effaced."

"Ok, what the fuck does that mean?" He shrugs.

"She shouldn't be showing signs of going in labor this early, to this extent anyway. If she continues to show progress, it worries me that little one is going to try to come early." Terror wraps itself around my throat that I may go into labor sooner rather than later. She looks at me. "Have you been stressed?"

My face falls. "Really?" That's a dumb question.

"Well, if we could, I would recommend bedrest at the hospital, but I understand that's not an option, so I'm putting you on bedrest here in the hotel."

"Bedrest? As in, I can't get up?" I'm already tired of being locked up, I can't sit in a bed for three more months!

"I MEAN, you can get up and move around, just don't exert your-self too much." She looks at the men with a pointed stare.

"What are you going to do when she has this baby? There will have to be public record of it, you will have to take her to a hospital."

"WE WILL WORRY ABOUT that when it happens," Zeek replies from the kitchen.

Doc rolls her eyes and begins to pack her things.

"JUST TAKE IT EASY. OKAY?"

"Yeah, I will." I sit up, pushing my shirt down.

"CAN we test to see who the father is?" Zeek asks.

Doc sighs, looking at my stomach. "We can, but there are risks."

"What kind of risks?" Zeek grunts.

"Um, off the top of my head. Ammonitic fluid could leak, and she could lose—"

"No." Mac stands straight, his shoulders tense. Doc looks at me with wide eyes and hands me a tissue from the box on the side of the machine.

"WHAT DO YOU MEAN NO? If we can find out if the baby is Gatz—"

"There's fucking risks! No way are we doing it, brother!" Mac's voice carries through the room. Swinging my feet over the side of the couch, I glare in their direction, angry they are deciding this without me. I am the mother, I should have the say so.

"CAN I speak to you in the hall?" Zeek's brows raise at Mac, his face red.

"Yeah, no problem!" Anger laces in Mac's voice and he stomps to the hallway slamming the door behind them.

"WHAT DO YOU WANT?" Doc asks, packing up her equipment.

I FLIP my hair over my shoulder.

"I don't want a test, I don't care who the dad is. The baby is mine regardless, and I love her." I shrug, the words pouring from my mouth without even having to think about it.

I love my daughter.

"THEN I WOULDN'T DO it then." She gives a curt nod, and I nod back.

"I'M NOT."

18

MAC

I slam the door behind me, knowing my ass is about to get chewed, and I'm ready for it. This testing on the baby is not happening. The hallway is musky, the smell of smoke from the casino drifting through the vents.

"WHAT THE HELL IS GOING ON?" Zeek turns, flicking his chin with his thumb. The dim lighting casting shadows upon his dark face.

"TESTING IS DANGEROUS, it's fucking stupid. Both dads are gone, so why does it fucking matter who is the father?" I shrug, getting to the point.

"WHAT IF IT'S not Gatz? What if it's neither of theirs and this chick is using us?" Zeek points out.

I SHAKE MY HEAD. "She's not like that." I've been trapped with her weeks, I would have picked up on her lying. Besides, what woman would want to be imprisoned like this unless she was in the position Simone says she's in?

"OH, I see what's going on." Zeek chuckles. A smug look crossing his face. I'm not going to like what he's about to say.

"What does that mean, 'I see what's going on?'" I mock.

"YOU FUCKING HER?" He tilts his head to the side. Son of a bitch!

I SHOVE HIM, pissed at his accusation.

"No, I ain't *fucking* her! You gave me a job to protect her and that baby, and that's what I'm doing." My nostrils flare. I've always been asked to be the tech guy, this is the first job that Zeek has given me outside of my skill and I'm not going to fuck it up just because his head is somewhere else.

HE TILTS HIS HEAD BACK, his chin lifting with conflicted eyes. He's not at all affected by my outburst, and it makes me want to punch him in the face.

"YOU DONE?" he asks.

INHALING, I realize I'm losing my fucking mind. I've never reacted like this to anything in my life. I'm the quiet fucker in the background watching everyone else's drama.

I turn away and run my hands down my face.

Glancing back, I look Zeek in the eye. Emotions I've never felt before filling my chest. These feelings foreign and uncomfortable. My life was balanced in hues of black and gray until Simone walked in beaming of color and drawing me in.

I LOVE a child that's not even mine. Protecting it is not a job anymore, but my own choice.

"I have kids, I have a woman, and I know a protective father and lover when I see one." Zeek points at me, but I don't respond.

"IF THAT BABY isn't Gatz's, you either claim her and the baby, or they're out, brother. This isn't a fucking charity."

I WIPE at the sweat on my forehead, so fucking mad my teeth are grinding into dust.

"WE HAVE A CLUB MEETING FRIDAY, show up." Zeek saunters off to the elevator, and the doors shut.

LIPS PURSED, chest tight I holler and punch the wall so hard my fist drives through it. Drywall dusting my wrist.

THIS IS why I keep my head in computers, my focus only on fucking people over. Caring for a female, this is a whole new world I'm not sure I'm prepared for.

THE DOOR to the suite opens, Doc standing there with wide ocean-colored eyes as she looks to the hole in the wall and my red hand.

"EVERYTHING OKAY?" Blonde hair that escaped her ponytail frames her heart-shaped face. She's smart and is a looker.

"PEACHY," my tone dry. I shove past her and grab the bottle of whiskey off the bar and head to my room. Not daring to look back at her or Simone. I need space. I need to figure out what the hell I'm doing. Simone and this baby have me so distracted I don't even know who I am anymore.

Next Day
Simone

Mac stayed in his room the whole night, he didn't even come out for his midnight sandwich like he does every night. I ate alone, my eyes on his bedroom door the whole time. It was our thing to eat a sandwich at midnight.

I'm worried about him.

SITTING on the floor in the sunlight casting through the window, I look through the baby name book. Placing the pen in my mouth I focus hard on the F section.

"Farrah. Faryl. Farzana." None of these sound right saying them out loud.

"SHOULDN'T you be in bed? Resting?" Mac questions entering the room. The sound of his voice makes my heart race and the baby kick. I hate how excited I get at the mere sound of his husky words.

"Rooster is outside if you need anything. I'm going out," Mac informs, not offering further detail. This being the first I've heard from him since the ultrasound, I don't respond. I don't want to seem desperate for his every attention. He's ignored me all night and day, and I don't want to seem too eager to learn where he's off to.

But I am. I want him to stay and help me pick a name out. I bet he'd pick one that I'm overlooking, one that is original and perfect.

I WANT to sit on the couch and watch TV with him, annoy him with my baby shows. To get into trouble and sneak out of the room again, to have him talk to me again. He has this tone that is smooth but scratches at the end with so much edge it makes my heart beat a little faster every time he says my name.

I DROP the pen from my mouth and lower my head. I'm a damn mess. We're a damn mess.

I LOOK out the window at the people passing by. My heart tugging with what Doc said yesterday. What am I going to do when I'm ready to have the baby?

HOURS PASS, and I eventually fall asleep on the couch watching re-runs of The Walking Dead. The door opening wakes me up, but that smell of melty cheese has me popping my head up over the back of the couch.

MAC SETS two pizza boxes down and rests his hands on the lip of the counter with his head hung. His distressed football shirt sweaty, his hair tousled in his face.

I OPEN my mouth to say something but then shut it. I'm upset he's been avoiding me, but he looks upset. I've never seen an upset Mac.

"I'M- I'm not good at this kind of thing." He shakes his head. "My mother died giving birth to me, and you Simone..." His head raises, haunted eyes taking my breath away like a breeze sweeping through a graveyard. "You're a loaded gun full of my skeletons I've been trying to run from my entire life."

MY BROWS FURROW WITH SYMPATHY, every mystery about Mac slowly falling into place. Scooting off the couch, I saunter over to him and gently place my hand on his shoulder.

"BEING BULLIED AS A KID. Homeless after my father was arrested. Outcasted as society's garbage." He waves his hand around. "I can handle all of that but send a pregnant woman my way and it dismantles the way I see everything," he scoffs, his eyes clenching shut.

"You were homeless?" I press for more information. "Until Zeek's father found me. Him and the club raised me." Having a bunch of brutal men raising you, it's no wonder Mac isn't great at showing his feelings.

"When I was a kid, I wasn't very popular either," I confide in him. "In fact, we aren't so different." He lifts his head, interested. "Our maid had an old-school Nintendo in her room, and I'd always go in there and play it. Kids from other families in the area thought I was weird because I wanted to be like Princess Peach instead of Brittany Spears." I laugh remembering how much I loved playing video games. Until my father found out and fired her that is.

He chuckles, lifting his chin, he bites at his bottom lip. "I'd beat your ass in Mario any day." Lightening the mood.

"I don't know about that," I raise a brow. He grabs a triangle box that holds a slice of pizza, and opens it, turning it toward me. I forget everything and focus on the triangle that has had my heart since I arrived here.

"You've been craving this pizza for a while, eh?" he changes the subject.

"Please look away, this might get ugly," I beg of him, picturing me devouring the pizza like a man. He grabs a slice, his teeth tearing into it viciously.

"Pssh. I'm a man, you and little peach haven't seen anything when it comes to eating pizza," he states with a mouth full.

"Little Peach?" I bite into the pizza, and it's so cheesy, sauce spilling into my mouth like heaven.

He juts his head toward my growing stomach. "Yeah, until you come up with a name, I figured, I don't know..." He starts backpedaling and it's the cutest thing ever.

"No, I like it." I smile, sauce all around my mouth. "For a nickname anyway, I have to find a real name soon."

He doesn't say anything, heading to the couch, he flips the TV on. Eyeing him from the counter, eating my pizza. He told me a lot tonight, a lot I've been dying to know but all it did was breed more questions. I wonder why his dad was arrested, and if anyone else knows about his mother dying while giving birth to him.

My heart skips a beat thinking what if I die giving birth, would Mac take the baby?

I close my eyes. No, I won't think like that. I'm going to be fine.

———

Sitting on the floor looking out of the window like I normally do, one of the books I got from the hotel when I was with Kane sits in my lap. I was reading one of the pregnancy books, but it made me anxious reading about everything that could go wrong.

HOPE IS STRONGER THAN FEAR, and I have to believe that the universe will turn in my favor when this all comes racing to an end. I rest my hand on my belly. Hope is the drug I've been living on for the past several months after all.

"WHAT IS THAT? I see you always reading it," Mac says from behind me. Leaning back on my hands, I look at him. He's at the kitchen island cleaning his gun, his laptop open right next to him. He's shirtless and has an unlit cigarette hanging from his lips. I wonder if he quit or if he's just not smoking around me.

"WHEN I WAS WITH KANE, I didn't have a view, TV, much of anything. So when the maid would find books, she gave them to me to read. This is one of them." I hold the worn book up.

"YOU LIKE READING?" He raises a brow, dropping the rag he was wiping his pistol with.

I nod. "Hmm, didn't take you for a reader." I find his assumption insulting.

"JUST BECAUSE I was born with a silver spoon in my mouth, doesn't mean I'm stupid." I roll my eyes. Actually, I never took to reading much, not until I was locked in that hotel room by myself day after day.

"I NEVER SAID you were stupid, just surprised you like to read. I don't come 'cross many women that like to read."

"THAT'S JUST IT, you've never met a woman," my tone snarky.

HE SMILES. "TOUCHÉ."

"ACTUALLY, to be fair, I just got into reading not long ago." My lips press into a fine line. "I only have a few books, but they're amazing. When I read them, it takes me on a new journey every time."

MAC PLUCKS the cigarette out of his mouth and looks at me with an unreadable look. It's almost brooding, but sexy. Alluring if you will.

"WHAT?" I laugh nervously.

HE SIGHS, looking down at his cleaning tools. The man's a mystery in every aspect.

His phone chimes and he picks it up.

"SHIT," he mutters under his breath. He stands from the stool, his low-slung sweatpants making my cheeks warm. They dip so low you can see veins leading down beneath the fabric.

"I've got a club meeting to go to. Rooster is being sent up," he informs. Leaning against the bar, his elbows resting on the lip of the granite he sips on a cup of coffee.

"Oh- okay." I look back down at my book. I hate being by myself, but hopefully he'll be back soon. I'd invite Rooster in for tea or something, but I've seen him through the peep-hole and he's kind of creepy looking.

Clouds suddenly blanket the sun, and I move to the couch to look the baby name book over again. I circle and cross out original names for what seems like forever.

God, who knew this was going to be so hard. Every time I find a cute name, but in the back of my head, I can hear kids taunting or making it into something mean and ugly.

A knock at the door causes me to frown. Nobody is allowed in here, and if someone did show up, Rooster would handle it.

"Open up, police department!" A series of loud knocks follow.

That's strange. Maybe it's a prank from the girls. Either way, I'll handle it.

Using my hands, I try and push myself up. My stomach in the damn way again.

"Coming!" I slowly make my way to the door.

Unlocking it, I slightly open enough to see whose there.

A TALL WOMAN wearing a dark blue pantsuit looks me up and down. The distaste behind her pupils sends hairs on the back of my neck on end.

Her dark chocolate hair highlighted with streaks of light brown hair pulls into a sophisticated bun.

"I'm Lieutenant Lopez, can I come in?" She fakes a smile.

"You have a warrant?" I know the drill. I've been raised to tell cops as little as possible.

She laughs before kicking the door open with her black high heel. I stumble, my pregnant belly nearly getting hit by the doorknob.

"ARE YOU SERIOUS?" I slam the door shut, pissed at her careless behavior. She can't just come in like this.

"So, you're the reason why Mac hasn't been calling me back?" she asks, pretending to be interested in the hotel décor on the walls. Her perfect red nails trailing along the granite of the counters in the kitchen.

"GET OUT!" I demand, not wanting to know what she means by Mac not calling her back. Everything about this woman is sending red flags off. She glances over her shoulder, her eyes falling to my stomach. Her face falls, and she turns on her heel. The tension in the room triples.

"WHAT THE FUCK IS THAT?" She points.

I RAISE A BROW, the shade coming from this bitch coming on strong. She's a crooked cop and sleeping with Mac obviously.
"Get. Out!" I repeat, pointing toward the door.

SHE STEPS AROUND THE CORNER, her heels clicking to the rhythm of my heart. If I wasn't pregnant, I would tear this woman apart.

FEET FROM ME, the smell of her perfume makes me hold my breath. Downfall of being pregnant is I smell everything.
"What's your name?" Her long thick lashes flick with a threat.
I lift my chin, my nostrils flaring.

"YOU THINK Mac and you have something special?" Her eyes fall to my belly. She thinks it's Mac's. "Don't kid yourself. He belongs to me, I have his pierced dick in such a vise that if he tries to fuck me over... I'll expose the club."

SHE POKES her sharp fingernail into my belly, and I slap her across the face. Nobody fucking touches me.

HER HEAD WHIPS to the side, her cheek blooming red with my handprint.

EERILY SLOW, she faces me. Her lips rolling.

"Get out, or I swear to God, I will kill you with my bare hands."

"ARE YOU THREATENING ME? I will throw you in a cell until you give birth to that little shit. In fact, I'll have that child in foster care before you can get your fat ass off the birthing table."

I don't respond, I can't. My shoulders lifting and rising with my heavy breathing. She's working me up to the point I can barely breathe.

I want to hit her, really hurt her but I can't move from the anger driving through my veins.

"GIVE MAC MY BEST, HMM?" Turning around, she leaves, slamming the door behind her.

I GASP, relief flooding over me. Grabbing onto the counter, I slink into the barstool trying to catch my breath.

A SHARP PAIN strikes across my stomach, and I whimper. I inhale a controlled breath, trying to calm myself but it's not working. Easing out of the stool, I waddle to Mac's bathroom. He has a tub, and maybe a warm relaxing bath will soothe my Braxton Hicks. Leaning over the rim of the porcelain tub, I turn on the faucet, and undress. Trying to remember to breathe slowly and at my control the whole time. That bitch got me so worked up, I pray I'm not going into real labor.

"STAY IN THERE, BABY." I rub my stomach.

THE WATER LINE halfway fills the tub and I step in, my hands holding my belly as I settle in. Water sloshes over the sides and I make a mental note to make sure I clean it up later.

I rub my stomach, my eyes closed, breathing through my nose.

WHO WAS THAT BITCH? Is she Mac's girlfriend? She obviously didn't know about me.

MOANING, I force that cop cunt out of my mind. Names, think of baby names.

My mind drifts into names starting with E, the woman in the blue pantsuit slowly forgotten. For now.

"SEE, everything's okay. Calm down little girl," I tell my baby.

19

MAC

Sitting at the club table, we discuss usual shit. Where to pick up merchandise, who owes us money, and where retaliation is needed.

Zeek looks my way, resting his head on his knuckles.

"Still no word on this Veer guy, I have every club in the area looking for him too."

I nod. My arm stretched out along the table picking at a piece of splintered wood. I try not to seem intrigued in what he's saying. Last thing I need is the boys busting my balls any more than they have, but I'm paranoid as fuck knowing this shit stain is out there somewhere.

"When the boys dropped by Simone's place, we were informed the father was found dead with a bullet to the back of the head, and we still haven't found the mother," Zeek's tone grim.

"You think the mother did it?" Machete from the end of the table. His reddish hair is slicked back again, and he's leaning over the table with a hand strangling a beer.

"Don't know." Zeek shrugs.

I sigh, knowing none of this is good news. None of which I want to tell Simone either.

Zeek slams the gavel down, ending the meeting. I crack my neck and step outside of the clubhouse. This Veer guy has me wound up tight. He could be around any corner, in any shadow.

He's good at hiding. Staring across the street, I notice a giant ad lit up on the wall of a Barnes and Noble quick store. The newest Nook spinning in the window, showcasing its newest features. Simone could really use that, it'd be better than carrying around a bunch of torn up books.

Maybe I should get her one. Wait, they have apps for book shit now I'll just set her up on that.

Machete steps up next to me, practically shadowing me he's so much bigger. He's like a fucking monster.

He pats me on the back, and I raise a brow at him.

"It's going to be ok. All of us have come to this point." He nods, but I'm clueless as what he's going on about.

"WHAT THE FUCK are you talking about?" I shrug.

"SIMONE." Her name slips from his mouth in a way that has me tense, like I should be the only one to say her name. I stare ahead, not playing into his games. "Life has a way of working itself out just when you start to think it never will, brother. Your lady is the path to foolishness, but that's when the fun begins," he winks.

"SHE'S NOT MY LADY," I clarify, not yet anyway. He chuckles as if I'm clueless.

"The hardest ones are the sweetest, aren't they?" His eyes gleam like an animal in the night, and he saunters off into the dark alley.

FOR AN ANIMAL, he's fucking smart. Simone's the most complicated, most teasing woman I've met. If I'm catching on to what Machete is saying, *she'll be worth it*. He's probably talking from experience. His ol' lady, Raven, was a hellcat before they both gave into each other's advances.

FINISHING MY CIGARETTE, I flick it into the wind, slide my tongue across my teeth and head into the casino. The sound of machines clinging and chiming in the background as I make my way up to the suite. As soon as the elevator doors open, Rooster is missing, and my hands roll into fists. He better not be inside, I'll kill him.

PUSHING THE DOOR OPEN, the lights are turned off, and I don't see Simone anywhere. My mind jumps from Rooster and Veer, worried one of them did something. Glancing in her room, she's not in there either.

"SIMONE?"

"In here!" Her voice carries from my room. Quickly I head in there, the sound of water splashing, I glance into the bathroom and see her in the tub. Naked. I turn my head quickly, not wanting to make her uncomfortable.

"ARE YOU OKAY? WHERE'S ROOSTER?"

"UM, JUST SOME BRAXTON HICKS. MAYBE?" Her voice strains. Uncaring of being a gentleman, I turn toward her, my face pinched in concern. I've read some of the books I got her and know Braxton Hicks is the body preparing itself for labor.

"SHIT, DO YOU NEED ANYTHING?"

"NO," she breathes heavily. Her face scrunches with pain, and I grit my teeth trying not to panic.

"Should I call Doc? What do I do for fucking Braxton Hicks?"

"NO, I think it's easing up."

SLIDING TO THE FLOOR, my back pressed to the tub, I try and think of something to get her mind off her pain.

"Do you like sports?"

"What?" she snaps out of breath.

"Sports? Do you watch any?"

"Mac," she says my name with irritation.

"My dad was a piece of shit, but Super Bowl Sunday was the one day a year he played the part of a father."

She quiets, and I replay the memories of sitting on the torn plaid couch, the big old TV that seemed to always lack signal right when our team would land a touchdown. Dad would cheer and wrap his arms around me like I meant something to him. It's the only childhood memory I cling to.

"What was your favorite team?" she asks. I knew I could hook her with talking about myself. For some reason, she's thirsty for knowledge about everything that I am. I'm not sure what to think about that.

I chuckle, my head lowering with embarrassment.

"The Cowboys are my favorite. They haven't been to the Super Bowl in years, but they will have their comeback. You just wait." My head turns slightly so I can see her beautiful eyes.

"If I have a kid one day. They will be a football fan."

She smiles, her hands sliding down over her belly.

"You'll have to teach us one day." Her sentence is an invitation to stick around after all this is over.

My chest constricts with an unbearable ache. Will I be around after she has this kid? Do I want to be? My dad's voice roars in the back of my head repeating how I'm a piece of shit, and I'm only good for killing genuine people. My mother.

　　I'm not any good for Simone and this baby. I'm really not, but I'm selfish and starting not to care.

"How are you doing?" I change the subject, needing this to go anywhere else.

"Better." She blows out a steady breath and sits up. Water sloshing over the rim of the porcelain. "Yeah, can you help me get out though, the water is starting to cool, and I feel like a beached whale." Her tone is off, little frown lines sketching around her face.

Holding my hand out to help her up, her wet hand slips into mine and my dick stirs in my pants. She's so soft and smells like wildflowers from the bubbles covering her skin. I want so badly to look her over, see her wet sultry body. Are her nipples hard? Does she have a little patch of pubic hair?

My eyes focus on the floor and not her. Out of my peripheral vision, she stands on her own two feet, so I snatch a towel from the rack and hold it out for her. Looking at the wall as she climbs out of the tub, wet fingers slide along mine as she takes the towel.

"Thanks," she mutters.

"Let's get you to bed, off your feet." I press along the small of her back. Ushering her to her room.

Pulling my phone from my pocket, I text Rooster, curious where the fuck he is while Simone dresses.

"Do you need any help with clothes or something?" I'm terrible at this. I don't want to make her uncomfortable with my hovering, but I also don't want to be a dick that stands back as she struggles. I need her to meet me in the fucking middle or something.

"Do you mind if I wear one of your shirts?" Silence fills between us as she waits for me to reply. Wearing my shirt seems simple enough. But it has me wonder why she wants it. Wearing shirts is relationship type shit, right? "They fit better is all," she clarifies.

I'm not sure if I'm relieved it's for that reason or pissed it's not for amorous reasons.

"YEAH, LET ME GO GET ONE," I finally agree.

HEADING TO MY CLOSET, I glance at my phone, nothing back from Rooster yet and it pisses me off. I could track him, see where the fuck he went and then go find him and make him eat gravel.

MY HEAD FALLS BACK. See, it's thinking like that, that has me wondering where the fuck my head is. Yeah, I want to hurt Rooster for fucking disappearing, but it's laced with emotion and not because he broke brotherly code.

STARING AT THE BEDROOM DOOR, my chest squeezes. Simone, I can't tell if you're breaking me or fixing me.

Simone

AFTER DRESSING in one of Mac's shirts, and a clean pair of pink panties I lay on the bed and cover up with blankets. My hair wet and dampening the pillow under me.

"DRESSED?" Mac asks, his knuckles tapping the door. My gentleman biker.

"Yeah."

Walking in, Mac's usual smoldering eyes have concern freckled in the irises. He sits on the side of the bed, the mattress dipping from his body and rests his hand next to my thigh. Looking at his hand, two of his fingers display large rings, and I get the sudden urge to hold his hand. Needing the contact, to feel if it's soft, or sweaty. Will his fingers interlock perfectly with mine, or will his hand be much larger?

When he's near me I feel. I feel like I'm home for the first time in a long time.

Wings that were carved into the flesh of my back unwrapped the day despair fell upon my shoulders. I lost everything in a matter of months. Instead of cowering in fear, I flew and I'm finding where I belong. My flock of butterflies may be of the darkest of colors, but I wouldn't trade them in for the brightest of wings.

"Why do I feel like something happened here tonight?"

I swallow, glancing up at him. It's scary he can read into my feelings so well.

"A cop showed up here," I begin to explain, and his shoulders tense. "She was tall and dressed in a pantsuit. She acted as if you two were a thing." I shake my head remembering how angry she was when she saw my stomach. "She threatened me and the baby and told me to let you know she stopped by."

Mac stands, his face red and shoulders rising and falling with his heavy breathing.

"Why would you open the door for her?"

I scoff. "Are you serious?"

"You shouldn't have opened the door, or you should have called me or something!" His voice rises.

"I'm sorry, I was busy trying not to have a baby on the floor!" I snap back.

He turns, pacing the room. His hands running through his hair back and forth.

"Does your club know you fuck a cop?" I can't contain the jealousy dripping in my voice.

Mac turns, his face unreadable.

"My club has a different view on the way we see law enforcement. You wouldn't understand," he mutters. Obviously not, their president's ol' lady is a damn sheriff.

I LAUGH, looking at my fingers. "Keep your friends close, and your enemies closer." I know exactly what he's talking about. He's screwing this girl to keep her on the side of the Outlaws.

"WELL, you better go run after her before the damsel in distress gets a warrant for the club or something." I sound jealous, but I can't help it.

HIS BROWS PINCH TOGETHER, his burning forest eyes narrowing in on me.

"YOU THINK I WANT HER. That I give two shits that she's hurt?"

"DO you care if you hurt anyone?"

MAC TURNS his head to the side. "Why do I get the impression you're talking about yourself?" His eyes hooded, his hand rubbing the scruff on his cheeks, I don't blink as I stare back at him.

HE CLIMBS ON THE BED, his hands on both sides of my hips. The smell of mint and cigarettes drifting around me.

"DON'T YOU GET IT, Pocahontas, all I'm trying to do is not hurt you."

PULLING my hand out from under the blanket, I finger Mac's chin, the scruff tickling the pad of my finger. An uncontrollable desire to be closer to him, to feel him deep inside of me has me scoot closer.

"HURT ME, Mac, hurt me so fucking good."

HIS EYES BLAZE with adrenaline and desire, that it almost has me second guessing the words I just spewed out of lust.

REACHING OUT, he traces the curve of my right side.

"YOU DON'T KNOW what you're asking for, Simone. I've been trying to stay away from you, because you deserve more than I can give you." His face wrinkles as if his mind just left this room and went to a dark past.

"I'VE BEEN PEDDLING the life of a sinner my whole life, Mac. I deserve everything I get in the way of karma," I confess.

His eyes snap to mine as if we both just surrendered our fates to one another. Like turning the lights off on your car and driving down a dark road.

THERE'S NO TURNING BACK, and no sight of the future.

"BEND OVER, SIMONE." His voice husky. My eyes widen, surprised.

"WHAT?"

HE TILTS his head to the side.

"DON'T PUSS out on me now." He starts to unbuckle his belt. "I said pull those panties down and bend that ass over."

MY NIPPLES BUD, and my sex pulses with what's about to happen. Within a few quick breaths, His jeans fall to the floor, and a long, thick cock bounces freely. The tip veiny and pierced with a silver barbell.

His strong stomach dipping into the finest V shape and happy trail of hair leading to a woman's fantasy.

Throwing caution to the wind, I push the blankets off me, shimmy out of my panties, and toss them on the floor. Mac presses his knees into the bed, kissing me deeply. His taste intoxicating me into a realm of pleasure. I inhale, taking in everything that is Mac. He's soft, but firm. Intimidating, but comforting. His fingers tickle my stomach as he fists the bottom of the shirt and pulls it over my head. My heavy breasts on full display for him.

HE STARES AT ME, skimming my naked body with hungry eyes.

"FUCK YOU'RE BEAUTIFUL, SIMONE."

I GIVE A HALFHEARTED LAUGH, and rest my hand on my stomach. I'm huge.

"No." He rests his hand on mine. "You are really fucking beautiful, pregnant or not. You're a catch, Pocahontas." His compliment has me blushing like an idiot. My cheeks warming of the pinkest petals any flower could present.

FISTING MY RIGHT TIT, I push into his hold for more. All I want is him to touch me everywhere. I want his fingers imprinting every inch of my body, and I never want it to end. His mutual thirst for my hands to be everywhere at once has us both groping and scratching at each other like a couple of teenagers burning with intimacy.

HIS LIPS SKIM MY NECK, kissing, tasting, breathing the scent of my skin inside of his body.

WRAPPING my hands around his neck, I strangle his soft hair, pulling his body closer to mine. My nipples glide across his hard chests like rocks on ice, and my sex drips with desire.

"DON'T STOP," I moan, my head falling back mid-ecstasy.

"Definitely not stopping," he grunts, hands all over my arched back, and lips on my neck.

TEETH NIP INTO MY COLLARBONE, and a mewl escapes my swollen lips.

His hands slide down and fist each of my butt cheeks, causing a breeze to sweep between my legs that has me practically begging Mac to take me already.

.

"YOU LIKE THAT?" he whispers in my ear.

I nod, the words I want to moan catching in my throat. I'm delirious, out of my mind and into my body.

HIS HAND SLAPS MY BACKSIDE, and my swollen lips part with pleasure. My skin blooming with warmth and a single handprint.

"TURN OVER," he demands.

KISSING HIM ON THE LIPS, I pull away and roll over on all fours. Hair in my face I peek over my shoulder. Mac's on his knees behind me, his eyes every shade of black. One hand fists into the bed whilst the other skims down my spine he dips in between my cheeks before slipping a large finger into my warmth.

MY HEAD FALLS BACK, my fingers digging into the mattress it feels that good.

"WHY DO YOU WEAR MY SHIRTS?"

I clench my eyes, my breathing labored. It's hard to focus on his question when all I want is him to take me. He pulls his fingers from my tightness, and my eyes open. I feel lost; disconnected. Glancing over my shoulder he stares back at me with hooded eyes.

"TELL ME, why do you wear my shirts. Is it really because they fit or is it something else?"

I LOOK BACK to the bed and exhale a nervous breath.

"I WANT to wear your stupid t-shirts, and hold your stupid hand because I want to feel you, is that what you want to hear?" I confess, my heart beating a mile a minute that he's going to run out of this room thinking I'm a clingy woman.

CRAWLING up the length of my body, his chest presses against my back. His lips on the shell of my ear.

"YES AND NO," he whispers, and he flicks my earlobe with his tongue. Our eyes meet, our breathing labored.

FISTING HIS COCK, he pumps it a few times before sliding it over my clit.

I MOAN, and it's not a modest moan. No, I sound like a trashy porn star.

Slowly, but way too fast all at the same time he pushes inside of me. My entire body becomes rigid as he fills me. Stretching me.

"FUCK, HOW ARE YOU SO TIGHT?" He groans, his forehead pressed into my back.

"DON'T STOP," I beg. Every hair on my body is raised, my nipples once soft swelling into hard throbbing buds.

HE PUMPS INTO ME, and pressure instantly races from my clit to my toes, making them curl and cramp. My body tingles, and the pulsing of my clit intensifies.

AGAIN, and again he slides in and out of me, hitting that little bundle of nerves that has me pushing for more, and pulling away because it's so intense.

HE WRAPS my hair around his hand, and pumps into me, watching his slick cock take me without mercy. His lips brush against the back of my shoulder, tasting and kissing every square inch of the soft skin.

"OH GOD, I'M GOING TO—" I clench my eyes, my nails chipping as I claw at the sheets. He speeds up, causing my tits to rock back and forth. His warm body spread across mine, his heartbeat syncing to mine, a burst of stars rocket behind my eyes, and I combust into a million little pieces.

MY JAW CLENCHES, I can't catch my breath, and my sex throbs so hard I can't help but cry out in pleasure and pain.

HE GROWLS, pressing his knees into the bed as he comes seconds after me.

SLOWLY I FEEL my body retain its normal blood flow, every little piece that was on cloud nine seconds ago pulling back into a whole.

HE FALLS NEXT TO ME, situating the pillow under his head. Slowly, I roll over onto my back trying to catch my breath. My body flushed, and so fucking sensitive I feel every stitch of the sheets around my legs.

"I DIDN'T HURT HER, did I?" he asks, resting his hand on the top of my ballooned belly.

"No, I think she's actually asleep," I breathe hard. He doesn't take his hand off me, and it's heartwarming. I can't help looking at his hard as a rock cock, it's dripping cum down the sides.

"MY REAL NAME IS RHETT," he confesses out of nowhere.

Holding my breath, I look at him, but he keeps his eyes forward. He's opening up to me.

"I've never told anyone that," he mutters with furrowed brows, almost as if it was painful for him to tell me.

"I like it," I whisper. I've never heard that name before. I grab his hand, and interlock my fingers with his, taking the risk he might pull away and ruin this whole night. He holds my hand, and I bite back the smile. His hand is bigger than mine, but it fits perfectly at the same time. It's hard to explain.

20

MAC

Laying on my side, I watch Simone sleep. Her olive colored face looks soft, her black lashes nearly reaching her cheeks. She's fucking beautiful. Lopez and Rooster have me irritated as fuck and I can't think about anything else. Slowly lifting off the bed, I decide to do something about it.

I GRAB my shit off the floor and walk into the main living area to get dressed. I can smell cocoa butter on my skin from Simone, and her eyes rolling in the back of her head while I was buried in her to the hilt flash in my mind. She was so soft to touch, smelled so good, and felt fucking amazing.

I've never had sex like that before. I was so close to her, needing to touch every inch of her. I don't know what made it different, but it was.

I TRY Rooster's number one more time, and he finally answers.

"'SUP, MAN?"

"WHERE THE FUCK ARE YOU?"

"AT THE CLUB, WHY?"

I HANG UP, and text Zeek to send a different prospect up here to watch the door.

I pace, fucking angry as I wait for someone to show up. I'm going to kill Rooster. Fucking strangle him and slam his face into my searing hot exhaust pipe. Lopez coming in here is a fucking risk, one that is not good for anyone involved.

A knock sounds at the door and my head snaps up.

PULLING THE DOOR OPEN, it's Felix, not a prospect. I step out and close it gently behind me.

FELIX PULLS his long hair into a bun as he eyes me with concern. Felix is the vice president of the club but is probably more level-headed than our own club president, if you ask me. I trust him though.

"I NEED to go handle some shit, can you keep an eye on things for a couple of hours?"

FELIX'S EYES pierce right through me with questions.

"SINCE WHEN DOES Mac have shit to go take care of?" he mocks. "Best Buy have a sale on computers?" He chuckles, taking a sip of his beer.

I ROLL MY EYES. "I don't buy computers, I build them, dumb fuck." His face goes blank. "I'll be back."

HEADING DOWN TO THE CLUB, I try and tell myself to act cool, handle it like an adult, but the matter of the fact is he moved from his post without telling anyone, and a fucking cop went inside the suite.

FINALLY REACHING the doors to the back of the casino, I push them open. The warm dry air making the back of my neck sweat as my feet stomp into the pavement. I can still smell Simone on me, I think I'll fuck her every day so I can smell like her.

"HEY, MAC BABY!" One of the girls coo at me. I can't remember her name, just the blonde crazy hair that reminds me of an eighties porn star. She's a regular fuck, but I'm not interested in the least bit. I hold my hand up, conveying my intentions. Fuck off.

IT DOESN'T GO UNNOTICED that for the first time I'm not wanting to get my dick wet by a club hangaround. Simone is definitely changing the way I see and feel.

THE DOORS to the club are propped open, probably for a breeze as it gets stuffy with so many bodies inside.

STEPPING INSIDE, the music of Zombie playing "Bad Wolves" vibrates through the speakers. A thick cloud of smoke hangs close to the ceiling, and a wave of bodies makes it hard to see anyone in particular.

I SPOT ROOSTER, his reddish hair pulled into a short ponytail, the bottom half of his head shaved. His face is sharp to the chin, and his lip is pierced with a multicolored hoop.

I CRACK MY KNUCKLES, any idea of being calm out the fucking door now that I see him.

"WHOA, BROTHER." Machete steps in front of me, his hand on my chest. His red hair is swiped back with sweat, and he's shirtless under his cut, showing off his detailed tattoos.

Noticing my aggression, he pats me on the shoulder, urging me toward the door. "You look like you need some fresh air." I shove him out of the way, not in the mood for one of his confusing lectures.

Pushing bodies out of the way, elbowing those that don't get the fucking clue I'm coming through, I slam both of my hands into Roosters back, making him stumble into a few girls.

"What the—" He turns around with a confused look, one I want to punch off.

"Where the fuck were you!?" I point at him, and his face falls. His hand holding a beer halfway to his mouth freezing.

HE OPENS his mouth to explain and I have no time to hear his lame ass excuses. Closing the small gap between us, I grab him by the lip ring and tear it out, the sound of skin ripping, him screaming, causing a lot of eyes to focus on us.

"Man, what the fuck?" he grunts, holding his hands under his bleeding mouth.

"You fucked up!" I seethe and slam my knuckles into his fat fucking mouth. He drops to the floor, and I'm on him in seconds, jabbing fist after fist into his ribs. Him leaving his post scared Simone into having Braxton Hicks. She was in pain and I wasn't there. I want Rooster to feel the pain she felt. Before I know what's happening, Machete and Zeek are on me, pulling me off the bloody fucker. I don't back down, I try and shove past them to get to Rooster.

"REIN IT IN, BROTHER!" Machete barks, tugging me backward.

BOTH ROOSTER and I are dragged out of the clubhouse away from the party, and nearly thrown on our asses from Machete and Zeek.

"WHAT THE HELL is going on here?" Zeek demands, his arms crossed over his chest. His hair is pulled up in a small ponytail, beads of sweat dripping into his dark questioning eyes.

WIPING the blood from my hand on my jeans, I stand. Adrenaline racing through me so hard, my knees wobble.

"ROOSTER LEFT his post today and let Lieutenant Lopez inside the suite where she threatened Simone and the fucking club," I inform.

BOTH MACHETE and Zeek's head snap in Rooster's direction.

"LOOK, man, she said she was with us, and that she had it from there! I tried to refuse, and she put a gun to my head and told me to go or else!"

"'OR ELSE,' always chose or 'else' when it puts your duty as a brother on the line." I point at him, my face red with rage. I want to kill him, fuck I want to so badly my hands are shaking.

ZEEK LOOKS at me with an unreadable look, probably because he's never seen me act like this before. I'm past losing my temper, I've gone off my fucking rocker.

"GIVE ME YOUR CUT." Zeek waves his hand at Rooster. That has me calm down for a second.

"WHAT? COME ON, MAN." Rooster's voice edges on the line of a child begging.

"YOU WANT to puss out when a gun is pointed at your head, I don't want you behind my back when shit goes down. You didn't mention anything to anyone about a cop showing up, and come to my club and drink my beer without a second thought. You're out!" Zeek waves his hand again, conveying he wants the cut.

"YOU HEARD HIM, give him your fucking cut!" Grabbing him, I jerk him out of the cut. Fucking pussy doesn't deserve to ever wear our colors.

"GET THE FUCK OUT OF HERE," Machete growls. Rooster lifts his chin with what pride he has left and saunters away from the club for good.

WHEN HE'S out of earshot, Zeek looks at me with narrowed eyes.
    "I knew this cop bitch was going to be a problem. What do you plan to do about it?"

SHAKING MY HEAD, I rub my chin. She threatened Simone and my club. Nobody gets away with that. My hand trembles as a complete thought out plan falls perfectly into place. My eyes light up, and I stare at Machete.

"I'M GOING to take care of it. Can I borrow Raven?"
    Raven is Machete's ol' lady, and is crazy as fuck. Death doesn't scare her, she harbors the grim reaper in her damn soul. The

more fucked up the situation, the better for her. It's like therapy for the psychotic.

"For what?" Machete questions, and Zeek rubs the black stubble on his cheeks.

"I won't hit a woman, let alone kill—"

"So, you want to borrow Raven so you can sleep better at night?" Machete sneers. I curl my fists, my nails digging into the palm of my hand. I don't want to punch Machete in the face, he's three times bigger than me, but he's really starting to piss me the fuck off.

I've seen my old man beat on enough women growing up, I don't have it in me to do it. I couldn't look myself in the mirror the next day without seeing my dad. But if it means keeping Simone and this baby safe... I'll take down every goddamn mirror in the casino and lick my wounds with a mouth full of Jack.

"Fuck it, I'll do it myself." I push past Machete, and Zeek grabs me by the arm. Stopping me.

"I respect you not wanting to hit a woman," Zeek adds with a sincere look. "You should take Raven. She's wearing our club colors after all, she can have our back when we call upon her," Zeek states, giving Machete a look.

"FINE, not like she'd let me live it down if she heard I took an opportunity for her to fuck some shit up," Machete scoffs.

"THANKS."

Machete looks at me with hard eyes, and I return the fucking look. He knows Raven is perfect for the job.

"IF ANYTHING HAPPENS TO HER..." He points at me.

"I WOULDN'T LET anything happen to Raven." My tone grim. Raven is crazy, if anything, I should be making him promise me that she won't let anything happen to me.

ZEEK POINTS AT ME, and I scowl. "I just want to point out this is the second time you've come in here knocking heads over this chick, Mac."

I LOOK TO THE GROUND, flicking my chin with my thumb. I don't want to go into details with him, because I don't exactly know what it all means either.

"WHAT IS IT?" Zeek presses.

Shaking my head, I wet my lips looking off.

"THERE'S SOMETHING THERE, I just- I'm just not sure if the club life is for her and the baby," I sigh.

"I GET IT," he nods.

BEING AN OL' lady in this club is more than making sure there's enough beer stocked at the bar, and riding on the back of a bike. You're down to ride and die with your man. Serving his club before anything else.

21

MAC

Raven steps outside of the club and looks my way. Fuck she's scary.

Her dark hair is pulled back tight, making her ominous eyes look demon-ish, and the way she wears a black fitted shirt and black cargo pants loaded with weapons, she looks like she's ready for the army. The army of the Devil that is.

I HEAD toward my bike but think better of it. We'll be taking a body with us tonight, can't take my bike for that job.

"You got a car?" I ask Raven.

SHE POINTS to a black Mercedes in the corner of the parking lot, her silence strong. I feel confident I picked her for this job. She's going to wreck this bitch.

"I'M DRIVING," I tell, not ask.

OPENING THE DRIVER DOOR, I slide in and she hands me the key fob to start it. The same song that was in the club plays through the speakers. "Bad Wolves."

TIRES SCREECH when we peel out of the parking lot heading toward our target. I know where she lives, so I can take the freeway, then the back way where nobody can see us.

SIDE-EYEING RAVEN as I drive down the freeway, she pulls her pistol out, checking it for bullets. Satisfied with that, she pulls her knife from the holder on her leg and eyes the blade.

MY BROWS FURROW with how equipped she is. She's ready for anything, and excited.

"SO WHEN WE GET THERE, just follow my lead," I explain to her. Her lips purse, and that unnerves me. I swear to God if she goes in there thinking she's running his show, I will pull her by her hair and lock her in her own fucking trunk.

STAYING BACK A BLOCK, I pull close to Lopez's house. One-story white house, with a palm tree planted in the front yard. Her car parked in the driveway.

"Ready?" I ask Raven. She smiles and opens her door to get out.

Following her, we head to the white house with red shingles. The shrubs outside dying, and walkway cracked from the heat. She's not much for lawn keeping, is she.

Stepping onto the patio, Raven tucks her back up against the house so she's not seen by Lopez, and I knock on the front door.

Seconds pass before Lieutenant Lopez opens the door. The smell of lemon and tea wafting around me. She's wearing a baby blue slip, her nipples hard and poking through the sheer material. Her hair is down, and she's makeup-free. Looks as if our little back-stabber was readying herself for bed.

"You've been ignoring my calls," her tone dry, and face smug. I shove my foot inside the door jamb and jerk the door open.

"I've been ignoring you because you're fucking nuts!" I point to my head to indicate how screwed up she is thinking we were anything than fuck buddies.

"Mac, what is wrong with you?" She stumbles back, and I invite myself in. Stepping inside, Raven marches in right behind me like a shadow. Her face stoic, and eyes drawn on the target.

"Who are you?" Lopez's voice wavers. Raven ignores her, and gently shuts and locks the door behind us.

"You've been a bad girl, Lieutenant Lopez." I act aloof, running my finger along the table next to her front door. A candle, a bowl for keys, and loose change scattered about. Her house really is nice. Black plush sofa, nice entertainment center that hugs an entire wall. The interior not matching her unkempt yard.

SHE HAS the taste more than a lieutenant of a police department can afford that is for sure. She's a dirty, dirty girl.

"GET out or I'm calling the—"

"COPS?" I finish for her and laugh. Her face falls, her hands searching behind her for something to protect herself as she stumbles backward. If she was going to call the cops, she should have before we came inside.

"YOU AIN'T CALLING ANYONE." Lowering my head, I let my eyes convey just how fucked she really is. She swallows, her throat bobbing as tears fill her eyes.

SAUNTERING TOWARD HER, she backs herself into a corner like an idiot. Everyone knows not to corner themselves. Her hands flat on the wall behind her, she lifts her chin; feigning confidence.

"WHAT'S THE MATTER, babe. You're not so tough now, are you?" I run the pad of my finger up her delicate throat. "You can only scare defenseless pregnant women, huh?"

Her eyes widen as if she now understands what my visit is all about.

"Is this- is this about Simone?" Her voice colored with surprise.

My eyes widen at the mention of Simone's name. Did Simone tell her, her name?

"How do you know her name?" Her tense body relaxes, a cocky grin spreading across her face.

"I know everything about Simone Ray." Her tone of voice drives the final nail in her coffin. I turn away from her, feeling my hands shake with the longing to dismantle her pretty little face.

"Don't- do not say her name." I wave my hand at her mindlessly as I step into the kitchen. I jerk the fridge open. "You don't deserve to say her name," I mutter, trying to distract myself with the contents of her fridge.

"She wasn't that hard to figure out actually." Lopez laughs under her breath, and this grabs my attention.

"What exactly do you think you know about Simone?" I chuckle, pulling out shit to make a sandwich. Every time my adrenaline pumps like it is, I get hungry. It's fucking crazy.

"I know why you're hiding her... fucking her, and she'll be gone very soon." Her threat seals her fate. I see black and rage.

DROPPING EVERYTHING, I round the counter and grab Lopez by the throat, shoving her against the wall.

"YOU FUCK WITH MY CLUB, you fuck with my girl, and now you can fuck with the reaper," I snarl.

Jerking her against the wall, I give Raven a look letting her know she can take over.

"IF I GO MISSING—"

"NOBODY WILL CARE. You'll be replaced at the department, and someone else will move into this house playing out their life. Maybe they will be smart enough not to cross an Outlaw," my voice dips with hostility.

"MAC, please. I just... I want us—"

I SMASH my lips against Lopez shutting her the fuck up and kissing her to her grave.

"THERE NEVER WAS AN US. Just a mediocre fuck, and you doing my dirty work," I whisper against her lips. Her eyes widen at my harshness, but it's the truth. What did she expect? For her to be my girlfriend or some shit. We'd never work. Turning away from her, I flick the dial on the stereo, the classical music she had on turning to Seether's "Let You Down."

RAVEN PULLS HER KNIFE OUT, and Lopez screams. Raven slashes it against her arm, playing with her prey, and Lopez falls to the floor trying to crawl away from Raven. Droplets of blood trail behind her as she tries to escape and Raven laughs, causing chills to rise along the back of my neck.

MAN, she's wicked.

"HIDE AND SEEK? I can play that." Raven cracks her neck, her face lit up like it's Christmas morning as she chases down her wounded animal.

NODDING my head to the music, I turn it up a little more to cover the hysterics echoing down the hall. Biting into my sandwich, I hear Raven tear into Lopez. Screams echo down the hall, and shit being knocked over bangs into the wall.

THIS IS A REALLY GOOD SONG, sad you don't hear it very much anymore. I take a bite of my sandwich and decide to see if Raven has everything under control.

MY FEET PAD on the carpet making sure to miss the blood trail, the pictures on the walls all sideways from Lopez falling into them dramatically. Finding the main bedroom, Lopez is on her back on the floor, tears streaming down her face as her eyes set on me.

"Shouldn't have fucked with my girls," I tsk, and Raven drives a bullet into Lopez's head.

Her body jerks and the look of the lost crosses her face. I feel nothing for the loss of her life, but I sigh in relief knowing she can't fuck with Simone or my club.

Looking over the room that looks like a scene from Stephen King, I shake my head.

"Damn, you made a mess," I say with a mouth full of lettuce and turkey.

Raven laughs, proud of her murderous artwork.

"I did make a mess, didn't I." She scratches her forehead, blood smearing across her face. "We're a good team," she states, putting her gun away. I nod, looking the bloody scene over. Crazy how I'm used to a dead body, but not used to feeling for another person. You'd think it'd be the other way around. Well, for a normal person anyway. Goes to show just because I'm the quiet guy out of the Outlaws, I'm still far from normal.

I sigh, my shoulders sagging.

"Time for clean up, I guess."

"I'LL CALL MACHETE TO HELP," Raven informs, pulling out her phone.

"GOOD, IDEA." Machete is a pro at making bodies disappear, and quick about it.

"Your girls, huh?" Raven side-eyes me, and it occurs to me during Lopez's final seconds I claimed Simone and the baby. "Can't wait to meet them." I inhale a ragged breath.

"I WOULDN'T JINX them with my ownership," I mutter, dropping my gaze to the stained carpet.

RAVEN STANDS STRAIGHT, her face stoic.

"YOU'RE JUST LIKE MACHETE, you know?" She shakes her head.

I'M NOT anything like Machete. "What's that supposed to mean?" I sneer.

"YOU SELF-SABOTAGE YOURSELF, just like he does. When anything good comes your way, you talk yourself into believing you'll screw it up, or don't deserve it," she explains. "Respect yourself enough to take the best of things without imprisoning yourself into accepting imperfections."

RUBBING MY CHIN, I look at the dead body on the floor. Her and

Machete are perfect for each other with their puzzling lectures. She's right in every aspect though, I am a pro at self-sabotaging. But I can't help it when I was brought into this world killing the only person that may ever care for me. My mother.

"THEY CALL IT ATELOPHOBIA—"

"I KNOW WHAT IT'S CALLED," I mutter, Tinker, our main club chick told it to me once.

I TURN, leaving Raven to make her phone call to Machete and me to finish my sandwich.

22

SIMONE

I wake up to the sound of the main door closing. I'm naked, and my hair is a knotted mess from epic sex earlier. God, I really needed that. I feel like I'm floating I'm so at ease and relaxed.

"Mac?" My voice heavy with sleep.

Grabbing the sheet, I hold it to my chest and slide out of bed to see what he's doing.

Just as I reach the doorway, I stop, my brows furrowing as a sharp pain presses into my abdomen. Dropping the sheets to the floor, and my eyes widen as a warm trickle drips between my legs like a crack in an old pipe.

"Yeah?" Mac replies.

I look up at him in a white panic. He's fully dressed and looks like he'd been somewhere.

"Mac...um." I look down to the floor, and water suddenly gushes down my legs. "Oh no, my water just broke." My voice wavers.

"Oh fuck!" Both of his hands swipe through his hair, his eyes on the mess around my feet. "Okay, don't panic," he breathes heavily.

"Don't panic, got it." I'm totally panicking.

He pulls out his phone with one hand, using his free hand he swipes it back and forth over the top of his head frantically.

"Zeek, it's happening, brother!" Mac hollers into the phone, obviously panicking. "Ok. Got it." He hangs up and is by my side in seconds. "Let's get you cleaned up and get some clothes on you."

"What are we doing?"

"Getting you cleaned up and to the hospital," he mutters. I don't argue, but fear inside my chest whispers Veer's name.

Going into my room, he grabs a towel from the bathroom, his shirt from the floor, and some clean panties and jogging shorts from my drawer.

He positions the shirt over my head, and I raise my hands to pull it on. I feel fine, so far there's no pain. He bends down and starts wiping my feet and legs down gently; drying me off. Tossing the towel over his shoulder, he holds a pair of my dark blue boy short panties open for me to step in.

"One foot at a time," he instructs, and I do. I let him dress me, because him taking care of me is a feeling I've never felt before. Cherished; if I have to label it.

Reaching out, I run my fingers through his hair, a smile on my face despite the slight pain starting to reside in my lower back.

"I'll be right back. Don't move." His voice firm as he stands.

"Where the fuck am I going to go?" I laugh sarcastically.

He jogs into his room, and I rest my head on the door jamb. Practicing breathing like I've seen in the videos. In. Out. In—

"Ok, every time you have a contraction, press this," Mac interrupts my deep breaths.

He hands me a fob looking thing with a red button in the middle.

"What's this?" I take it from him. It's lightweight and looks like something that would go to locking a car.

"It will time your contractions precisely."

My mouth parts and I look up at him with doe eyes.

"You got this for me?"

"I made it," he shrugs, a boyish grin fitting his face.

"Really? You made this?"

My eyes fill with unshed tears, he made it. He freaking made me a device.

A sharp pain throbs in my back and I press the button like I might break it. My knees buckling beneath me. Ok, it's getting worse. I take a deep breath, my body shaking from the pain.

Mac's hands are quickly on my hips, the smell of him blanketing me.

"Ok, just breathe through it, baby." His voice almost soothing. I nod, inhaling through my nose, but it's not helping with the pain at all. The videos lie, the books fib. This shit hurts!

The front door opens and Zeek, Jillian, Felix, Alessandra, Machete, and Raven are all standing there staring at me. The whole crew, all here for me.

Jillian rushes to my side, the sight of another woman comforting.

"If her water broke, we need to get her to the hospital now!"

"Shit!" Zeek turns where he stands, looking at the floor for answers.

Raven hustles to my other side, wrapping her arm around me. She smells of bleach oddly.

"Come on, let's get you down to my car."

Mac steps in, pushing their hands off me.

"I got this, just—just lead the way," he barks at the women. Both of the girls look at each other before cautiously stepping out in front of us and heading toward the elevators. Mac is protective and panicking. It's cute.

My finger bites down on the device as another contraction rips through me like an earthquake splitting concrete.

My jaw clenches, and I groan, trying to keep up with the crowd, I have to force my feet to walk through the pain.

"Let's take the back way, we don't want people staring," Zeek states in a calm voice, his boots stomping onto the floor loudly.

Hunched over from the last contraction, Mac keeps his arm tucked around me tightly. I feel like nothing can get between us, that we're safe. Inside the elevator, it smells like stale smoke, and there's glitter sprinkled all over the floor. The song "Him & I" by G- Eazy & Halsey plays.

"I like this song," Alessandra states, and everyone just gives her an odd look.

"What?" She shrugs with doe eyes, and Felix just chuckles.

Mac leans down, his eyes in line with mine while rubbing my back.

"I got you, and I'm not letting anything or anybody take you out of my sight, Pocahontas. Do you understand?" His determined eyes stare into mine deeply. I could drown in them, like a little girl twirling in a forest caught on fire. Embers and ash blanketing around him.

He is so serious, it makes me nervous that someone is actually attempting to take me from him.

He presses his lips to my sweaty forehead, and I close my eyes. Taking it all in.

I'm escorted outside a back entrance, the air outside making me hot and irritable. Pressure slowly builds in my abdomen, and I stop where I'm standing. My bare feet burning on the hot asphalt.

"Another contraction," I breathe heavily.

I grit my teeth and press the button on the device Mac gave me.

"Come on!" Zeek waves us on.

"Fuck off!" Mac shouts at him, his hand on my face while I push through it. "You got this, baby. Take a deep breath, here." He fists my hand. "Squeeze it as hard as you need."

Intertwining my fingers with his, our eyes silently locking as I tightly grip his palm.

Pressure builds, my body feeling like it's being ripped apart from the inside. Sweat drips down my face, my chin trembling from the terrible pain.

Before I know it, the contraction has passed, and we're moving toward the car.

Mac helps me into the back of the seat, Raven and Machete are in the front, and Zeek and Jillian climb on Zeek's bike with Felix and Alessandra. That's when I notice a couple of other motorcycles revving up beside them.

"What are they doing?" I ask, looking at the men and women climbing on the motorcycles.

"Escorting us, making sure we don't have any surprises before we get you to the hospital."

I look at Mac, surprised at the great lengths everyone is taking to get this baby safely into the world. I clench my eyes shut. I won't cry.

"Are you having another contraction?" Mac whispers in my ear.

I shake my head.

"I just... I've never had anyone do so much for me before." A tear slips from my eye, and I quickly swipe it away. My mother and father have done things for me because they're my parents, but they've never shown such loyalty. Not like this.

He presses his forehead against my clammy temple, his arm wrapping around me and pulling me close. I lean into him, drinking him in like a cold glass of water.

"Get used to it, I'm... I'm claiming you, Pocahontas and I'm going to give you everything I can."

Wrinkles form on my face. "Claiming?"

"Yeah, claiming you as my ol' lady."

Raven gasps, and they look at each other in knowing.

"It just kind of happened." He smirks.

He lays his hand on my belly.

"You make me quiet and loud at the same time. Fast and slow, hard and soft. When I'm not with you, I feel nothing and though that used to be my normal, I find it scary as fuck now. I need you and this baby in my life."

My eyes bounce back and forth between his. Our fingers interlocking into one.

The car pulls into the emergency drive of the hospital, and everything happens so fast.

Motorcycles roar and park all around us, shielding us from any citizen.

Mac gets out of the car, and just as my feet hit the pavement, he's swooped me up and is jogging us inside the hospital doors.

Inside the hospital, a whoosh of air from the opening doors blows my sweaty hair from my face, the smell of stale hospital food and anesthetic filling my lungs.

A young nurse runs to us, a stethoscope bobbing around her neck.

"How far apart are the contractions?" she asks.

Another nurse brings a silver and blue wheelchair and Mac sets me in it, pulling out his phone.

"Five minutes apart," he informs.

"OK, so about five minutes," the nurse mutters.

"No! I said five minutes, and that's what it is!" Mac corrects sharply, and the nurse looks at him like he's lost his mind, but I have to keep from smiling.

"Easy brother." Machete rests his hand on Mac's shoulder.

"What's – what's your name?" The nurse shakes her head from Mac's outburst and readies her pen on a clipboard.

"Simone Ray," I grit through a contraction, my nails piercing the rails of the wheelchair. Closing my eyes, I try to breathe through it, but I'm going to call bullshit on this whole breathe through the pain crap. It's not working, and the pain is getting so much worse I'm about to hurt someone.

"How far along are you dear?" the young nurse asks me.

"Uh, thirty weeks." I have to think as the pain nailing me in the stomach is distracting. I open my eyes, looking at the woman with dark curly hair and bright red lipstick. Her face pale as she stares back at me.

"That's early." She blinks at me as if I have all the answers as to why I'm having the baby pre-mature, but I don't. In fact, her blank stare only makes me terrified that something is going to go wrong.

Mac steps in front of me, my shield from horror. "Yeah, so let's do something about it besides stand here and stare!" Mac barks, making the nurse jump in her place.

"Right, call the doctor," she tells the front desk. "And let's get her hooked up to see where we are." The nurse starts to push me away from the group and I drop the button and reach for Mac's hand. I don't want him to be far, I need him close. He grips my hand and doesn't let go.

We're pushed into a small room down the hall. There's a bed, machines along the wall, and on the right side of the room there are two windows overlooking the parking garage. Mac helps me onto the bed with stiff white sheets, and nurses from all over hook me up to wires and devices. It's as if everything moves in slow motion as they undress me and run about the room getting me ready for the doctor. But, my hand stays in Mac's the whole time, our eyes never breaking.

"I'm scared," I mouth. It's too early, what if she's not ready? What if I'm not ready?

He drops to his knees, his chin resting on our locked hands.

"Everything is going to be fine. I know it, you have to believe it too. Little Peach is going to be just fine, and so are you." He squeezes my hand, his fierce eyes looking darker than ever. As if the fire in his eyes has been doused and ashes float about his irises. He's scared something is going to happen to me or the baby and to be honest, I am too.

"So, you're just shy of eight months?" a male voice asks entering the room.

Looking to the door a man with thinning hair and a white coat looks at the chart the nurses have put together.

I nod, my stomach tightening with another contraction. Pursing my lips, I blow a breath of air and try not to rip Mac's fingers apart.

The doctor scratches his wrinkled face, his dim blue eyes shining with concern. My heart skips a beat, this isn't good. I shouldn't be in labor.

"Ok, let's see what we have." He grabs a stool in the corner and positions himself between my legs. Shifting on my back, I stare at the ceiling lined with tiles. I hope he can't tell I had sex not but a few hours ago. Wait, is that what made me go into labor? "Bend your knees, placing your feet at the end of the bed," he instructs, interrupting my thoughts.

Clearing my throat, I do as I'm told, my sweaty palm squeezing Mac's. The doctor inserts his fingers, and it takes everything I have not to push. Squeezing my eyes to the point I see swirls of colors, I wait for him to pull his fingers out of my cervix.

"You are one-hundred percent effaced, and fully dilated, dear." His words make my chest sink with more fear than I can take in.

"What does that mean? Can we stop the labor?" My voice wavers, but I know the answer to my question based off the books I've been reading. I'm having this baby early.

"I'm afraid not." He shakes his head, a nurse steps up beside him helping place gloves on each of his hands.

He confirms my fears, pending doom makes my heart race, my eyes filling with warm tears.

Suddenly a very sharp pain squeezes my entire stomach, as if Freddy Krueger himself is inside my uterus clawing to get out.

"OH MY GOD GET IT OUT!" I scream, my face red, and eyes as wide as saucers. "Give me some medicine for the pain. I need it. Get it," I demand, snapping my fingers. My whole body slicked in a cold sweat and my hips are numb from so much agony.

"Simone, it's too late for that, I need you to sit up, okay?" His controlled voice is not helping me panic any less.

I glance at Mac, and he's already helping me sit up before I can silently consult with him about what we should do.

"OK, I need you to give me a couple of big pushes." The doctor rests his hands on my knees, focusing on my vagina.

"Wait, it's too soon to push. These things take hours. I read that." I shake my head, needing more time. This is moving too soon. Too fast.

Suddenly another sharp pain slices through me, cutting my excuses off. My hips bare down, and I push without me even having to think about it.

"Yeah, not happening tonight, dear. We're having this baby now. Now push harder!"

Squeezing Mac's hand like a vise, I push so hard my toes curl into the bed. Sweat drips down my face, and my pelvis feels like it's being ripped apart. Out of breath, I relax, panting for air. I can't push another second.

"I can't breathe, I can't catch my breath. It's so hot in here."

"You're doing great!" Mac encourages, his face pale as he dabs my forehead with a white cloth. Where'd he get that?

"Oh yeah, if I'm doing so great she'd be out!" I snap at him, pushing my hair from my face. I can't do this, it hurts so fucking bad. I feel like my pelvis is a wishbone at Thanksgiving dinner.

Mac presses his lips to my temple and kisses me, his mouth lingering on my skin. That one kiss brings me back down to earth, and I finally take the breath I've been needing.

"OK, one last push Simone, and you get to meet your baby girl."

This is it, the moment I've been waiting for. This moment is the one that has led everyone here, and even people I care about to their death. My heart aches thinking about Gatz and Kane. They lost their lives for this little girl's first breath, and it will not go in vain. I can do this. I will have this baby, and she will be beautiful, smart, and loved more than anything.

This little girl was the best thing I ever did for myself. She made me a mother and a warrior. She's stopping the wave of falling dominos and giving us a new life.

Then again, I wouldn't have come to this point without Mac. He's cared for us both, protected us, and loved us. He's put himself before his club, and himself. I trust him more than I've ever trusted anyone. We need him in our new life, to show us the path of being strong, and free-willed.

"Yes." I nod. Mac looks at me with bewilderment.

"I didn't say anything."

"Yes, I'll be your ol' lady. We'll be your girls." I smile, and Mac smirks the most handsome, sexiest, mischievous grin I've ever seen.

Making me and my baby girl his is the best thing I could do for us.

"Let's do this, babe." He presses a chaste kiss to my cheek, and I nod in agreement.

"Come on, Momma, let's push!" the doctor hollers, tapping my leg.

Taking a big breath, tears streaming down my face. I push, I push so hard I see stars, my legs shake, searing pain slices through my pelvis, and all of a sudden, a huge relief pulls from my insides and I fall back onto the bed out of breath.

The sound of the cutest girly cry fills the room, and I can't stop the tears from falling down my cheeks.

"Oh, she is beautiful, Momma!" the doctor congratulates. My eyes hazy, I breathe in, but it's shallow and not quite filling my chest. I try again but feel nothing but a burn in my lungs.

"Simone?" Mac is in my vision, but he's blurry and unfocused.

"Something... something's wrong," I whisper, gasping.

"Ok, Mom's in distress, I need you to step back, Dad." The doctor pushes Mac out of my face, and I hear metal falling to the ground. A table being knocked over, and commotion all around me. A nurse puts a clear mask on my face, pumping oxygen as fast as she can, and suddenly the doctor is yelling, "She's losing blood!"

I reach out, wanting Mac's hand. Needing it to bring me back down to earth but feel nothing but air. "She needs her daddy, where's Mac," I say into the oxygen mask, half conscious. But nobody answers me. Everyone's moving around, panicking and I can't move, or can't think. There's nothing, and I slip into a blanket of darkness.

23

MAC

I'm shoved into the hallway by two nurses trying to explain to me why I need to be out here instead of in there with Simone, but I can't hear them. I'm unhinged and on a mission to get back to Simone's side. If I'm in there, I can protect her. Why I think that, I don't know, I have no experience in medical. I just need to be beside her.

I shove at them, trying to get back to her but as soon as I get rid of one woman, the other is in my face.

ROARING like a lion whose lioness has been taken from him by a headhunter, I jerk and thrust my hands through the nurses. Determined to get to Simone even if I have to hurt someone. I promised her I'd be by her side.

"BROTHER!" Zeek's voice cuts through the chaos, and I freeze. His voice grounding me back to the reality of where the fuck I am. My head trembles with emotion racing through me like poison.

"I'M GOING to call security if you can't get ahold of yourself, sir!" a young nurse with black hair hollers in my face. My eyes fall to hers, then her name tag.

"Shelly, fuck you," I push through gritted teeth. Her eyes widen, mouth parting at my crude behavior.

"THAT'S NOT NECESSARY, we got him," Machete informs, stepping in between me and the nurse. Shelly shakes her head and hurries back inside to Simone.

MACHETE TURNS, eyeing me warily. "What the hell has gotten into you? They're trying to help her!"

"Oh fuck her!" I wave him off. "She's acting superior because she got on a pair of fucking scrubs. I need to be in there with Simone, what if she dies like my mother and I'm not there!" I point at the doors, and by the blank stare on everyone's faces, I realize what I've just said.

"FUCK," I mumble, hanging my head.

"YOU NEED to let them do whatever they need, especially if there's a problem," Zeek states, patting my shoulder. Glaring in his direction, I shake my hands out, the ache to slam them into something itching up my wrists.

"SHE'S NOT YOUR MOM, she's going to be fine," Zeek whispers, and I close my eyes. I'm trying to believe him, but it's hard to when I feel like everything bad in my life is due to me ever being born.

Ever since I was a little kid I've had it in my head that maybe if my father was by my mother's side when she gave birth... she'd still be alive. Crazy, I know.

"Come on, let's get some coffee or something while we wait for an update," Machete suggests, and I refuse. I'm not leaving this fucking spot.

"The last thing he needs is caffeine." Zeek narrows his eyes at me, and I return the fuck you look.

Instead, I pace outside the doors to Simone's room, my hands pulling at my hair, fidgeting. It's taking too long. Something is wrong. I should go in there.

"What's taking so fucking long?" I holler at Zeek who is looking a housekeeping magazine over. He opens his mouth to say something but shuts it. Nothing he has to say is going to calm me down, and he knows it.

"I've never seen him like this, should we do something?" Raven whispers to Machete, but she sucks at keeping a low voice because I hear every word.

"Yeah, give him a tranquilizer dart in the ass cheek," Machete scoffs, his arms crossed while glaring at me.

I shouldn't have claimed her, this is my fault for getting too close. I'm bad luck.

"I know what you're thinking, and stop," Zeek interrupts my thoughts. My boots screech to a stop, and I scowl.

"You don't know shit," I sneer.

"You're thinking about your mother again." His face softens, and the back of my neck begins to sweat. How can I not think about my mother at a time like this.

"What happened to your mother?" Raven asks from a waiting room chair, a cup of coffee balancing on her knee.

I shake my head. "Nothing." Nobody needs to know my sob story, it doesn't change anything. I'm bad luck, it's in my DNA. Period.

Zeek sighs, pushing himself off the brick wall of the hospital. He grabs me by the shoulder and pulls me in close. His fingers digging into my leather cut.

"We all have been where you are, maybe not in this particular situation, but the place where we don't think we deserve anything good."

Scratching my forehead, I close my eyes.

"You're starting to sound like Raven," I sigh.

"Well, then she's one smart bitch." Thumb and finger rubbing the stubble on my cheeks, I exhale.

Does an outlaw ever deserve anything good? An outcast that breaks all the rules is bound to have karma breathing down their neck, waiting for the moment to hurt them at their weakest point.

FINALLY, the doctor steps out of the room, his coat covered in blood and my knees suddenly feel weak at the sight of it. I've never felt ill at the sight of blood, but right now I feel like I might faint.

"YOU'RE THE DAD?" He looks to me. Everyone looks to me, waiting for me to claim Simone and the baby publicly.

"YEAH," I reply, my eyes watery.
Zeek's eyes widen.

"THE BABY IS FINE, she's a tough little thing. Her stats are near perfect and I've seen babies full term come lesser than her—"
"And Simone?" I interrupt.
"Simone has lost a lot of blood due to a placental abruption. We had to do a blood transfusion, and stabilize her, but she's doing okay. We're keeping a close eye on her right now," he explains, but he might as well be speaking Spanish.

"PLACENTAL ABRUPTION?" I ask, not sure what the fuck that is.

"IT's where the placenta detaches from the uterine wall early and causes bleeding. We have the bleeding under control right now, but if it doesn't stop, we will have to remove the uterus. A hysterectomy."

I TURN, my hand on my forehead as the strangest sound spills from my lips. Relief and heartache rolled into one sigh. She's okay but may never have another child.

"WOULD you like to see your little girl?"

I TURN BACK AROUND, my hand on my mouth. My little girl.

IT RINGS AROUND in my head and implants itself. I'm responsible for this little girl. I have to be her daddy, because if I don't... who will? Gatz and Kane aren't here, and I won't let anyone else be her daddy because nobody can do the job better than me. Nobody.

"YES, I want to see my daughter." The words come out smooth, and they sound right.

I FOLLOW the older doctor around the corner, past the front desk to a large finger-smudged glass. There are little tubs full of babies wrapped in pink and blue blankets, but I spot Little Peach instantly. She's darker skinned than the others, just like her momma, and has just the cutest amount of dark hair on her head. She's the cutest one in there.

A NURSE HOLDS a stethoscope to her chest, as she cries bloody murder. My chest constricts, as if hearing her cry through the glass alerts something in me to go to her.

"CAN I HOLD HER?" A tear slips down my face, and I brush it off. I feel like a pussy crying, but I can't help it. Look at her.

"YEAH, LET'S GO IN." He steps to the side of the glass to a metal door, and presses in a code into a keypad, unlocking the door. Stepping into the secure room, the smell of baby soap and the sound of crying babies is overwhelming.

THE DOCTOR STEPS up next to Little Peach's tub, and I follow him. She's so small, her skin nearly translucent.

A nurse wraps her tightly in a pink blanket and holds her to me. I hesitate, I've never held a baby before. Looking to her with panic, I convey just how fucking scared I am to hold her. What if I drop her? What if I'm sick and I don't know it?

SHE SMILES and presses the crying little girl to my chest.

"Just support her head here." The nurse places my elbow just right under her head. "And snugly here." She pushes my hand under her body.

LOOKING DOWN, I draw in a tight breath at the sight of Little Peach. I'm holding her, and not dropping her. Her round face and small puckered lips are the most delicate thing I've ever seen.

"HEY LITTLE ONE." My voice cracks with emotion, and she looks up at me with goo applied around her eyes. She stops crying, and I can feel her heartbeat against my arms.

"She recognizes your voice," the nurse says with a big smile.

"What?" I look at her with watery eyes.

"THE BABY, she knows your voice, that's why she stopped crying. She feels safe." She nods.

And just like that, I'm wrapped around this little girl's finger. We stand their quiet, looking at one another. She brings her fingers to her mouth and begins to suckle and it's the cutest thing.

MY EYES FALL to a mark on her chest now that she's removed her arm from the blanket. I turn my head trying to get a better look at it. Is it a scratch?

THE NURSE SEES me staring with concern and steps over to me with furrowed brows. Using her finger, she pushes the blanket down a bit.

"OH, that's just a birthmark, or a stork bite. It might go away, but some don't." She shrugs like it's no big deal. But it is a big deal. That birthmark is identical to someone I know.

I SWALLOW the sudden lump in my throat and stare at the mark. Gatz had a similar birthmark to this one. A horseshoe-shaped birthmark.

THIS IS Gatz's little girl for sure. She's an Outlaw.

A DARKNESS FALLS outside the display window, and I look up. My boys with their women, are standing there in leather and smiles watching me. I smile, back holding my daughter.

IF YOU ASKED me months ago where I'd be... I never would have said here. I'd never would have guessed I'd lose control of my emotions and become unhinged to a woman and unborn child that isn't even mine.

MY FATHER USED to tell me I'd never survive a day in the real world, but I'd like to see that motherfucker last a night in mine.

I'LL NEVER BE HIM. I will be the best man I can be in both of my girls' lives.

24

SIMONE

Waking up, I feel stiff. There are pads wrapped around my feet that inflate and deflate every few minutes that are annoying the hell out of me. There's a drip in my arm making my forearm ache, and I feel extremely sleepy and cold.

The smell of blood and iodine makes my head hurt, and I wince from the harsh light beaming above my bed.

Looking around the room there are machines all over, and a TV on the wall, with a lone wooden rocking chair in the corner that holds Mac holding our little girl. Our little girl. I smile, liking the sound of that.

My heart beats at the scene before me. His leather cut hanging off the back of the chair as he holds her like she might break, his intense eyes looking down at her like she's his whole world. Teaching him how to be soft, and strong at the same time.

The doctor walks into the room, his eyes holding shadows of tiredness under them.

"Ah, you're awake." He grins in my direction.

Mac looks my way and lights up in a way that has me glow

like a love-struck teenager. Standing from the chair, he comes to my side of the bed.

I try and push myself up, but my abdomen feels like it's been sliced open and I wince. Letting myself fall back on the bed.

"She's gorgeous, Simone, you have to see her." Mac bends down, positioning her in my right arm. The sight of her has me gasp, she's more beautiful than I would have ever imagined. Having her in my arms distracts me from the foreign pain across my belly, or why exactly I look to be in an ICU room, and not a postpartum room.

Seeing my little girl for the first time, it takes my breath away. Everything fades as I take her in. Her nose is small, and pouty lips adorable. Her fingers tiny, and skin soft. My eyes fill with tears, a sob trembling from my lips. She raises her arm, and my eyes fall on a birthmark on her chest. My lips part as my brain takes me back to the night I conceived her.

A spot on his bicep causes me to turn my head sideways as I focus on it. It's a birthmark in the shape of a horseshoe, it's unlike anything I've seen before, then again, I'm high. I reach out to touch it, just as he leans down and kisses me.

Coming back from the memory, I continue to stare at the birthmark in awe.

Gatz had the same birthmark. She's... she's Gatz's little girl.

"So, we ran into some complications, Simone." The doctor sits at the end of the bed, breaking my moment of bliss. Glancing up at him, I remember blacking out right after delivery.

"You had a placenta abruption and lost a lot of blood. Unfortunately, we could not stop the bleeding and had to do a hysterectomy I'm afraid." His face frowns, and my chest constricts with the information.

"I'm sorry, what?" I half laugh, the information not quite settling.

Mac's head falls, his hand searching mine under the baby,

squeezing tight. Looking at his hand, it starts to sink in. They did a hysterectomy.

"What?" My voice cracks with emotion. A hysterectomy means I can't have any more kids. I can't have a big family or give a sister or brother to my daughter.

A warm tear falls down my cheek, and I sniffle looking down at my little baby girl.

"I'll give you guys a minute," the doctor mutters, leaving the room.

"Hey." Mac squeezes my hand. Glancing up through unshed tears I try to keep it together.

"It's okay, she's all you need."

I sob, shaking my head. "What if you fall in love with me and want to have kids one day. What if we want to give her a sister or brother?" I shrug.

A finger slides under my tear-stained face. Fierce forest burning eyes digging into mine.

"I already love you, and this little girl may not be my blood but let me tell you something about bloodlines. The heart decides what it need and wants, not blood. My brotherhood, that is my family. You and this baby, are my future and my now, none of which are my DNA. Doesn't stop me from loving all of you."

My wet eyelashes flutter. "You love me?"

He grins. "I do. What I know of love anyway, it's all for you. You're the most beautiful thing in my heart, Simone."

I laugh like an idiot. "I love you too. Since you've been around, I smile more than I used to, ya know?"

His boyish charm that only I've gotten to see, lifts his face.

"I know," he replies arrogantly.

Looking down at what I made, the first thing I've ever done right.

"You and her, you're my salvation." I roll my lips onto one another. I've run from hell and felt the heat of the flames on my neck, but it was worth it in the end. I've found my peace with a man that is the sexiest geek I know and would do anything for me. I have the most beautiful little girl anyone could ask for. It doesn't get much better than this.

Mac rests his head against mine, his hand on my back.

"Mine too. Mine too."

We sit in silence, watching our little one coo and play with her fingers.

"I need to name her," I sniffle, remembering I haven't found the perfect name yet.

"Catori," Mac suggests. It's cute, really cute actually.

Wrinkles form on my face. "Catori?" Why didn't I think of that one?

"It's Native American and means spirit." I know it means spirit, but how does he know that?

"Did you look it up or something?"

"I might've been looking at names ever since you found out she was a girl." He glances up at me with a boyish grin.

"I love it." I knew he'd have the perfect name. "Catori it is."

"You can give her my last name you know." His suggestion nearly whispered.

My head snaps up, my eyes watering all over again. He wants to be her dad, like really be her dad.

"You want to give her your last name?"

His shoulders rise with an inhale.

"I do. I want to be her dad." His voice firm and concise. He takes Catori from my arms and holds her close to his chest. The look in both of their eyes makes me sob. He's so tough, but with her he appears to be a big softy.

"You do?"

"I need to be in her life just as much as I need you in my life, Pocahontas." He glances at me, but briefly before looking back at Catori.

"I don't even know your last name." I silently laugh, my fingers playing with the fabric of the sheets. I know his first name is Rhett, and his nickname is Mac, but as far as I know... he's never told anyone his last name.

"Lockhart." I glance at him, but he doesn't break eye contact with Catori. "My name is Rhett Lockhart."

"Catori Lockhart," I whisper, petting her chubby little arm. "I love it."

And just like that, we became a family. Mac rebuilt the woman I am. Took the broken bricks and remolded them into something that resembled a strong independent building.

25

SIMONE

I stayed in ICU for a night and then was moved to the maternity ward for two more days before we were released. I slept most of the time as I was recovering from my surgery, and Mac took care of Catori the whole time. He refused to let her out of his sight and wouldn't let the nurses take her back to the nurse's station. They had to weigh her and observe everything with him by their side. He aggravated every doctor and nurse that came in to check on us both. Hovering over them, making sure they were doing everything that was needed for me and Catori. I loved it though. I never had someone hover so much over my care, and it was nice.

Zeek and Jillian come to visit, and Jillian ran straight to Catori. Mac frowns at her, holding her tighter.

"Really? You're not going to let me hold her?" Jillian pouts.

"Let her hold her, she's fine!" I snap.

"She's pre-term, she can't get sick!" He narrows his eyes at me.

"I know she's pre-term, I had her!"

"Guys!" Zeek steps in between us, his brows raised.

Jillian steps to the wall and squirts some hand sanitizer the hospital offers into her palm.

"Look, germ-free!" She holds up both hands and smiles.

Mac glares at me, and I scowl in return.

"Fine," Mac groans. Turning, he places Catori in her arms, but not before he makes sure she holds her perfectly right.

"Oh my, she's beautiful!" Jillian gasps. "Oh Zeek, we need another!"

Zeek's face pales before he scoffs.

"Heard you had a rough delivery," Jillian whispers, standing next to my bed. I shrug, looking at Catori.

"We're alive, that's all that matters."

Jillian smiles. "Damn straight."

Zeek steps up to my bed, crossing his arms. Something obviously on the tip of his tongue. Crossing his arms, his shoulders rise.

"Anybody been in here to ask you questions?"

Mac's head snaps in my direction.

"What do you mean?" Mac asks defensively.

"The Devil's Dust, Kane's club, they want Veer badly, so I was just curious if they've sent anyone here to ask her questions yet," Zeek informs, his rough tone making Catori upset.

I shake my head. "No, nobody has asked or said anything."

Zeek gives a curt nod. "Good, don't." The warning in his voice is not missed, Jillian eyeing me and silently conveying for me to agree.

"Why?" I can't help but need more than just that before I agree.

Zeek rubs his chin, looking Jillian and Catori over.

"Veer killed Gatz, and we called that Veer's blood way before the Devils, that's why." Giving me a once over, he heads to Jillian, looking Catori over. The Outlaws want Veer for what he did to Gatz.

"I'm not standing in *anyone's* way... just as long as Veer fucking pays for what he's done."

Whoever gets him first, gets him.

THE DAY OF RELEASE, Mac brought a frilly dark green dress with him and dressed Catori in it.

"That's my favorite color," I smiled.

"I know, that's why I got it." He grinned. That's right, I did tell him that was my favorite color.

"You don't think she should wear pink?"

He gives me an awkward eye.

"She'll have enough pink crap her whole life, this dress is perfect for her first day in the real world."

I laugh, looking Catori over in her dress. She's so cute in green.

"One more thing," Mac mutters, placing the purple dragon Gatz got her, next to her.

I gasp, tears filling my eyes.

"I may not be able to fill your daddy's shoes, but I'll be the second best," he tells Catori, and I can't control the sob that trembles from my mouth. God, when will these hormones go away?

"You're all set, we just need to make sure you have a car seat, and she's buckled in correctly before leaving," A nurse enters the room handing us some papers.

"I- I don't have a car seat." Panic sets in, they're going to take Catori, find me as an unfit mother.

"No, I got one," Mac casually informs the nurse.

"You did?" My eyes dart to his. "When did you do that?"

He opens up a large cabinet next to the bed and pulls out a blue and pink car seat by Eddie Bower.

He places it on the bed next to me, and I rub my finger along the suede material.

"This morning."

"This looks expensive," I mutter.

"It has the best crash ratings and is most compatible with any vehicle." Mac gently places Catori in her car seat, and his lecture on the specifications on the car seat make me go deaf. He's going to be the most protective, annoying dad; I can see it. I love him and want to slap him.

A male nurse enters the room with a wheelchair, and Mac helps me out of the bed. The weight on my stomach causes it to sting and feels like it's ripping apart. Sitting in the chair, I can't help but sigh with relief.

I'm wheelchaired out, and Raven and Machete await outside the front doors of the hospital with Raven's car. Motorcycles on each side of the car to escort us back to the club.

Mac buckles Catori in, and I swear he checks it five times to make sure it's buckled in right.

Slowly climbing in next to Catori, Mac on the other side we pull away from the hospital.

"Slow down Raven, fuck!" Mac yells at Raven.

"I'm like going three over, chill out!"

They get into a full argument about how fast the car should be going with the amount of weight inside the vehicle. Even Machete jumps in on the argument.

I feel camouflaged in the moment. Catori and I, blending in with our new life. As two bikers covered in tattoos hash out what the speed limit should be when driving a baby back to a clubhouse.

I feel safe and comfortable for the first time in a long time. I'm laughing, and an amazing man is holding my hand that truly loves me and isn't bound as a family obligation to care about me. It's his choice to want to be with me, he wants to be in mine and Catori's life.

A mansion filled with the most expensive things and people who are blood-related wasn't a home.

This is home.

I know without a doubt every person in this car will protect me and Catori, even if it means taking a bullet to do it.

26

SIMONE

A rriving at the clubhouse, Jillian is outside with Alessandra, big smiles on their faces. I can tell by the look on their face they're up to something.

"Mac?" Shifting in my seat, I poke him in the arm before pointing at the two women smiling like they have planned a party or something inside. I'm in no shape for a welcome home party.

Mac opens his mouth and then shuts it. "I told them no," he breathes heavily.

"You mean you knew about this?" I hush-whisper.

"They texted me about it, but I told them you'd probably be tired."

"Girl, you better get used to Jillian doing what she wants." Raven laughs from behind the wheel. I sigh, knowing she's right. Jillian is a strong-willed woman, all of the ol' ladies are actually, but their care for one another is not lost between the lines of being independent. I learned that the day all three of them came to my room when I was at my lowest.

FORCING A SMILE, I lift my chin. I might as well accept my fate. We're all ol' ladies after all. I'll just make an appearance and then head up to the hotel room. I'm exhausted, and not sure I can stand very long with the incision on my lower stomach.

RAVEN STOPS THE CAR, and Mac helps me out of the car. Every move tears and pulls at my stomach and I wince. I should have taken a pain reliever before I left the hospital.

"TAKE IT SLOW." He rests his hand on my back, easing me out of the leather seat.

"I'M GOOD," I exhale through the pain, and stand up straight. Mac bends into the car and unlatches the car seat from the belt. His bicep flexes, his shoulders rising when holding the weight of the seat with one arm. A biker holding a baby car seat does things to a woman that are unfair.

BITING MY BOTTOM LIP, I force myself to look away. Four weeks. Four weeks until we can have sex again and it's going to be the hardest four weeks of my life.

Mac

WITH THE CAR seat gripped in my palm, Jillian and the girls come running at me to see the baby.

Jesus Christ. I hold Catori up high, nervous they're going to smother her to death.

"MAC." Jillian scowls, raising her brows, and I raise mine in return. She has it in her head I should just give her the baby whenever she wants, and that's not fucking happening.

A HAND CLAPS down on my shoulder and I take my eyes off Jillian to find Zeek staring back at me with questioning eyes. He needs to talk, shit. Leaning into Simone, I tell her, "Go inside, check out whatever they did, and I'll come rescue you in five." I kiss her on the cheek and point at Jillian. "Jillian, do not take your eyes off her." My tone of voice threatening. She gives me the bitch eye before helping Simone inside.

I Follow Zeek away from the crowd, and he glances down at Catori, rubbing the scruff on his cheeks.

"SO YOU CLAIMED Simone as your ol' lady, huh?" He doesn't sound surprised, or the least bit worried.

SWITCHING the car seat into the other palm, I nod. I claimed Simone before I knew it was Gatz's child, and I regret nothing.

"YOU NEED to keep her up in that suite until we find Veer, brother.

Especially now that there's documentation of her giving birth here in the state," he says, watching the women go inside the club.

"WELL, get me a good fucking prospect to keep guard at the door," my tone dry.

ZEEK'S EYES snap to mine. "I'm trying."

"What about Bishop? He's ready!" I encourage. The kid is bred for this kinda shit.

ZEEK RUBS AT HIS CHIN, annoyed with my persistence. "You know the women want him to get his GED. Not many of us Outlaws can say we've finished high school."

I give Zeek a knowing look. It would be good for Bishop, the best gift we can give a brother.

"GO GET your chick and go rest," Zeek nods. "I'll take care of the giddy fucking women with their ovaries about to combust." He shakes his head, and I can't help but laugh.

STEPPING INTO THE CLUB, it looks like a fucking she-shed. There's pink ribbon, and pink balloons, and just fucking pink everywhere. I find Simone, sitting on a stool and unwrapping a stroller. I can tell she's in pain but trying to mask it for everyone else's sake.

"You guys, this is too much. Thank you!" She smiles up at everyone, her face glowing. She's unwrapped a few gifts since I've been outside. A crib, some clothes, diapers, and formula.

The club really came together for her, for us.

Simone's face creases and her hand rests on her stomach. She's really starting to hurt. I shove through the group of women, and to her side.

"Okay, Simone needs to rest you guys. We can bring up whatever you want later, but she needs her pain meds, and Catori needs a diaper change I'm sure," I interrupt.

Raven rolls her eyes, resting her elbow on the back of the bar.

"You going from changing oil to changing diapers there, Mac?" She busts my balls. I flip her off and help Simone up from the stool.

"Oh, I'm fine." Simone acts coy, but the way she's gripping my hand, I can tell she's grateful I intervened.

Machete and Zeek following us up, but Simone starts to slow down, her pain level escalating. With hesitation, I hand Catori to Machete. "Don't you dare hand her to anyone else!" I demand.

"You better watch your threats, brother," Machete scowls. Glancing down at Catori, his face softens, eyes widening as he takes the car seat, fear dilating his pupils. He has a kid, but not this small, he missed out on the newborn state with his son.

Positioning my arms carefully behind Simone, I pick her up. She doesn't even resist, she wraps her arms around my neck and rests her head on my shoulder. She's exhausted, and in pain. I wish I could take it all away so she could enjoy Catori.

"I got you," I whisper, kissing her forehead.

Finally, in the suite, I take her to my room. Fuck that sleeping in separate bedrooms shit. I place her pain pills on the side table and fill a glass with tap water.

Grabbing the bottle, she takes a pill out and takes it quickly.

"Rest, I got Catori," I tell her.

"Mac, no. You've done too much." She tries to sit up to argue, but it's not up for debate.

"I got this, sleep now. 'Cause we might have to take shifts if she wakes up tonight," I explain. I'm tired as fuck and will be needing to crash at some point. Seeming satisfied with taking turns, she lays back down. Pulling the blankets over her, I leave the room and shut the door.

I FEEL DIFFERENT. Caring so much for her and the baby comes so natural but how? Looking at the floor, I bite my lip.

"YOU ALL RIGHT, BROTHER?" Zeek asks, breaking my dissecting of this emotion rolling through me.

"WHY DID you give me the job to protect Simone?" I can't help but ask. He knows my back history, he knows how my mother died.

HE FUCKING SMIRKS, resting his hand on the counter. "'Cause, we all broke to a woman better than us, it was your turn."

MY EYES WIDEN, so many questions and words on the tip of my tongue. Machete laughs like a fucking idiot and hands Catori to me before he follows Zeek out of the suite.

SIGHING, I look to the baby, who's looking up at me with doe eyes.

"DO YOU LIKE SANDWICHES? I feel like I need a sandwich, or I might kill a brother," I tell her.

27

SIMONE

Waking up groggy as hell, I find Mac beside me spread out on the bed passed out. Rolling over on my side, I find his hand gripping a white baby monitor tightly. He's lying on his back his bare tattooed chest facing upward, and his dark-colored sweats hung down low outlining his cock. He must not be wearing any underwear the way the material outlines it so perfectly.

MAC DADDY IS AMAZING. He's done so much for me, and I feel like I've done nothing.

Biting my lip as I contemplate how I can pay him back, I run the pad of my finger over the blue vein lacing down his hip. All men love blowjobs, right? I've never given one, and I might suck at it, but I'm willing to try for him. His pants slowly begin to rise as I trace his veins ever so slowly, it excites me to know my touch affects him. Shoving my hand down his pants, I pull his fully erect cock free from his boxers. The barbell pierced through his head shimmers from the moonlight coming through the window.

Man, he's so big and thick, it makes my mouth water just looking at it.

MY EYES SLIDE up his hips finding him still asleep. Lowering my head, I flick the head of his length with my tongue, then slide it along the shaft. He tastes of salt and musk filling my mouth. He stirs, and I take the plunge - I shove as much of his hard, throbbing cock into my mouth as I can. His barbell hitting the roof of my mouth, I gag but don't stop.

A FERAL GROWL vibrates his chest, his fingers tightening into my tangled hair with excitement.

"FUCK YES." He thrusts his hips upward, the thick head gagging the shit out of me. Sheathing my teeth with my lips, I suck and bob, and suck and bob. The soft velvety skin of his cock sliding in and out between my lips with ease. His body tenses and rises off the bed. Having him come undone with the power of my mouth is a rush I've never had.

"OH MY GOD, Simone. Just like that," he whispers huskily. His fingers in my hair lifting and lowering my mouth just how he likes it.

MY NIPPLES ACHE, demanding to be freed from this heavy shirt and my clit throbs for rough attention.

AS IF HE reads my mind, he slips his hand under my shirt and tweaks my budded nipple. Soft moans ripple through my swollen lips as I close my eyes and suck him like he's the best popsicle earth has to offer.

"FLIP, FLIP!" Mac warns. Before I can let his length leave my mouth, he has me on my back, shirt raised above my heavy tits, and is spraying white beads of cum all over my chest. It's warm, and silky and covers the mounds of my chest like icing.

HAIR IN HIS FACE, mouth lax, and eyes dark and hooded, he looks at me in silence. Brushing the hair from his face, I smirk. Happy I can please my man.

"MY TURN," he breathes heavily. My eyes widen in panic. I have a pad the size of a man diaper on, he can't go down there.

"I- WAIT!" I try and stop him, my struggle making my incision burn. "The doctor said at least four weeks!" I remind him.

"I'm not going to fuck you, not yet anyway." He winks, and my stomach knots. He's going to run for the hills when he sees what's hidden in these panties.

HE SHIMMIES DOWN MY UNDERWEAR, and I smack my face with my hand. I bet I'm covered in blood. My bloody pad the sexiest thing he's seen, I'm sure.

"I DON'T NEED A TURN, I'm fine," I assure him.

"LOOK AT THAT CLIT, swollen and ready for only me." The admiration in his tone has me drop my hand and look at him with awe. This man is surprising me every day, how is he not grossed out?

LOOKING DOWN AT MYSELF, I notice there's no blood on me, thank God.

STICKING his thumb in his mouth, he sucks on it hard. Dark dominating eyes pinning me where I lay.

A CHESHIRE CAT grin spreads across his sleepy face, and his dexterous finger swirls my clit into a bundle of stars and pressure. My fingers claw at the sheets, my mouth parting with how fast the pleasure was brought upon. God yes, I needed him to touch me. Clenching, and holding my breath I try to keep myself together, so I don't wake the baby.

"LET IT OUT, I want to hear you moan. I want the fucking neighbors to know my goddamn name!" he bites his bottom lip. My body feels like it's teetering on the side of a cliff, pleasure and satisfaction just beyond the ledge. Warm fingers pinch my left nipple causing a spark of pain to ricochet down my torso. Taking the jump, I free fall over the side of the cliff and exhale a loud, blissful moan. "Rhett!!!"

HIS FINGER RELEASES MY CLIT, and goosebumps rise up my back. Opening my eyes, I take a deep breath, shifting my body into the soft mattress.

The tingles subside, and I'm brought back down to earth and reality. My feet landing softly on the ground as Mac pulls my panties back up.

HIS EYES NARROW in on me with an unreadable look. I hold my breath curious if I did something wrong. Was I too loud?

"You said my real name." I can't tell if he's mad or if he liked it, though. I couldn't help saying it, it was the first thing that came to mind when I was in the moment.

"Does that bother you?"

A PANTY MELTING grin spreads across his face. "You make it sound strong and sexy. Say it again." A quick lift of his chin encourages me to do exactly what he asks.

"RHETT," spills from my swollen lips, flirtation coloring my voice.

HE NODS APPROVINGLY. "I'd kill a man for saying my name before as my past of being bullied in school turned it into something ugly. But when you say it... all I can think about is you saying it again." His brows pinch together like he can't make sense of the situation.

"IT'S A NAME REBORN," I laugh. I think we both have been reborn, and we owe it all to Catori.

"How are you feeling?" He changes the subject, lying next to me. I snuggle up next to him, the feel of his sweaty hard body next to mine making me sleepy again.

"Mmm, I'm good now," I reply in a daze. My body suppressing its pain and living in the moment of heavenly bliss. We both close our eyes, and Mac throws his arm over me, pulling me even closer. My cheeks ache from smiling so hard. I've been through hell to get here, but it was all fucking worth it.

The baby monitor suddenly crackles, and the sound of soft cries echoes through the room. My eyes pop open, and I sigh loudly.

"I'll get her," I state, sitting up.

"No, I got her, go clean yourself up, and I'll make a bottle." He slips out of the bed, pulling his pants up and I grab his wrist before he can leave me.

"Do you believe in fate?"

He gives me an unreadable look, so I feel the need to explain myself more. "I've been through the darkest streets, did business with the worst kind of people, and talked the language of the sinners, but in the end... I think it was to end up here with you. Does that make sense?"

He nods, his hand interlocking with mine.

"Fate may predict the future, but it's how we play the cards that we're dealt that makes the difference." Letting go of my hand, he takes a step backward. "I wouldn't go thanking fate for me in your life just yet, Simone. I'm sure to fuck this up, that's what I do to things that are too good in my life."

I blink, the thought of losing him scary.

His lips press into a fine line, an arrogant look fitting his face. "But, I'm the best card player I know, so I'm giving the deck I was handed hell before I let go of my girls."

"I know you will," I smile deeply.

He steps out of the room to make a bottle, and I'm left staring at the back of the bedroom door.

That's the one major thing Mac and I have in common.

We fuck everything up. I mean, that's what led us to the here and now.

Because I fucked everything up, trying to fix everything.

I just hope the never-ending fall of dominos have run its course and I can be happy now.

28

ONE WEEK LATER

MAC

"Oh my God, it's yellow. Is it supposed to be yellow?" My nose scrunches up while I stare at Catori's diaper. Maybe we should Google it, but the last time Simone Googled something we were running to the emergency room for nothing but a clogged nose. They gave us this blue sucker thing and sent us on our way.

Catori continues to cry hysterically, hating having her diaper changed and I get anxious. I hate hearing her cry, it makes me so upset knowing she's upset.

"HANG ON, I'm getting the bottle from the steamer and I'll look." Simone turns from the counter with the bottle in her hand. "Fuck that's hot!" Her face contorts in pain, and she drops the bottle, causing milk to explode all over the floor and counter.

JUMPING UP FROM THE FLOOR, I race to Simone to check on her. Before I can reach her, my bare feet slip in the milk. Just as I'm about to wipe out, Simone grabs onto my arm to keep me from falling and we both fall together in warm spilled milk.

SHE LOOKS AT ME, and I look at her as Catori continues to scream her heart out.

"DID YOU BURN IT BADLY?" Reaching for her hand, I flip it over and inspect her red palm. I knew I should have made one with a cooling system for the outside of the bottle. These store-bought ones suck.

SIMONE'S EYES begin to water with tears, this last week has been fucking brutal. We've had little to no sleep, hardly any time together, and I don't know when the last time I showered was. Being a parent is not fucking easy. Those books lie out of their ass saying it's easy with just a few steps to make a child stop crying.

Scooting closer to Simone, I wrap my arms around her, milk dripping from my hand onto her hair. We're a mess.

"WE'RE GOING TO NEED A SHOWER," she laughs, leaning into me.

"You should see Catori, she has crap all over her back. We all need showers." I grin. Maybe we're all messes.

"WHY DON'T you go for a ride and take a break, babe."

ANGRY, I fist her by the chin making her look directly at me. My eyes narrowed in at her glossy browns.

"I SIGNED up for this shit, and I'm not going anywhere. I'm her dad, and I'm not going to run out when it gets tough." Her eyes bounce back and forth between mine, fighting tears. I claimed Simone and am not running out on her just because our baby might have colic, or I haven't gotten to ride my motorcycle for a week. That last one is killing me though.

"You're too good to us," she pouts, grabbing my hand. I scoff in response. I need to find Veer so I can truly be the dad I never had. I want to get us a place with a big yard that Catori can play in with an ugly ass dog of some kind.

"Why don't we do a date night?" I suggest before really thinking what the fuck I just offered. I've never done a date, what the fuck do I know about being romantic. Her face drops, her head shaking.

"I can't leave Catori—" I slap my hand over her mouth, her interrupting irritating me.

"I'll go out and get Chinese, we can chill on the couch, maybe light some candles and shit." I shrug, trying to do the best I can, given my limited resources.

"I know it's not really a date..." I start backpedaling. She hates it, why did I offer this?

Her milk spotted hand reaches for mine, pulling it free from her face revealing a smile.

"I'D LIKE THAT. I don't know when I had a full dinner last." She looks to the floor, and relief causes my tense shoulders to relax.

"You can ride your bike to get dinner too," she points out. I nod, a big grin on my face now. Fuck yes! Maybe I'll have Machete roll with me, get some brother time in before baby language becomes my first tongue.

"DO YOU HEAR THAT?" Simone looks at me with wide eyes. I listen but hear nothing.

"She stopped crying," I reply with wide eyes.

WE BOTH STAND, and find Catori playing with her poopy diaper, it's all in her hair and face.

WE BOTH SIGH, Simone sinking onto the counter with exhaustion.

"ROCK, PAPER, SCISSORS?" I suggest. Simone laughs and readies her hand for the ultimate challenge. This game is something we both have relied on when it comes to Catori and her diapers, and puke.

"ROCK, PAPER, SCISSORS." I slap down a rock, and she plops down a pair of scissors.

"YES!" I hiss, my hands in the air like I just won a championship game.

Simone growls, rounding the island in the kitchen.

"Come on poop princess, it's time for a bath," Simone sighs.

"I'll get the baby bath filled, though you might think about getting in the big tub in with her." I scrunch my nose at her, the smell of cooling milk not pleasant.

Simone

Laying Catori down in her crib in my old room, I turn the baby monitor on and slowly step out.

"She's asleep," I breathe heavily. I could use a nap, maybe some wine, but tonight me and Mac have plans to just relax. Just us. I can stay awake.

"Nice. I'm going to run and get our dinner, Jillian is going to come up and keep you company until I get back," Mac informs, slipping his arms through his leather cut. I haven't seen him put it on in over a week. Seeing the dark leather claim his back makes him look dangerous and sexy.

His hair is slicked back with just a few strands falling in his face. A dark blue shirt and black jeans hugging his legs well.

"Stop looking at me like that, woman. We have three weeks before I get to fuck you, and it's killing me." I jump, startled I was caught staring like a horny woman. He hands me the remote, his eyes hooded. "Find a movie for us but make it a good one."

"WHAT'S A GOOD ONE?" I frown.

"I DON'T KNOW, not a chick flick." He shrugs. "Anything besides Baby Genius, please."

I laugh at his dramatic tone. Mac read that Baby Genius is great for soothing newborns, so we've been watching a lot of that lately.

It puts me to sleep.

A KNOCK at the door has Mac turning around to answer it and I flip the TV on to see what movie to buy.

"HEY, THANKS FOR COMING," Mac says.

"ARE YOU KIDDING, I could use a break myself. I have two kids, you have one." The familiar voice of Jillian sounds from behind me.

DROPPING the remote on the couch, I turn around to greet her.

"HEY!" I smile.

SHE HAS her hair up in a messy bun, a white shirt, and gray sweats with white shoes. She looks comfy, which is good because

I didn't dress up for company. I'm wearing one of Mac's torn rock band shirts, and a pair of sweatpants myself.

"Where is the baby?" She grins wildly. The woman has baby fever bad, I bet she's fucking Zeek like crazy.

"Catori," Mac reminds her of the name and Jillian scowls in response.

"She's asleep, but I'm sure she'll be awake soon," I explain, pointing to Catori's room.
"Still not sleeping through the night?"
"Not at all," I sigh.

"All right, I'm out." He points at Jillian. "Watch everything."
"Go, everything will be fine!" she insists, waving him off.

Mac gives me a kiss on the lips, nipping at my bottom lip.

"I'll be right back." He winks, and my chest swells. I want to tell him to hurry back, but I want him to enjoy his ride.

Both of us girls sit on the couch, and Jillian begins to explain when she had her twins, it was a nightmare. No sleeping, bathing, or sex.

I SHAKE MY HEAD. "I couldn't imagine having two babies at once."

Then again, seeing I can't have any more kids I guess I'll never know.

WE GROW SILENT, and she rests her arm on the back of the couch.

"You know, I have to be honest. I never thought Mac would settle down. Then again, I've never seen Mac the way he is around you." Her brows raise.

POKING the stray string from the couch I laugh nervously.

"He wasn't a ray of sunshine when I met him, trust me." I recall how crude he was, and how we fought constantly. I don't really know what to say about Mac. When we met he was quiet and brooding, but slowly he came around and I see parts of him nobody sees.

"HOW'D YOU AND ZEEK MEET?" I ask, curious how she tamed the Outlaw of all Outlaws.

She looks at the ceiling, her mouth open as she begins to tell me. "Uh, well. I tried to arrest him."

MY EYES WIDEN, a laugh ripping through my throat.

"I WOULD HAVE PAID to have seen that." I can't imagine someone the size of Jillian trying to take Zeek down.

"IT DIDN'T GO SO WELL." She giggles with a scrunched face.

"I bet not. So how'd the club take it when they found out about you two?" I can't help but get the scoop, I live for gossip. I mean a sheriff and a biker, that is as taboo as it gets!

"They hated me, but they came around because Zeek made them," she shrugs.

KNOCKING on the door has us both frown.

"SOMEONE ELSE COMING?" Jillian asks.

I SHAKE MY HEAD. "No, last person that showed up uninvited was one of Mac's hos." My tone painted with hatred.

JILLIAN SUDDENLY STANDS, her body going into defense.
    "Well, I'm a pro at telling hos off. Let me take care of it."

JILLIAN STANDS, and heads to the front door. Grasping the baby radio, I lift it to my ear to check on Catori, but I don't hear anything. She's still sleeping.

STANDING, I take the opportunity to go to the bathroom while Jillian tells off whoever is at the door. Shutting the door behind me, I sit on the cold toilet seat and do my business. My bleeding has let up a lot, so I'm down to normal pads now. Which is great because the other pads made it hard to walk.

A BUMP in the other room makes the picture on the bathroom wall shake.

NARROWING MY BROWS, I nervously squeeze the toilet paper in my hand.

"JILLIAN?"

NOTHING.

WIPING, I quickly stand, and hurry out of the bathroom to see what's going on. The front door is open, and nobody is in the living room.

My head snaps in the direction of the baby's room.

"CATORI..." I breathe with panic. Racing to her room, I shove the door open, not caring if I wake her. Standing next to her crib is Veer. I gasp, my knees wobbling at the sight of the man that keeps me awake at night has Jillian at gunpoint. On the floor next to them is another gun, it must have been what the commotion was about. Jillian tried to fight him off.

MY CHEST TREMBLES as a ragged breath gets caught in my throat. Veer is just as intimidating as I remember. His shadow on the bedroom floor creeping around my legs and stealing the very breath from my lungs.

29

SIMONE

Veer's white button-up shirt is without so much as one wrinkle, and his black slacks perfectly fitted.

He runs the hand holding the gun over his black hair, a blinding smile punching me in the stomach.

I turn quickly to grab my phone off the charger on the side table just outside the room, and Veer tsks, halting me.

"Looking for this?" He has my pink iPhone dangling from his hands. He drops it to the floor and slams the heel of his leather shoe right into the screen. Cracking it into pieces.

Fuck.

"I've been looking for you, Simone."

"HOW DID YOU FIND ME?" I can't help but ask, anger and terror battling in my chest.

"WELL, it wasn't easy. I came here first and killed one lover only to find you not here. Then I went to the other lover from a different club, to find out you weren't there either. "But alas a broken-hearted cop reached out in attempt to hire me to do her dirty work to off an entire club, and in return, she'd give me your whereabouts, but she went missing before we could become accomplices. So," he takes a deep breath, looking back into the crib. "Good ol' birth records gave me everything I needed to find you in the end."

"PLEASE, DON'T HURT HER," I plead, my eyes filling with tears. My body trembles and the fear in my chest is so heavy I can hardly breathe.

HIS HEAD SNAPS in my direction, the disgusted look pulling at his face makes my knees tremble with fear.

"HURT HER? She shouldn't be here, Simone! You broke the unwritten laws of our marriage agreement! You made me look like an idiot!" His face turns red, his voice shouting. That's when I realize this is all about pride and he's not going anywhere without me by his side.

I'm a statement, and he'll stop at nothing to show everyone he knows that he's a man of his word. I hang my head, knowing if I fight him he'll kill anyone in his way.

"PLEASE, if you just let her go... I'll- I'll go with you." A tear slips down my cheek. The idea of not having Catori in my life seems bleak, but I'd rather not have her next to me, than her be gone forever.

"SIMONE!" Jillian hisses, but I can't look her in the eyes. She doesn't understand, if I don't willingly go with him, he will kill Catori and her. I can't let anyone else die because of me.

"WHERE IS YOUR MOTHER? Is she here?" He changes the subject, throwing me for a loop. Like my submission means nothing to him.

"WH-WHAT? NO," I reply confused.

HIS FACE TURNS TOWARD MINE, his dark snake eyes causing a chill to race up my neck.

"WHEN I KILLED YOUR FATHER, she ran. I figured she'd be with you. She deserves to die for your betrayal," he sneers.

"YOU- YOU KILLED MY FATHER?" The words sound foreign spilling from my lips. My actions have caused so much spilled blood.

A MANIACAL LAUGH wracks his whole body, the sound making my limbs shake with terror.

"He let you become a whore! I don't take breaking a contract lightly," he growls. As if I'm not a person but an object. "You're mine, and you will learn how to be my wife if I have to beat it into you. You will redeem my last name with honor!"

"SHE'S NOT GOING ANYWHERE with you!" Jillian seethes through gritted teeth. He waves the gun at her, but she seems unfazed by the threat. Her face lax and eyes conveying boredom.

"Jillian," I warn. She has no idea what kind of man she's dealing with, Veer will shoot her without warning.

Her eyes fall to the gun on the floor and a fearing chill bumps up my back.

She dives to the floor reaching for the spare gun, and Veer jerks as a loud boom echoes through the room. Jillian's body suddenly going limp. Oh my God, he shot her. Catori cries, and I scream at Jillian's lifeless body on the floor. Reaching for the wall to hold me up, I try and hold in my sob.

"YOU DIDN'T HAVE to do that!" My voice cracks.

"Yeah, but she was really getting on my nerves," he chuckles. Not able to take my eyes off Jillian, blood begins to stain the surrounding carpet under her body. Her back rises taking in a shallow breath. Oh my God, she's alive.

SHAKY MOVEMENTS, I fall to Jillian's side, trying to turn her over to see where she's been shot.

"YOU'RE OKAY," I lie. I have no idea. All I can think about is how cold and shaky I suddenly am. Her thigh has a massive amount of blood dripping out of a hole in her sweatpants. That's where she's been shot. Looking on the other side of her leg there's no exit wound.

I DID ENOUGH in medical school to know that if I don't slow this bleeding down, Jillian won't make it long enough for Mac to find her.

RIPPING MAC'S SHIRT, I attempt to wrap her leg tightly with it. My hand under her thigh, Jillian grips my fingers and I freeze from her sudden strength. My eyes dart to hers, and she nods, shoving something into my palm.

SPREADING my gaze across her limp body to my hand I realize she's giving me her phone.

Veer looks at Catori, his gun waving around and I quickly shove the phone down my shirt.

MAYBE I CAN GET a break to call Mac and tell him where I am, or maybe he can use one of his computer programs he loves so much to trace it.

"GET UP!" Veer suddenly barks, and I jump where I kneel. His voice shrill and terrifying.

"GET UP, or I will pull this fucking trigger!" he threatens, turning the gun to the crib. A blood-curdling scream makes my throat raw. Instantly, I climb to my feet, my hands outstretched to stop him from pulling the trigger.

"PLEASE DON'T, I'm up and listening," I cry in a hoarse voice. I'll do anything for him not to hurt Catori. Anything.

"YOU MADE A FOOL OUT OF ME," he seethes. His hand tightening around the trigger of the gun. "Look at her, she's not even full Native American!" he insults.

"STOP!" I scream. "Don't hurt her. I know, I'm sorry. Just, please. Let's go," I coax, waving him toward the door. Trying to get him away from the crib and away from my baby girl.

HE LOOKS at Catori with disgust, and my heart sinks to the pit of my stomach. Doom swallowing any hope that Mac and Catori sparked in my cold heart that my life may be different. He's going to kill her and if he does, he might as well kill me too. I've caused so much chaos with my actions, ruined lives even. But losing my little girl will put a bullet through my brain. I'll be a living vegetable. Breathing, but not surviving.

"PLEASE VEER, I will go with you if you just let her live. She doesn't have anything to do with my betrayal," I explain. "She's just a baby."

SCRATCHING his temple with the barrel of the gun, he contemplates my offer. Looking at Catori as if she is a baby for the first time rather than a bastard child.

"YOU WANT TO GO WITH ME?" God no, but I will go anywhere if it means Catori is safe.

"YES, let's go. We can get married, we can still do everything you wanted. Just let her go." Every word is sharp glass to my throat, but I'm scared to death he'll hurt my little girl if I say the wrong thing.

WAVING the gun from the crib, he points it at me and I freeze.
"Get your shoes on. We're going home. Wife."
Vomit fills my mouth hearing him call me wife. Swallowing, eyes teary, I glance at the crib.
"Can I say goodbye?"

HE LOOKS at the crib before finally nodding.

QUICKLY, I erase the space between me and crib. Catori's in a pink elephant sleeper, crying hysterically. Placing my palm on her chest, she begins to calm down. I situate the purple dragon next to her, and she settles.

"Hey there," I whisper. "You be strong, okay?" I sob, trying to paint her face to memory. The smell of her baby soap, and the feel of her heart beating against my palm. I impregnate my mind with every detail of my little girl.

Tears down her face, she looks up at me and it brings me back to when my mother had to walk away from me for my own good. Ordering me to run for my life. I wonder if it was just as hard for her as it is for me.

"I'm doing this for your own good, but know that I love you, and always will." My voice wavers, tears slipping down my chin and dripping on her bedding.

"Time's up, let's go. We'll have babies. Children meant to be in this world." He growls, and I squeeze my eyes shut, the truth of me having a hysterectomy on the tip of my tongue.

If I tell him, it will just make everything worse. I need to control myself and get him away from Catori.

He tugs on my arm, pulling me away from the crib. I step over Jillian lying on the floor and find my shoes next to the couch. Slipping them on one by one with trembling hands.

Mac will look for me, and if he can't rescue me, he will be the best dad to Catori any girl could ask for.

M̶Y̶ H̶E̶A̶R̶T̶ B̶R̶E̶A̶K̶S̶ in my chest, and I can't breathe. I feel light-headed, as if someone is squeezing the life from my chest with their bare hands.

Snot and tears dripping down my face I remind myself I'm doing this for Catori.

LOOKING at the lamp on the side table, thoughts about bashing it against Veer's head wavers in my mind, but one wrong move and he'll kill Catori for sure.

I CAN'T RISK IT.

STANDING, I lift my chin, trying to be strong like my mother.

LETTING my daughter and Mac go is the hardest thing I've ever had to do. Like a little kid lifting the lid to a jar full of beautiful rare butterflies.

Mac

SHOVING the grease stained bag of Chinese food in my saddle bag, I listen to Machete go on about how him and Raven have been fucking like mental patients gone wild. With his red hair flying in the wind he looks mental right now.

"I TIED her to the bed and painted a picture with hot wax on her back and if she guessed the picture wrong, she got a spanking." Machete slapped his palm with his other hand, a wild grin on his face.

I JUST SHAKE MY HEAD. They're into some kinky shit.

STRADDLING MY MOTORCYCLE SEAT, I start it and rev it up. Excitement buzzes through me needing the silence and solace the wind and the motor of my motorcycle have to offer, along with my brother by my side on the black pavement. It's a peace I can't explain.

THE WARM AIR of the summer feels good against my sweaty skin, every time we hit a stop light, my boots on the ground to balance myself, beads of sweat instantly form on my back. I need it though, it's better than the air conditioner of the suite.

A CAR PULLS up beside me, a young woman with blonde hair looking my way before she quickly darts her eyes forward. Her shoulders tensing with fear. I smirk at her cowardly demeanor.

SEEMS our name still upholds our reputation.

PULLING UP TO THE CLUB, I back my bike into its spot and turn it off. Exhaling a long breath, I climb off my motorcycle and grab the food from my bags. The smell of hot noodles and crab rangoon making my stomach growl.

"THANKS FOR RIDING with me man, I needed that," I state, buckling up my saddle bags.

"NOT... NOT A PROBLEM, BROTHER," Machete replies, distracted with his phone in his palm. The way his face contorts into concern, I know something is wrong. Raven must have grabbed the wrong nipple clamps or something.

WITH A LIFT of my chin I ask him, "What's up?"

"ZEEK HAS BEEN BLOWING my phone up," his tone distressed.

SETTING the food down on the seat of my bike, I tug my phone free and see four missed calls from Zeek. My hands become jittery with anxiety.

"HE CAN'T GET AHOLD of Jillian," Machete reads a text out loud. My head swoops upward to where Jillian and Simone are in the hotel as if I can tell what's wrong from down here. The feeling of fingers digging into my heart, push my feet forward. Leaving the Chinese behind, I sprint inside the casino, past gamblers and half-naked women serving over-priced cocktails, to the private elevator to our suite.

MACHETE beside me in the elevator, he tugs his machete from his boot, and I pull my gun from my waistband ready for whatever may go down. This is what I'm trained to do, yet I feel like a loose cannon ready to spray bullets and pray they hit their target.

"I SEE the vein in your neck pumping, brother. Take a deep breath," Machete schools.

"Fuck you, your chick isn't up there," I growl in response.

I SHOULDN'T HAVE LEFT Simone. It was too risky leaving her without Outlaw protection. God, I hope they're just being stupid with the TV too loud or something. Deep inside my gut though, I know they're not. The sharp coldness on the back of my neck, and the knot in my stomach silently telling me something has gone wrong.

THE ELEVATOR DOORS SLOWLY OPEN, and I slide through the opening needing out now. Entering the hallway, I notice the front door to the suite is wide open. I was right, something bad happened. The sound of Catori's screaming from inside her room makes my blood chill to the bone, and the grip on my gun tightens.

"SIMONE! CATORI!" I run to the sound of her crying and into the baby room. Jillian is laying on the floor, blood pooling around her while Catori cries in her crib.

Rubbing my chin anxiously, I step over Jillian and Simone's

cracked phone to check on Catori. She's crying hysterically, her dragon right next to her. I frown, knowing for a fact someone placed it next to her. Simone and I made sure it was in the corner of the crib watching over her. The only people to know it means anything is Simone, and I thought she must have moved it. I place my hand under her and pick her up. Spinning her in the air, I check for any injuries, but she's clear of any wounds. I sigh with relief. Thank fuck.

"Easy baby, Daddy's here," I soothe her, pressing her to my chest. I kiss her head, and she quiets some. Her baby smell and soft touch what I needed.

I bend at the knee next to Jillian's body, pressing two fingers to her neck.

"Is she alive?" Machete asks, coming into the room, his voice cracking with concern. The same question hangs heavy on my mind as I try to look for a pulse. She's the club's queen, if she dies the club will lose a part of its soul. Our president will lose his fucking mind, bringing all of us to insanity.

Faintly I feel the vessels in Jillian's neck beat against the pad of my finger.

"She's alive, call 911."

BEFORE MACHETE CAN PULL his phone out, Zeek and Felix are flying through the front door of the suite, yelling Jillian's name. He must have given up trying to call her and headed over here himself.

"IN HERE!" I inform.

ZEEK MARCHES IN, his hair a fucking mess, and he's wearing just his leather jacket and some jeans. Looks like he was at home relaxing when he started to become worried about Jillian. Felix's hair is down, his Harley shirt on backward, and jeans smeared with Dorito dust.

ZEEK FALLS to the floor next to his queen, his face pale. For the first time in my life, my president looks lost as to what to do next. It makes me feel vulnerable. Zeek always has the answers and strength for any situation, and right now... he's fucking lost.

"OH MY GOD," he mutters. "Jillian, wake the fuck up!" He shakes her with a trembling hand. Regret smothers me in a dark remorse. I never should have left these girls here by themselves. I bet Veer fucking waited for me to turn my back. Makes me wonder how long he's been watching Simone, waiting for his chance to strike.

RUBBING MY NECK NERVOUSLY, I notice something wrapped around Jillian's bloody thigh. A piece of my shirt to be exact. Simone must have done it to slow the bleeding, good thing too or she might have bled out.

"WE NEED to get her to a hospital and now," I tell Zeek. He knowingly gazes at me, he hates the hospital but knows we don't have a choice.

"AN AMBULANCE IS ON THE WAY," Machete informs us, already making the call.

STANDING with Catori tightly pressed against my chest, her warmth and heartbeat somehow keeping the little bit of sanity I have in check.

"I'm going to check the camera I installed in the hallway." I hooked it up after Simone came home with Catori.

"VEE—" Jillian crackles from the carpeted floor. I freeze, looking down at her.

My brows pinching together I scowl at Zeek. "What'd she say?"

JILLIAN COUGHS, her eyes closed.

"V-VEER!" she replies with more clarity this time. My neck tenses as hard as rocks, my hands coiling into fists at the mention of that fucker's name. I knew it!

I was right, Veer finally found Simone. But why didn't he take the baby? Looking down at Catori, her eyes are closed, her cheeks wet from crying.

"Where would he take her?" Felix asks, kneeling next to Jillian. Him standing in the back looking everything over, I almost forgot he was here. I exhale a ragged breath, not having a clue where this creepy fuck might take her. I should have given Simone a pin with a GPS device on it, something Veer never would have seen. Why didn't I think of that?

I hang my head trying to think where Simone is.

"I don't know." The complex words slip out with grief laced around them. Sliding both of my sweaty hands in my hair. I silently pray to God he doesn't hurt her, he better fucking pray he doesn't hurt her. Catori needs her mother. Fuck, I need her. She pulled emotions out of me and gave me strength to withstand any storm life relinquishes me. Without Simone, I'll become numb and suppress any wave of emotion, I'll be of no use to anyone, let alone Catori.

"Jillian's phone is missing!" Zeek proclaims, grabbing my attention from Catori.

Wait, maybe Simone has it. My eyes widen and fall to the floor next to Jillian, my mouth next to hers.

"Did Simone take your phone?"

"DUDE, BACK UP!" Zeek becomes protective, but I brush him off and ask Jillian again. I need to know if Simone took her fucking phone. It might be the only thing to find her.

Zeek shoves me in the shoulder, but I don't budge. My eyes glued to Jillian for any sign or signal she can give me about this damn night.

SECONDS PASS, and she doesn't respond. She's out of strength to answer me, and I'm running out of time and patience.

JUMPING TO MY FEET, I jog to my laptop sitting on the coffee table in the living room. Placing Catori down on a cushion, I barricade her in with pillows while I work.

BRUSHING the chip crumbs from the keyboard, I pull up my handy programs.

"YOU REALLY THINK SIMONE HAS IT?" Felix asks over my shoulder.

I TYPE Jillian's number into my computer as fast as I can and pull up a GPS map.

"I FUCKING HOPE SO," I mutter, my focus on the screen.

A MAP DISPLAYS on the screen, and a little red dot finally pops up on the left side.

SHE MUST HAVE TAKEN it when she was fixing Jillian's leg because it shows the phone outside the casino. It will take a while for the GPS to exactly pinpoint where she is though. Anxiety causes my neck to pulse nervously. Shaking my hands out, I stand and begin to pace, wishing my programming was better. I always want it to be better, that's why I'm always working on it. Learning new back-doors and adjusting my codes. I can get better results with this program, but it takes longer to get them.

DROPPING MY HEAD, I take a deep breath. I can work with this, I can still save her. I just have to be patient.

"LAS VEGAS EMT!" Three women race inside the suite with a stretcher, and I stand quickly. One's short and chubby, one tall and built with muscle, and the other of medium build.

"IN THERE." I point to the room where Zeek and Jillian are.

STEPPING UP BEHIND THEM, I watch as they look Jillian over, and talk to Zeek about what happened.

"INTRUDER, we're looking into it. Can you just fucking get her to the hospital!" Zeek snaps at them hatefully. He won't tell them who it might have been, because in reality, they won't do anything. Cops will come and ask a bunch of stupid fuck questions, and then leave. That will be the end of it.

No, we will be the law tonight.

THEY INSPECT Jillian's wound and place her on the stretcher, Zeek and Felix by her side.

AS THEY PASS ME, Zeek stops in front of me. His brows furrowing, jaw clenching.

"GET THE OL' ladies up here to watch Catori, and take whatever men you need to find Simone," Zeek demands. He grips my shoulder, his eyes becoming ablaze.

"I'D DO this quietly if you don't want the Devil's Dust getting in the middle. They've been blowing my phone up wanting the man's head who killed Kane. I'm giving you first dibs. So when you find him, don't fuck it up." Zeek gives me a commanding look, and I nod accepting.

WHEN I'M DONE with Veer, he's going to be coyote shit in the desert. There won't be enough of him to worry about putting a toe tag on him.

30

SIMONE

Riding in the back of a stretch limo, Veer watches me from across the seat. His hair is disheveled, but still shining like something out of an eighties movie. The overwhelming smell of sandalwood and cigar smoke smothering my senses.

"HOW OLD IS SHE?" Veer tries to make small talk as if he just didn't take me away from my kid. As if he didn't aim his gun at her and try and kiss her with a bullet of death.

"DON'T. Don't you ever bring her up," I snap. Vindication coloring my voice. His shoulders lift as he swipes at his slacks as if he has crumbs on them. Rolling my nails into my palm. I seek for a form of pain to release my rolling emotions.

"ONE THING you will learn is respect. Your father lacked that tool in raising you, but no fret." His snake eyes snap to mine and I hold my breath, my throat feeling like sandpaper when I swallow. "You will learn it."

SLIDING into the seat next to me like a slick cobra, he grips my hand. His touch cold and unfriendly just like a serpent. He squeezes my knuckles together, my fingers popping from the harshness. My mouth parts with pain as I pry his white knuckles one by one from my sore fingers, his eyes never leaving the side of my head as he conveys just how determined he is to make me obey him.

FEELING TRAPPED BY HIS CLOSENESS, I shuffle closer to the door and gaze out the window with tear-filled eyes. My lungs burn with the urge to ugly cry, my cheeks burning with remorse and regret. My heart sinks as we drive farther and farther away from my whole world.

MY ONLY ESCAPE from this man is the blanket of darkness my eyelids have to bring. Leaning my head against the cool glass, taking a shaky breath I close my eyes. The breath of the cobra sitting across from me keeping me on edge, it takes me forever to fall asleep.

THE CRUNCH of gravel under the car's tires has me stirring in my seat. My neck aches and my legs are stiff from being bunched up for so long.

The smell of cigar smoke reminds me where I am, and who I'm with. I bolt upright. Veer's smug smile greeting me while a cigar dangles in his left hand; his legs casually crossed. Mac would never cross his legs. A roiling heat in my stomach sparks, reminding me just how much I hate Veer's face. I look out the window needing anything else to look at and I notice it's daylight, we've been driving all night. I've been away from Catori all night.

WORRY SNAKES itself around my heart, and I nibble on my bottom lip thinking if anyone has found her or fed her. She needs a diaper change by now, will Mac remember to put the rash cream on her?

"WHAT ARE YOU THINKING?" Veer's smug voice cuts right through my worry, and contempt boils back to a full flame.
    I ignore him.

LOOKING OUT THE TINTED WINDOW, a large mansion made out of white stone approaches. It's bigger than my parents'. Trees with the greenest leaves I've ever seen frame the acreage, and two medium sizes Indians carved out of stone set the pathway to the biggest set of front doors I've ever seen.

"THIS IS YOUR HOME NOW, Simone. Maids, chefs, a heated pool, fully stocked library, anything you might need you will find it right here. You'll never have to leave the estate," Veer brags, and it takes everything I have not to roll my eyes. I've had all this before, and call me crazy... but I don't miss it. I long for the view of tourists walking by, and the feel of being independent. Making my own food and folding my own laundry... it was something nobody could take away from me.

CIGAR SMOKE ROLLS around my head and I cough, waving it away from me.

I miss the smell of mint and leather, the sound of Mac click-clacking on his keyboard.

DRIVING INTO THE ROUND DRIVEWAY, a white man with a black suit waits for the car to stop. A butler it appears.

THE CAR ROCKS us to a stop, and the man opens my door. Giving Veer a brief glance, I step outside. The fresh warm air making me inhale it in my lungs so deep I almost cough because I forget to exhale.

"SMELLS BETTER THAN VEGAS, doesn't it," Veer rasps from behind me. His cool breath on the back of my neck rancid and reminding me of death. I step away.

"WELCOME HOME, SIMONE." A belittling laugh laces through his welcome, and my legs jerk with acute shock. This is real. I'm never going to see Catori or Mac again.

MY BOTTOM LIP TREMBLES, but I breathe through my sullen emotions and begin the climb up the stairs to the mansion. Every step forced like a baby colt on a lead for the first time, I have to pull and drag myself to move forward. The wild spirit in me not wanting to be tamed or imprisoned.

THE LARGE DOORS creak and scream as they open, the smell of dust and incense inviting us inside the house of riches.

There are immaculate paintings on every wall, covering every inch. It reminds me of the Harry Potter movie that Mac and I watched one night while eating sandwiches. In the movie, the school had paintings on every square inch of the walls, overdoing it surely.

My eyes sweep from the paintings to the gold banister leading to the second story with ivory carpet lining the stairs.

Is that real gold?

The pitter patter of Veer's expensive shoes causes my throat to close up, forcing a cough to pull from my chest. I turn on the heel of my foot and stare at him dryly.

"I'M TIRED. I want to go to bed. Where's my room?" I can't bite back the bitterness in my tone, the uncontrollable violence I feel toward this man confuses me. I've felt a lot of things in my life, but the emotions this man pulls from my chest could be compared to a voodoo doll from the devil. It's unpredictable and vile.

VEER CRACKS HIS NECK, his dark lashes framing his ominous eyes like a monster in the night stalking his prey.

"YOU DON'T WANT to sleep with me?" The sound of his voice sends shivers down my back. Opening my mouth to reply, I shut it quickly as anything I have to say will surely fuel him toward his natural behavior of something dark.

NOTICING MY TERROR, the corner of his mouth tugs into a crooked grin. "I figured we'd sleep in the same room," he mutters with a softer tone. My brows furrow, if I sleep next to this man... I'll suffocate him with his goose feathered pillow. I've never seen myself as a murderer, but I would bathe in this man's blood for taking away my daughter.

AS IF HE can read the anger in my eyes, he clears his throat.

"I PRESUME until we say our vows and consummate our marriage on our wedding night, you can sleep in the room across from the master bed." His left shoulder shrugs. "We will be married very soon though, so don't get too comfortable."

"GREAT, WHERE'S IT AT?" I ignore his attempt of reminding me of my obligation to be his wife. If I dig deep, when I think about marrying Veer, I see a black widow spinning a web around a male spider, ready to devour his guts.

HIS FACE REDDENS, his mouth parting as he looks to the marbled floor unhappy that he didn't get a response out of me about marrying him.

"IT SEEMS you living with bikers these last few months has made you... an idiot?"

"Excuse me?"

"Look at yourself!" His hand waves at my attire. Glancing down at my torn shirt and sweatpants I roll my eyes. "Because I'm not in a designer brand, I'm an idiot?"

"Yes, and the way you hold yourself and talk... it's trashy so stop it now!" The order in his voice makes me jump where I stand. My nostrils flaring at his continuous insults. It's not trash to hold your nose at the level of everyone else, wearing a t-shirt instead of designer polo is not tasteless.

Taking away materialistic things in my life, I've learned to live like everyone else in this world, and that's what I'm doing regardless of what thread count my bedsheets may be. I'm happier this way. I don't have to please anyone.

"Piss off. I'll talk and act however I feel." I lift my chin in defiance. Veer raises his hand and backhands me. I stumble onto my knees, my hands catching me just before I faceplant the floor. A searing burn races across the apple of my cheek. The side of my face throbs with the beat of my heart, swelling blooming across my cheek.

My hysterectomy incision burns from the sudden movement, and I hiss from the pain.

Veer steps forward, his polished shoe stepping onto my hand.

Closing my eyes, the day I was a little girl playing with chalk on my parents' patio, blurs behind my dark eyelids.

JUST AS *I set the chalk down a shiny shoe slammed on my hand. Pressure and a piercing sting slithered up the bones in my fingers.*

"Ow!" *I cried, trying to pull my palm out from under the foot. Using my free hand, I pulled at my wrist until the prisoned fingers freed. With heated eyes, I looked at the person who purposely stepped on my hand.*

IT'S A BOY. *The sun shined behind him casting a shadow amongst me and the colors on the sidewalk.*

"RESPECT ME!" he roars, bringing me back to the now. I don't say anything, I don't have the strength in me to fight a second longer. Leaving my daughter behind has taken everything from me. Pulling the sole of his shoe away from my red fingers, I pull my hand to my chest and stand. Feeling numb, I look away not sure what to say or do. The little bit of bravado I had, he slapped into the wind.

"BILLIARD, please escort Miss Ray to her quarters for the night," he instructs his butler. "It's best we take some time to settle into our new situation apart." He straightens his tie, looking down at me like dirt on his shoe.

HOLDING my sore cheek with my sweaty palm, my face shakes

with anger. My teeth clashing into one another like icebergs ready to crack. I want to kill him.

"RIGHT AWAY." The man's throaty voice vibrates his Adam's apple.

STEPPING PAST HIM, Veer snatches my hand from my face. The feeling foreign and making my stomach churn.

"I'LL SEE you at dinner. Tonight." Pulling my hand free, I wipe at the artic feel his fingers left behind.

"I'd rather starve." I snarl and step away.

I SAID I wouldn't run from him, I never said I would cooperate with him. Ever.

No matter how many backhands, punches, or abuse he bestows upon me. I'll never love him, not like Mac.

INSIDE MY ROOM, I slam the door shut and slink to the floor. Tears spring from my eyes, and my nails claw into the plush carpet. No matter how far away from Veer I am, a dark presence looms over me, reminding me what he took from me. Clenching my eyes shut a kaleidoscope of heartwarming memories of Mac and Catori swirl with color in the back of my mind.

WHEN I WOKE up in the hospital and Mac was holding her. Him changing her diapers; feeding her. I can't help but think about what our life would be like if Veer never showed up.

WE'D MOVE to a house outside the city, have a big swing set in the backyard. Catori walking to Mac who's on his bike in our perfectly paved driveway to kiss him goodbye before he leaves for a club run. We could've really been happy. I'll never forget them, the ache in my chest will never stop until we are reunited once again.

SOBBING, I swipe at the tears staining my face and look around the room. It's huge compared to the rooms I've stayed in of late. In the middle of the space is a step-up platform to a king size wooden canopy bed. Blankets bright white and clean of any lint drooping over the sides.

The windows behind it are draped in golden silk, and across the room a dresser holds golden hair brushes and combs with one large spotless mirror across the back of it.

It's as if Veer is trying to compensate for something with all the money he's spent on his house. Who needs a golden brush?

Standing on wobbly feet, I inspect the room further, the smell of money making me ill. I long for the smell of baby puke and leather. I hiccup, feeling alone and cold without Mac and Catori. There's a piece of me that's missing, and I'll never be whole again without them. My heartbeat will be one beat short, my body temperature a few degrees off, and my focus always on what they might be doing at that exact moment.

My mind drifts to wander, what *are* they doing right now?

SHAKING my head of the rapid thoughts, my finger drifts across the white embroidery on the luscious comforter drowning the bed, as I head to the large window.

RAYS of sun shine down on a red barn with the most beautiful horses I've ever seen prancing around; their heads held high.

I SNARL AT THEM; their noses in the air remind me of Veer.

I don't want to ride a fucking horse. I want to ride a motorcycle, with Mac. I never got to ride with him come to think of it.

TEARS FILL my eyes at the sudden thought.

THE DOOR SUDDENLY OPENS, and I swing around to see who it is.

A LITTLE OLD lady wearing a black and white uniform with white trim waddles in. Her curly hair lacing around the ruffled headpiece across her head.

"OH GOOD, I was hoping you were still awake. Here's a change of clothes, my dear." She sets down a silky baby blue pajama set on the end of the bed and wipes her sweaty palms on her maid's outfit. "If you need anything else, just let me know." Her thin lips press into a smile before her brows raise. "Oh, and I'm Miss Fowler." She gives a quick bow and waddles out of the room.

SHE'S A HANDMAID, I had one until Dad fired her.

SAUNTERING TO THE BED, I unfold the top of the pajama set. It's the perfect size and made of the most expensive silk I've seen in a long time.

Scoffing, I toss them on the floor and opt for Mac's shirt I'm still wearing and the sweatpants. Climbing onto the bed, my hands and knees press into the expensive material as I squirm myself to the middle. The cut across my stomach pulls with my stretching, I can't help but wince in reaction. I'm so tired. I'd do anything to hold Mac's hand right now, to hear Catori cry from the other room. The silence of this place is deafening and making me insane.

THROWING the sheets and blankets over my head, I consume myself into complete darkness as I begin to cry again. A hint of mint has me pause my sobbing, the smell of Mac making my heart almost beat normal again. My wet lashes blink rapidly, and I grab the shirt I'm wearing and pull it to my nose. The smell of minty sweat smothers my pain for just a second before tears pour from my eyes.

WILL I ever see the two people I love most again?

31

SIMONE

"M iss?" A pudgy finger pokes me in the arm, waking me from an ocean of blankets and sheets. Untucking my arms from the material, I pat it down to find Miss Fowler looking at me from the edge of the bed. Her gray eyes wide as saucers, and brows lifted to her hairline.

"YEAH?" I croak.

"IT'S TIME FOR SUPPER. Veer has requested your presence, and to wear this." She holds up a white and golden sequin dress, and my mouth drops. "He asked to meet him down in the dining room in ten minutes."

"YOU GOTTA BE FUCKING KIDDING ME," I scoff, sitting upright on the mattress. Miss Fowler scowls, turning around and laying the dress across a white accent chair in the corner. She must be team Veer.

GIVING me a look over like I'm a thug, she leaves the room.

HMM. Maybe Mac's language has rubbed off on me a little.

MY STOMACH GROWLS, reminding me it's been over a day since I last ate. I'd starve and die just to prove a point but there's a sliver of hope that Mac will come to save me, so I shouldn't give up too soon.

Throwing the blankets off me, I shuffle out of the bed and stretch. Gazing at the dress, I decide to look at it a little closer. Picking it up I can already tell it's going to be itchy and uncomfortable.

I DON'T MISS WEARING this kind of crap.

I DROP IT.

I'M NOT GOING to be told what to wear. The baby blue pajamas on the floor grab my attention though, and I smile. Those look comfy enough for dinner.

PULLING out of my wrinkled clothes, I dress in the pajamas. The silk is so soft and light it feels as if I'm wearing nothing but air.

STEPPING OUT OF MY BEDROOM, I look down the hall, my hands braiding my hair down my shoulder as I look around. I'm not sure where the dining room is. Clinking of dishes downstairs causes my feet to head down the steps. My hand slides along the cool golden banister, my bare feet not making a sound on the thick carpet. It's so white and clean, I wonder how many times they have to shampoo it.

THIS IS DEFINITELY NOT a place for children. Catori would have this place in a frenzy in less than two hours. Butlers running for bottles, maids cleaning up puke and poop.

A SMILE BREAKS through my sorrow just thinking about it.

ROUNDING THE STAIRCASE, a door next to it is open. Peeking inside, I see a large dining table with candlesticks lined down the middle. I guess I found the dining room.

CROSSING MY ARMS, I push my feet forward. The smell of meat and mashed potatoes making my mouth salivate. Inside the dining room, there are abstract paintings along the walls. A dining table that is the length of the room with high back chairs framing it covered in delicious looking rolls, salad, and fruit. Taking my seat at the far end of the table, my ass presses into the memory foam seat. I feel out of place being here, hell, I don't even remember the last time I ate at a table.

"Aɦ, ʏᴏᴜ –" Veer stops mid-sentence, his face contorting into anger. "What are you wearing?"

Bɪᴛɪɴɢ ʙᴀᴄᴋ ᴍʏ sᴍɪʟᴇ, my eyes drop to the china on the table.

"Sᴏᴍᴇᴛʜɪɴɢ ᴄᴏᴍꜰᴏʀᴛᴀʙʟᴇ," I mutter with a light shrug. It pleases me to know he noticed my defiance.

Hᴇ ᴜɴʙᴜᴛᴛᴏɴs ʜɪs sᴜɪᴛ ᴊᴀᴄᴋᴇᴛ, sighing as he takes his seat at the opposite end of the table.

"Hᴀᴠᴇ ʏᴏᴜ sᴇᴇɴ ᴍʏ ʜᴏʀsᴇs?"

I sᴛᴀʀᴛʟᴇ at the strange question, my eyes lining the table until meeting his black soulless irises.

"Sᴏᴍᴇ ᴏꜰ ᴛʜᴇ most thoroughbred horses in the states are on my land, and I've broken them all. I will break you too." He points his fork at me threateningly. A rise in my body temperature has me shift under Veer's intense stare.

"Wʜᴇɴ ᴛʜᴇ ʜᴇʟᴘ brings you something I've requested you to wear, I expect you to wear it then. Those pajamas were for your nap, not dinner!" he snarls. "Have some damn respect." His fist slams on the table, rattling the dishes, and I tense where I sit.

SANDPAPER LINES MY THROAT, and I opt not to say another word for now.

IN BETWEEN THE SILENT STARES, two servers wearing white pantsuits rush inside the room with silver platters, placing them in front of each of us.

"Thanks," I mumble, pulling the top off. Roasted lamb and mashed potatoes waft in a delicious steam in front of my face.

GRABBING the knife and fork to my right, I tear into the meat and begin eating. The meat literally melts in my mouth it's so tender. Flavor bursting with every chew, I can't get enough.

"DO you not say grace before you stuff your face like a pig with the bikers?" Veer asks hatefully, his voice echoing through the room.

IGNORING HIM, I bite into another chunk of meat. Ideally, I would set my silverware to the side, apologize, and say grace as my mother has raised me better, but the more I disgust Veer... the better.

"YOU WILL LEARN when I ask you a question, I expect an answer." His voice laces around my throat and squeezes the independent woman defying him. Our eyes locking as I fight his attempt at making his idea of the perfect wife.

A TALL WOMAN wearing a black dress, sashays into the room, her long lashes fluttering at Veer. Her blonde straight hair curves at her sharp jawline and her pouty lips smile at Veer.

"I'VE GOT our best wine, Veer," she informs, her voice thick and lustful.

"THAT'S MY GIRL." He grins, his teeth scraping across his fork. Goosebumps chill my skin at the sound of it, it's one of my pet peeves.

FILLING his crystal glass with blood colored wine, their eyes never break. They're obviously screwing each other, why doesn't he just marry her? Make both of our lives easier.

"HERS TOO." Veer points to my glass. Looking at me, her face goes sour. Lifting the bottle away from Veer's crystal, she heads my way, filling my glass only halfway. Snatching it from the table, I take three huge gulps. The sweet red wine filling my mouth and causing it to pucker at the same time. My taste buds argue if it's sweet or bitter.

WHEN SHE LEAVES, I can't help the sudden bravado bubbling within me, again. I've lost everything, what else do I have to lose saying what I think? Doing what I feel? I'd blame it on liquid courage, but surely it hasn't had enough time to affect my thinking just yet.

"WHY DON'T you just marry her?" I ask, cutting into the lamb once more.

"SHE DOESN'T HAVE a last name worth anything, you and I together will change history and make a wealthy future." His callous tone pisses me off. Sliding my tongue along my teeth, I stare him down. I can't help but wonder how his parents raised him, how does a man like this sleep at night?

"SO, it doesn't matter if you like me or not, you just want—"

HIS LOUD SIGH has me pause. Setting his fork down, he scowls down the table.

"I WANT YOUR DNA. Your blood is worth a lot to our families and slapping the Walsh name on it is priceless. Who I fuck"—he waves his hand to where the wine girl just left—"is not your concern, I assure you." Picking up his fork again he begins to eat like a prince on a throne. Small petite bites, little chews.

MAC ATE SANDWICHES like they'd literally jump from his hand if he looked away. He ate like a man.

WAIT A SECOND. Did he just say he's using me to make babies, and he will continue to screw whomever he wants? Well, the joke's on him, I can't have any more children.

"YEAH, THAT WILL NEVER HAPPEN." I purse my lips, shaking my head at his bizarre outlook on where this relationship is going.

HIS SILVERWARE DROPS on his plate, the clanking causing me to startle. My eyes bolt to his. His chair pushes back with haste, falling to the floor. Standing from his seat, he stomps my way.

SWALLOWING the food in my mouth, I casually look up at him, trying not to shrink into my seat from fear. He disgusts me on so many levels it's easy to replace my terror with anger. His back-woods way of how a woman should act in a marriage fuels a side of me I've never felt before.

Hatred. Violence.

A VEIN THROBBING in his neck has my eyes slide to his throat. I envision that little vein being slashed open and bleeding out with every pump of his heart.

HIS HAND SUDDENLY DARTS OUT, gripping my chin painfully. Wincing, I shift in my seat my toes curling into the floor to ease the bruising he casts upon my skin.

"YOU'RE MINE. You were mine when we were kids, you're mine now, and always will be. You will do what ask when I ask it, and fuck when I want to fuck."

"NO," I push out through flushed cheeks.

"No?" His head turns to the side.

"I wouldn't touch you when we were kids, and I won't now." I remind him of when he tried to kiss me when we first met, and I kneed him in the balls.

Challenge sparks in his eyes, and my nostrils flare.

Bending down, his lips purse as if he's going to force a kiss upon me. Blinking, a burning sensation drives through me. Possessed with rage and a broken heart, I clutch the fork in my hand, hold my breath and scream as I thrust the tongs of the fork right into the throbbing vein in his neck. His lips a hair's length away from my own he freezes while I push the silver in as far as it will go, his body tensing. Blood trickles from the prongs of the fork, spilling onto my sleeve and soaking it into a design like one of the paintings on the wall.

"I'll never kiss you," I whisper, our eyes locked on one another.

He swallows, the look of shock coloring his face as he stumbles back. He jerks the fork out of his neck and blood spurts out all over his perfect carpet. He falls to the floor gasping, choking, and crawling for the doorway.

SITUATING myself back into my seat, my shaky hand reaches to the empty plate next to me. Grabbing a clean fork, I stab the last piece of lamb on my plate, chewing it while Veer gasps for his very last breath.

SOMEONE WATCHING MIGHT SAY I was in shock, or maybe I wasn't. Maybe, I was determining my future for once as I finished my meal while my enemy bled out on the floor.

A BANG SHAKES the walls of the mansion and staff screams, running through the dining room for shelter. I'm sure security is here to take me out for killing their king, so I take the moment to drink the last drop of my wine in my glass. Savoring the expensive taste before I'm kissed with death.

"DEAR LORD, please watch over Catori and Mac. Keep them safe. Great Spirits watch over my family. When life fades, as the fading sunset, my spirit may come to you without shame." I recite parts of the Great Spirit Prayer. I whisper every prayer, and to every higher power I know to keep the ones I love most safe while I'm gone. For the men about to come in and kill me will take that power away from me. I'll never be able to protect them again.

ONE WARM SOLID tear slips down my cheek, my hand shaking with the glass of wine.

32

SIMONE

M y eyes focus on the doorway over the top of my glass waiting for men dressed in suits and weapons to enter.

Instead what enters has my skin warm to an overheating temperature.

Mac and his men race into the room, guns raised, and I nearly choke on my wine.

MY HANDS TREMBLE UNCONTROLLABLY, eyes filling with tears, the glass slips from my hand, bounces off the table, and shatters into a million pieces.

"MAC?" This can't be real. Veer poisoned me, I'm seeing things.

"POCAHONTAS," he breathes as if he's been holding his breath since I left, his eyes taking in the gruesome scene.

I'm not dreaming. He's real!

JUMPING FROM MY CHAIR, it knocks back onto the floor. I step over Veer's body and rush into Mac's arms nearly knocking him over. Hard, warm arms wrap around me, pulling me into the smell of mint and leather. The scent comforting me into believing I'm going to be safe and I'm going to see my daughter again.

MY FINGERS CLAW into his leather cut, pulling him closer, my face in the crook of his neck. I can't feel him enough, smell him any more than I am, but I'm going to fucking try. My heart resumes beating, my body temperature warm instead of cold, I feel whole again having this man in my arms.

"YOU'RE SAFE, BABY," he whispers in my ear, holding me tightly. Telling me exactly what I needed to hear since I left Vegas.

"DAMN, WHAT HAPPENED IN HERE?" Machete asks, stepping past us.

Mac pushes me a step back, his eyes curious but I don't want to talk about. The scene before them says everything.

"WHERE IS CATORI? Take me home, Mac," I cry, ignoring their curious eyes. I'm not a murderer, a bad person. Veer made me into the monster I became, showing me what I'm fully capable of. "Take me to our little girl," I whimper, my voice wavering with emotion.

His gaze sweeps from Veer's body to mine, his lips more inviting than ever. I smash my mouth to his, my tongue taking in his taste of salt and beer. He kisses me back, his tongue massaging my own, his hands gently pressing against my cheeks as he deepens the moment.

"I'M TAKING YOU HOME, where you belong," he whispers against my trembling lips. Opening my eyes, his pupils dilate as they set on the cut on my face where Veer hit me.

"What the—"

I TURN my head away from him.

"I TOOK CARE OF IT," I mutter, hurt and anguish painting my voice a color I don't recognize. Everything that has happened here I just want to forget. None of it matters, I just want my daughter now.

"LET'S get you out of here, baby."

I nod, so ready to escape this place.

"UM, you can't ride out of here in that." Machete points to my pajamas, and I remember there are blood stains all over it.

HOLDING MY ARMS OUT, the baby blue pajamas something from a horror movie.

"I UM- I HAVE something I can change into." I remember the dress upstairs. It's over the top, but it doesn't have blood spilled all over it.

MACHETE BENDS AT THE KNEE, inspecting Veer's body a little closer.

EYES FLUTTERING, my fingers trembling as I recall my loss of control. I killed someone. I took a life with my own hands. I've never been a violent person, but something dark raced through my veins at that moment and I did what I had to do. As a mother, and as a woman.

I'LL NEVER BE a doormat to such a vile man.

"GO CHANGE, and Machete and I will take care of this." Mac kisses my cheek, but my fingers refuse to let him go. I don't want to leave him, he just got here.

"GO WITH HER, I got this, brother." Felix pats Mac's shoulder. Felix is such a good-looking man, his man bun, and large biceps, a kryptonite for any single woman. Alessandra surely has her hands full with that.

Looking into Mac's eyes, I plead for him to go with me to change.

"OKAY," he agrees.

I STOP, looking over the uneaten food laid out on the table.

"OH, ARE YOU GUYS HUNGRY?"

MACHETE SNIFFS the chrome bowl of potatoes and then dips two fingers in before plopping them in his mouth.

"SEE, violence doesn't just make *me* hungry." Mac points at him, wrapping his arm around my neck as we head up to my room for clothes.

Mac

"IS JILLIAN OKAY?" Simone asks, undressing from those hideous blue pajamas.

"Uh, yeah, Zeek took her home after they pulled the bullet out and gave her some blood." That's what he texted me anyway. I've been hell-bent on finding Simone to go see either of them at the hospital.

SITTING ON THE BED, the fucking bedding is so fluffy my feet don't even reach the ground. This place is immaculate, better than I could ever give Simone.

"JESUS, this guy was loaded, why would you wanna be with me when you could have all this?" The sentence falls from my mouth before I can catch it, but it's a question that needs to be asked. I can't offer her and Catori half of this shit.

SIMONE TURNS AROUND with her hands on her hips, her bra and panties the only thing she's wearing. My chest rises as I take her cute little ass in. I missed her so goddamn much. I thought I was going to die with every passing second I was on the road trying to get here as fast as I could. Every minute I thought that something bad was happening to her, made me speed even faster.

"YOU THINK *THIS* IS LIVING?" she scoffs, and my eyes trail up her torso back to her eyes. "This doesn't make me feel like I do when I'm with you. This"—she waves her hands around—"is making up for a life of loneliness, and let me tell you something, it doesn't fucking work! It's just a fancy prison." She takes a deep breath, her hand rubbing her collarbone.

"I DON'T LOVE BEING HERE or any of this stuff if it's not with you and Catori." Her voice softens, and sucker punches me right in the chest. "I told you before, I wanna hold *your* stupid hand, and wear *your* stupid shirts. Nobody else's."

A BOYISH GRIN spreads across my face, and I suddenly need to touch her. It's one thing to hear it, but I wanna feel it.

SAUNTERING UP BEHIND HER, I trace my finger down her spine, little peach fuzz tickling against the pad of my finger. Her flirtatious eyes peek over her shoulder and my dick rises.

SHE YANKS a dress off the floor and steps slowly into it.

"CALL ME CRAZY, but I'd rather wear leather than this stupid ball gown." She shakes her head, shimmying her shoulders, the sheer fabric falls into place. This woman is marriage material, I tell you.

SLIDING my hands down her sides, my dick dances in my pants. Fuck, she's getting thin and curvy as hell and it's turning me on to see every inch of it in this dress.

PULLING her braid from her shoulder, I pull my cut off my shoulders and grab her arm, helping her into it.
   Smiling eyes meet mine as I help her put it on. Clutching her shoulders with my hands, I force her to turn around and look in the mirror.

"ANYTHING LOOKS GOOD WITH LEATHER." I wink at her reflection in the mirror, and she giggles. "When we get home, you'll have your own cut, babe."
   "Yeah?" Her eyes light up, and that reaction means so much to me. Knowing she wants the world to know she's my property.

I'M GOING to fuck her with so much disrespect when her doctor gives her the clear.
   My tongue, cum, and fingers will be on every inch of her skin.

"What are the guys going to do with Veer?" she asks, taking my mind off her sexy ass. I open my mouth to tell her but decide against it. There are some things that need to remain club business, and this is one of them. It's not that I don't trust Simone, I'm protecting her. Protecting her from the mental damage and guilt that comes with being in the brotherhood, and from anyone who thinks she might have details of club shit.

"We have to make a pit stop in Vegas," is all I tell her, hoping she'll be asleep when we take care of it.

"Let's roll!" Machete roars from downstairs.

Smacking Simone's ass, we head out of the room and downstairs, my hand wrapped around her tightly. The entire staff of the mansion is tied up on their knees with pillowcases over their heads. The boys work quick.

Simone's eyes widen as she looks everyone over. "We couldn't take any risks with someone calling the cops or ID'ing us," I explain.

Clutching her hand, I take her outside to my motorcycle. Raven is standing guard just outside, her gun raised and ready to fire. She's fierce and determined. I tried to make her stay behind, but it's almost as if she thinks she's patched in as a brother or something. Always down for some action.

"Easy, Tomb Raider, we're out of here!" I tell her in passing. She lowers her gun and smiles at Simone. Starting my bike, Simone climbs on behind me, her fancy dress and heels making it hard for her. When she wraps her arms around me tightly, my cock throbs at the recognition of her touch. It's scary how addicted I am to her, how crazy I become without her.

They say meth is the most dangerous drug out there, freely sweeping the streets on its own will, but I don't think it has anything on love. It's more dangerous and out of control than a street drug.

Machete whistles casually as he and Felix carry a large garbage bag into the back of the truck; Veer's dead body. Simone doesn't look away, it's almost as if she needs to see it to believe he's really gone. Reaching back, I squeeze her thigh in reassurance that nobody will ever hurt her again.

A loud groan sounds from the bag and Simone nearly screams.
"Fuck!" Growling, I pull my gun out and climb off my bike. Stepping to the bed of the truck, Machete backs up, letting me climb up into the back. The bag moves and grunts.

Pointing the gun at the round end of the trash bag, I fire one single bullet and the groans fade instantly.

"Damn it, I'm really going to have to bleach my truck now," Machete mutters. Gun still aiming at Veer's body, a small hole in the plastic allowing blood to spill out, I feel much better knowing I delivered the final blow to his existence.

HOPPING OUT, Simone is looking the other way with her hand covering her mouth.

PUTTING MY GUN UP, my hand on her lower back I kiss her neck.

"I TOOK CARE OF IT, let's get home to Catori."

SHE NODS and climbs on the bike after me.

MACHETE GETS INTO HIS TRUCK, and Felix gets on his bike beside me. Pulling out of the mansion driveway, we leave behind more than just a crime scene, but life Simone gave up to be with me.

WE LAST a few hours on the road, and I notice Simone starting to shift, her hold on me lightening. For someone who doesn't ride often and with her still recovering, long hours can be straining. Veer took Simone down south to his mansion in California, and it's a good few hours away from where we reside.

I pull over to a secluded gas station off the freeway to give her a break, we need to fill up anyway.

THE LITTLE SHITTY gas station's yellow and blue paint is chipping away with every gust of wind, the gas pumps old and rusty.

"WHY ARE WE STOPPING?" Simone asks as soon as I turn the engine off to my bike.

"NEED GAS, and why don't you climb in the truck for a while. Stretch out?" I suggest.

"NO, I DON'T—"

Pressing my hand against her mouth to shut her up, her eyes go wide.

"Go. Rest. I'll be right behind you." I'm not giving her the option. I don't want to be apart from her either, but with her just having surgery a little over a week ago, I know she's in pain.

HER BODY SULKS, and she stares at me with a death look as she slowly begins to climb off the leather seat. Taking her hand, I help her off. When her heels hit the ground, she winces, her hands on her knees as she bends over.

"YOU OKAY?"

"IT'S JUST MY..." she waves to the general area of her cut.

"YEAH, see. Come on, let's get you in the truck for a while."

"FUCK THIS IS A DRIVE!" Machete yawns, climbing out of his truck and stretching.

"SIMONE IS GOING to ride with you, she needs a break," I tell him.

"YEAH, CLIMB IN." Machete shrugs, uncaring. "I'm getting jerky."
Walking her to the back of his truck, I open the door. The smell of new car rushing about us.

GIVING SIMONE A KISS, she nips my lip and smiles weakly before climbing into the back seat. My hand on the bottom of her back, I do my best to help her in.

"I'LL BE RIGHT BEHIND YOU," I assure her before shutting the door. I hate being without her, but she's in so much pain she needs a break.

"DRIVE LIKE YOU HAVE SOME SENSE!" I point to Machete who is walking out chomping on dry meat.

FILLING OUR TANKS, and grabbing some snacks, we're back on the road in no time. I'm ready to see Catori. Alessandra, Felix's ol' lady stayed back to watch her, and that alone makes me nervous. Alessandra is a firecracker and does whatever she wants. I'll kill her if she does anything stupid with Catori in her care.

33

MAC

Night falls upon us as we drive for miles and miles. Finally, just outside of Vegas, Machete takes a right to a side road and we all follow. Stopping in the middle of the desert, he keeps his truck running and climbs out. Putting my bike on its kickstand, I go to help. This is my mess after all.

"SIMONE AWAKE?" I ask, not wanting her to see this.

"NOPE, both of them are out. Perfect time for this," he grunts. Dropping the tailbed, he drags the body out of the back. No matter how tough Raven is, Machete does his best to protect her.

VEER'S BODY falls to the ground hard, the trash bag still wrapped around his corpse when Machete pulls his blade out and starts hacking at limbs.

"Jesus!" I jump away, not wanting to be bladed into pieces. Blood and bone fly everywhere, so I take a step back and watch the crazy fucker do what he does best. I swear he was a butcher in his past life.

GLOWING EYES CIRCLE US, foxes, coyotes, snakes. It's as if they know it's feeding time. They stay a perfect twenty feet away from us, not one of them coming any closer as they wait for their meal.

"You BETTER HURRY before our friends get impatient," Felix informs from his bike, noticing the animals circling us as well.

"THEY'LL WAIT," Machete states, out of breath.

"You DO THIS OFTEN?" I can't help but ask, and I get a maniacal laugh in return. I'm not sure if it's a good thing he feeds the starving wild animals, or a bad thing he's feeding them body parts on a regular basis.

IT DOESN'T EVEN TAKE him twenty minutes before he's completely sawed the man up, and is chucking pieces of the body out to the desert animals. The sound of growling and chomping making my bones chill.

MACHETE ROARS, thumping his chest like a wild animal himself, and I worry he's going to wake Simone. I don't want her to see this shit, and he knows that. She's not like the rest of us.

THERE'S a place between good and bad, and Simone is right in the middle of that. I want to keep her there, right within my reach.

"KING KONG! Can we drive home now?" Felix whines.

MACHETE LAUGHS, throwing his bloody blade in the bed of the truck, and climbing back into the cab.

STRADDLING MY BIKE, I start it and follow him back to the club. I'm just glad all this is fucking over.

Simone

VEGAS LIGHTS SHINE through the back window, waking me from my sleep. This dress is so uncomfortable my back is soaked in sweat. I can't wait to get it off. Sitting upright, I pull at the suffocating fabric for some relief.

THE SIN CASINO comes into sight, and I nearly start crying, the uncomfortable dress forgotten. I'm going to see Catori in a matter of minutes. Raven sits upright in the front seat, glances in the back seat with tired eyes and smiles. Her black hair is a mess, and she has bags under her eyes.

"You excited to see, Catori?"

"God, yes!" The words fall out as if I'm saying a prayer.

Machete pulls in the back lot of the casino, and I don't even wait for the truck to stop before I'm jumping out and running into the casino. Adrenaline rushes through me, my heart racing like I'm on drugs. I need to see Catori now. I need to know she's safe, feel her against my skin, and hear her cries.

"Simone!" Mac's voice has me stop near the blackjack table, and I wait, letting him catch up.

He grasps my elbow and pulls me in the opposite direction.

"This way!" He escorts me to a black elevator to the side, men in leather cuts guarding it. It's a private elevator that will take us straight to the room.

Stepping inside, he presses the button to the top floor and locks his fingers with mine as we descend upward. His fingers interlock with mine perfectly, both of our palms sweaty. The song "Rock-abye Baby" by Clean Bandit plays through the speakers.

My heart is drumming in my chest so fast I can't catch my breath, my tongue dry and feeling like sandpaper in my mouth.

The doors finally open, and I hurry into the hall finding Bishop with a gun pointed at us. His surfer looking hair swept in front of his determined eyes as he aims at us. But I don't stop in my pursuit. He's going to have to shoot me to keep me from entering that room and getting my baby.

"I got it from here," Mac tells him, and he drops his gun, taking a step back.

"Just want to be safe," Bishop whispers, and Mac gives him a brotherly pat on the shoulder.

Mac pulls his key out and unlocks the door. Pushing it open with both hands, tears fall down my face, my bottom lip trembling with the adrenaline rushing through me as I step inside.

THE FAMILIAR SMELL of the suite greets me as Alessandra, Felix's ol' lady, rocks Catori in the main room. Her ol' lady leather cut greeting me, and her dark hair in a messy ponytail spilling around her face.

WITH A SMILE, she whispers to Catori. "Look who's home!"

MY ARMS OUT WIDE, I strut to her. Alessandra gently gives me my baby, and I press Catori into me closely. I can finally breathe, and I inhale the smell of her baby soap. The feel of her soft skin and the sound of her little snore when she sleeps has me crying.

GOD, how can you love something so much, so hard. It's not fair. It's blissful as it is hurtful.

MY KNEES GIVING OUT, I slip to the floor with Catori tightly in my grasp.

"I'll never leave you again. I swear." I sob into the top of her black hair. Regret for leaving her floods my body. Regardless if I was saving her, it hurt so bad to leave her behind.

"Thanks for watching her, Alessandra." Mac sits on the couch, watching me and Catori reunite.

"Absolutely, she was amazing." Alessandra's voice cracks with exhaustion.

Running the pad of my finger over Catori's chubby little cheek, I pray to the gods, thanking them all for bringing me back where I belong. I don't deserve happiness, but I'm so thankful for it, I'll spend the rest of my life making it up to everyone around me.

"I'm going to go, catch a ride home with Felix," Alessandra informs.

"I'll walk you down," Bishop states, standing in the doorway with a weapon in his hand. He seems more at peace with a gun than a textbook.

Sniffling, I look up at her with swollen eyes. "Thank you. Thank you so much!" I tell her, trying to pull myself together. She winks, tears in her own eyes from our homecoming.

LIPS PRESSED INTO A THIN LINE, I rest my head on Catori's. I love being a part of an actual family who has each other's back. I will forever owe them for this and look forward to the day I can repay my debt.

LOOKING DOWN AT CATORI, she never wakes. She's out solid. God, she's so beautiful. Lacing my finger around hers, our matching toffee skin, I feel our heart beat as one. We sit like that tangled up on the floor for at least an hour. My incision hurts, and this dress is killing me, but I don't want to move. For I'm afraid if I do I'll wake and this will all be a dream.

THE JAR of butterflies I let go won't be free, but dead.

"LET'S GO LAY HER DOWN." Mac rubs my back and my head snaps in his direction.

"I CAN'T PUT HER DOWN," I whisper.

"LET'S put her in our bed then, I don't want to be away from either of you." He stands, holding his hand out to me. Looking down at Catori, rocking her, I think about it.

RAVEN ENTERS THE SUITE, dressed in all black with a rifle in her right hand. My eyes bulge at the sight of her. I swear she's G.I. Jane's sister.

"I'M KEEPING GUARD, mind if I grab the couch?" She juts her chin to where Mac was sitting. I open my mouth to speak, but I can't form the words. This woman hardly knows me and yet is going out of her way to protect my family.

"NOT AT ALL," I wave toward the cushions.

GLANCING DOWN AT CATORI, her hopefully dreaming of lambs and kittens makes me agree to lay her down somewhere where she's more comfortable. I'm exhausted myself. I might have slept a lot the last few days, but without Catori next to me, it's as if I haven't really slept at all.

"LET'S GO LAY DOWN," I whisper, kissing her forehead.

"YES, go lay down. I got this!" Raven insists, plopping down on the couch with more weapons than I've seen on one woman.

INSIDE THE BEDROOM, it's just like I left it. The sheets a tangled mess from me and Mac trying to sleep.

I lay Catori down in the middle of the bed and step out of the uncomfortable dress, I grab a shirt from Mac's closet and slip it on. The smell of it making me bring it to my nose and inhale. I'm home.

CLIMBING in on my side of the bed, I keep my hand on Catori's chest. I'm too scared to close my eyes for I fear I might blink and she'll be gone. My eyes are glued to her, watching her chest rise and fall as she sleeps. Mac is on the other side of her, his arm thrown across us both, staring at me closely.

"I LOVE YOU," I whisper. He shakes with a silent laugh, glancing at Catori before me again.
"I love you too." His brows furrow, and I frown.
"What?"
"It's just... It's weird to say. I've never said it to anyone. Ever."
Swallowing the tears that threaten to spill, I grab his hand and lay it on my arm. How did I fuck everything up, only to have it all fall into place perfectly?

THIS MAN LOVES a child that's not even his own blood and it goes to show that bloodlines don't mean a damn thing. It reminds me of what Mac said about life handing you a deck of cards, I thought he was crazy. But, he's right. It doesn't matter which cards come from what deck. You can still play the game with them.

LIFE GIVES us blessings disguised as accidents but the truth of it is... it's those accidents that lead the pathway to something bigger.

YOU JUST HAVE to hold your breath and hold on for the ride.

34

6 WEEKS LATER

SIMONE

L aying Catori down in her crib with her yellow binkie stuck in her mouth, Mac steps up behind me, his hands on each of my hips. Soft seductive little kisses tickle the back of my neck, his lips skimming every inch of my skin. I draw in a quick breath, for some reason I'm nervous. This is the first time having sex with him without being pregnant. Will it feel the same? Will he still find me attractive?

TURNING WHERE I STAND, the look in his eyes make the self-conscious whispers fade. His eyes are determined, hooded and intoxicating. Gripping me by the thighs, he picks me up, and takes me into our room. Plopping me down on our bed, my legs and arms spring about everywhere. Within seconds, he's on top of me, my bent knees allowing him in between, my fingers on his strong bare shoulders. His hot sticky breath warms my skin, the swell of his cock pressing against me. A familiar shiver bumps up my back with excitement and need.

"I'VE BEEN WAITING for you, Pocahontas," he whispers against my cheek, his face against mine. I can't respond, I'm so worked up I'm already breathing hard.

SLIPPING A HAND UP MY SHIRT, he fists my tit and nips at my collarbone. His sharp teeth making my head loll back into the mattress. He's in the zone, desire fueling his next move before he knows what it is.

"ARE YOU WET?" His throaty voice does me in, and I begin to pull at his low-slung jeans.

Sitting back on his knees, his smoldering eyes watch my fingers unbutton, and unzip his jeans.

SHIMMYING THEM DOWN, I'm surprised he's not wearing boxers, his veiny cock falling out. I grab it, fisting it just under the head. A little bead of pre-cum presents itself and I rub my thumb over the velvety skin, my finger moving across the slit of his head and barbell in a circular motion.

GROANS ROLL UP HIS CHEST, and it soaks my panties. He's so fucking hot, rugged, and smooth at the same time. Rolling his head, he enjoys me playing with his length.

I FLICK the head with my tongue, and the barbell bobs from me swiping at it. My mouth still on his cock, I lift my arms and scratch my nails up his abs and the little bit of chest hair before I drag them back down. He hisses, trails of red in the wake of my nails.

"HOLY HELL, woman. You're going to make me blow my load all over your face." Grabbing a hand full of my hair, and stares down at me. "I fully intend on blowing that cunt out tonight, so stop," he exhales, his dirty talking has me biting my bottom lip in anticipation.

HE PRESSES AGAINST MY CHEST, making me fall back.

Lowering himself between my legs, each of his hands tug at my sweatpants. Goosebumps race down my thighs, and my toes curl into themselves as he pulls them off my ankles and onto the floor.

HIS HEAD DIVES between my thighs, his hand slowly tickling its way down the soft skin. Using one finger, he sweeps my panties to the side not bothering to take them off. My legs are spread wide, and I can't see his face to tell what he might be thinking. I shift, uncomfortable in this position. Warm, amazing pressure swirls around my clit. My body arches and my eyes roll into my head. It feels so good and wrong at the same time. His tongue flicks and swirls at various speeds, he sucks gently and then hard.

"Yeah, you like that?" he groans against my wetness. He's so arrogant, and yet I find it so sexy. I squeak in response and lick my bottom lip as I enjoy every second of his hot mouth on my pussy.

Two fingers slip into my dripping sex, and my body feels like an egg that's been cracked and whipped into a concoction. I can't move, so many things are happening at the same time. A wave of pleasure sparks through my pussy, causing me to yell out, grab at my hair, and stiffen at the same time.

MY SEX BECOMES sensitive instantly after coming, and I jerk my hips away from Mac's swollen lips.

Lifting his head, his intense, smoldering forest eyes hold mine. I'm breathless and languid. Completely vulnerable in this position as I'm spread out before him. A bright blush heats my skin as I stare back at him.

"I'VE NEVER DONE THAT BEFORE," he admits licking his swollen lips.

SITTING UP ON MY ELBOWS, I eye him suspiciously.

"Bull! No way someone that good, has never done this before."

"I'll take the compliment, but porn is the true hero here," he chuckles. "You're dangerous, Simone. Your magnetism holds no bounds to what I want to do to you," he continues.

I fall back onto the bed, and a blush spreads across my cheeks knowing I was Mac's first at something so intimate.

I can't help but feel special having something to hold over all the women he's been with.

"READY FOR ANOTHER ROUND, POCAHONTAS?" Lifting my head, I gaze at him. He's on his knees in between my legs, pumping his dick with his hand. My mouth parts, unsure if I can handle another exhausting orgasm. "I'm not done with you yet." His voice changes to something rough and possessive. I love it. Fisting my maroon laced panties, he rips them. The elastic the last thing to go as it snaps against my thigh, leaving a slight sting to my skin.

BEFORE I CAN COMPLAIN about his roughness, he's pushing inside of me burying himself to the hilt. His head stretches me, his cock filling me. He feels so different now that I'm not pregnant. It hurts and fills me with so much pleasure at the same time.

"TAKE YOUR SHIRT OFF." He juts his chin at me, slowly pumping into me.

Lifting my back off the bed, I pull my top over my head, my heavy breasts falling free.

LEANING down his hot mouth envelops my nipple, his tongue licking its way up to my mouth.

He kisses me deeply, his hand replacing where his mouth was seconds ago.

Fondling my tit, he swirls his hips, his cock hitting me just right. Damn, I missed him, us, being connected.

"I COULD LOOK at you like this all night," he mutters, staring down at my flushed naked body.

PULLING OUT, a coldness rushes over my nipples making them hard as glass. He slaps my ass. "Flip over!" he demands. Quickly, I'm flipping over onto my chest and he spreads my ass cheeks. I tense.

"NOT THERE, NOT YET!" I glance over my shoulder. A boyish grin tugs at his bee-stung lips, his eyes entertained by my inexperience.

"We got all the time in the world, I'll take it slow... for now." Hand at the base of his cock, he's pushing back inside of me, and I relax knowing I'm not getting it up the ass. Yet.

His arm wraps around my front and gripping my chin. Stretching my neck to an uncomfortable position, he fucks me hard.

"You're mine, Pocahontas, I will fuck every inch of this gorgeous body, and then do it again just because you want me to," he breathes into the back of my head. I moan, his dirty fucking mouth making me wetter. He lets go of my face and suddenly pressure pushes into the bud of my ass. I tense, but I can't stop as everything he's doing feels so damn good. His sweaty hips pound into my ass cheeks as a finger slips inside. I can feel the jiggle of my breasts and hips every time we make contact, but it feels so good I can't make myself care enough what I look like.

"Fuck you look good with my cock inside of you and my thumb up your ass."

I whimper, moan, and take in every thrust he gives me.

HIS COCK SLIDES in and out, in and out, slowly building me to a point of breaking into a million little pieces. Like a comet hitting the atmosphere.

I FALL face first into the bed, my hips in the air. With his hand in my hair, my legs open up even wider for him as I continue to combust. My eyes clench as little spasms swim through my entire pelvis.

"RIGHT THERE!" he grunts, driving hard into me three more times. Warmth fills me, and it arouses me even more feeling him drip out of me with every thrust. Pulling himself from me, he falls on top of me, our bodies sticking from the sweat, we try and catch our breath.

ROLLING TO HIS SIDE, he fists me by the hips, pulling me into the crook of his body. I'm hot, but too exhausted and worn out to move. I've never had sex like that before. My body is spent, and it can't even lift itself to use the bathroom to clean up.

"FOR A CLASSY CHICK, you sure like dirty shit in the sack, babe." He chuckles behind me. I open my mouth to disagree, but my first time was a threesome and I did like his finger in my ass. So I close my mouth and cuddle closer to him.

————

A KNOCK on the door has me stirring awake, and Mac gets up to answer it. I smile, he's only wearing his boxers, his tattooed back displaying his club's colors sexily. Turning my head to face the wall, I close my eyes to fall back asleep. My body sore in all the right places.

Voices sound from the other room, and I find it hard to go back to sleep. Hushed tones has me sitting upright in the bed.

"WHO IS IT?" I grumble, but instead of Mac responding, he walks back into the room with an ashen look on his face and grabs his jeans from the dresser. My heart sinks, goosebumps racing across my arms.

"YOU NEED TO COME OUT HERE." He rubs his chin anxiously.

GRABBING A SHIRT FROM THE DRESSER, and some gym shorts, I finger my hair and step outside the bedroom.

ZEEK TURNS, and my mother stands in the kitchen looking everything over. Her dark hair braided down her back and a gold headpiece dangles from her forehead, matching her red and gold gown.

"MOTHER?" The word wavers as I take in what's happening. My mother is standing here in the suite with us. Where has she been? She turns, a slight smile tugging at her pink lips.

"SIMONE."

"H-HOW DID YOU FIND ME? Where were you?" My mind races with questions that have been in the back of my head since the day I ran. I never thought she'd find me. I thought about trying to find her but wasn't sure if she was running from something bigger than Veer.

"WELL, when your father was murdered, I ran and hid. I never stopped moving. I didn't know where you went, but I've been searching hospital records in the surrounding states, knowing you'd be giving birth soon, and I hit a mark here in Vegas, and got lucky," she shrugs. Tears fill my eyes, and I rush to her, throwing my arms around her in an embrace.

SHE SMELLS of spices and herbs... just like I remember. Clenching my eyes shut, I squeeze her tighter, not realizing how much I really missed her.

"I'M SO SORRY SIMONE, I never should have let your father do what he did." She cries into my shoulder, and it takes me aback. My mother is so strong, to see her break down it truly shows how much regret she harbors.

"WAIT, you had something to do with setting her up with that psycho!" Mac pulls us apart, trying to protect me. His face contorts into anger, stepping in between us.

"AS SOON AS I saw the kind of man Veer was, I knew I had to intervene, and I did," she explains, her strong demeanor back in place.

I TUG at Mac's arm pulling him out from in between us. "She's right, Mac, if it wasn't for her, I'd never have even had Catori." Veer would have hurt me purposely to lose the child, or even killed me. "She helped me escape." Briefly looking at me, his brows narrow with uncertainty.

"IT'S NOT uncommon for arranged marriages, Mac. Doesn't make her a bad parent," Zeek butts in from leaning against the kitchen counter, his eyes hooded. "A lot of cultures do it."

MAC POINTS AT HIM, his jaw sharp and flexed. "Piss off!" Zeek rolls his eyes, looking the other way. "Right, let's not take advice from a man with two kids and a girlfriend."

"DO YOU HAVE A PLACE, where are you staying?" I change the subject, curious how she's been getting around.

"YEAH, I just checked into a room here at the casino," she informs, her hand playing with her diamond earring as she takes in the suite. She may have left my father, but she didn't leave her money behind I see.

"SO YOU NAMED HER CATORI?" She looks back at me with an approving grin.

"YEAH, MAC CAME UP WITH IT."
   She gazes toward Mac, sizing him up. Surely, she can't complain considering we worked with men just like him.

"SPIRIT, I LIKE IT," she finally says, smiling at Mac.

IT OCCURS to me mother hasn't even seen her grandchild. A knot forms in my stomach at the sudden thought that she may not want to see her. She's not full Indian, and that was something that mattered to my father.

"Do you want to see her?"

Mother's toffee colored face lights up, and she nods with glossy eyes.

"WAIT, ARE YOU SURE SIMONE?" Mac's concerned face has my chest bloom with warmth. No matter what, he's always protecting us. Catori's going to hate him when she's a teenager.

"DUDE, chill, I patted her down when she came in," Zeek says in passing, and my eyes widen.

"You patted down my mom!"

Mac grins, and Zeek shrugs me off like it's a no brainer.

"HE DID, AND I WAS IMPRESSED," Mom points out, approving. "You can never be too safe," she nods with a pointed finger.

SIGHING, I grab her hand, and I lead her into Catori's room. I was finally able to let her sleep in her crib just last week. I know Veer is gone, but the void in my chest I felt when I left her behind is a feeling I'll never forget.

ENTERING THE ROOM, the walls are decorated with maps and worlds. A destination theme that the ol' ladies came up with. We told them we were waiting until we moved into an actual house, but they weren't hearing it. I love those women.

Catori's little feet kick and twist her Paris blanket, her cooing making me smile.

SHE'S awake and blubbering away.

MOTHER STEPS up to the wooden crib and looks in. She gasps, covering her mouth as her eyes fill with tears.

"OH MY GOODNESS, she's so beautiful," she sobs. "Can I hold her?"

"Of course?" I wave her on.

Reaching into the crib, she holds Catori's fingers. Their skin color nearly identical, it's tan and glowing.

"I'M GRANDMA," she whispers to Catori. I've never seen my mother smile so big. A hiccup of delight catches in my throat, and I press my hand to my chest to calm myself.

MAC STANDS in the corner like the protective father he is and watches closely.

"I HAD HER EARLY," I inform. Mother looks at me with curious eyes. " I—I can't have any more children," I mutter. Sympathy wrinkles her face before she gazes back to Catori.

"SHE'S ALL YOU NEED. She's everything," Mother approves. "She was worth every bloodshed, and bullet casing."

"I KNOW," I agree, knowing I'm very lucky.

THE END

EPILOGUE

6 MONTHS LATER

Mac

The sun is out today, its rays blasting into the leather cut on my back. My boots press into the soft ground, causing me to shift as I watch Catori smell the tulips her and her mother picked out today. They're white with the greenest stalks.

Catori falls on her butt, her green dress that ties behind her neck lifting with the light breeze dancing around her. Tucked under her arm is a stuffed purple dragon Gatz gave Simone when she was pregnant. Sweat trickles down my neck it's so hot today, why won't a breeze hit my way. Looking up at the trees, the leaves are not moving in the least, in fact, there's not a draft of wind anywhere except for where Catori is sitting. Almost as if her daddy is speaking to her from the grave. She babbles, her fingers digging into the etched stone of her daddy's headstone.

PUSHING OFF THE TREE, I bend down to pick her up.

"Who's ready to go home and play on their swing set?" I tickle her, and she giggles, slobber dripping down her chin from teething. Those two teeth have caused many sleepless nights.

"Tell Daddy bye-bye," Simone encourages, waving at the grave stone. Taking Catori's hand, I try and move her chubby little fingers into waving goodbye as we head to Simone's SUV.

I bought it for her to get around in after an investor bought my invention for the labor button I made Simone. It ended up buying us a house outside of the chaos of Vegas too.

The guesthouse out back is where Simone's mother stays. She comes in very handy when we need a sitter. She even asked to come to a club party next week, which surprised Simone and I both. She's in for a real treat when my boys get going with drugs and booze.

Her mother is strict but very determined. We don't see eye to eye on a lot of things when raising Catori, like religion, but we are when it comes to her safety.

I'm not worried though because Simone and Catori are mine, and I can get rid of the bitch of a mom real quick. I'm sure the coyotes are waiting for their next meal.

Sliding into the back seat, the leather is hot from the sun. Simone climbs behind the wheel and I look down at Catori as we drive off. Her cheeks are red from getting too hot outside, and I make a mental note to put sunblock in her diaper bag.

STICKING HER FOOT OUT, she tries to stick it in her mouth, and I laugh, pulling it away.
"That's dirty, don't eat that."

SHE GIGGLES, and then goes stoic.

"DADDY."

MY FACE FALLS, and Simone slams on the brakes, rocking us to a hard stop.

"DID SHE JUST SAY...?"

"SAY IT AGAIN FOR DADDY." I tickle her big toe, and she babbles a toothy grin, kicking her body straight in her car seat with excitement. She's such a squirmy thing, so full of life.

SHE LOOKS TO THE WINDOW, a peace brushing over her. Catori's beautiful brown eyes glistening with the sun as she stares intensely at the tinted glass.

"DADDY," she babbles softly. Simone and I look at the window, curious if she's just looking at it, or if she sees her daddy Gatz.

GRABBING HER SOFT HAND, I know for a fact her daddy will always be with her, as will I. Taking her gaze from the window, she focuses on my rough fingers and continues to say daddy to herself.

"DADDY. DADDY. DADDY."

SHE'S DONE the same thing every time after we visited Gatz's grave. She'd babble daddy to me, and to something off in the distance.

SHE KNOWS who her daddies are, and for that she will always be protected by the Outlaws.

SNEAK PEEK

Sin City Book 6

Bishop

Leaned over the bar, I stare at the textbook in front of me. It's all fucking garbage if you ask me. I want a drink, a blunt, anything but this crap.

The club is having a party, so the music is loud, and the smoke rolling around me in a fog, but Tinker... she stands clear as daylight bent over the counter handing out beers. Her short shorts rise up her ass, and that black crop top shows the supple bottoms of her breasts.

Fuck me.

I adjust my cock and shift on the stool.

"Hey!" Zeek stabs his finger into the binder of my textbook, and my eyes dart to his. "Titties don't pay for school, boy!"

I roll my eyes and pick my pencil back up to work the word problems. I was taken off the streets and from a local gang and placed in the hands of the Outlaws. They treat me better, and the work here is nothing I'm not used to. I came from California to take care of my mom, I miss the waves. Out here it's nothing but desert and cactus, dry as hell. But, this club treats me well, gives me a bed at night, and helps me take care of my mom. This is the path for me, and I can't screw it up.

The ol' ladies want me to get my GED, and Zeek fell into that line of shit telling me if I got it I would get my prospect rocker. I guess because I can handle a gun and deal drugs they are trying my lack of book smarts rather than street smarts for my part of the club.

Glancing at Tinker, beads of sweat form on the nape of her neck. She's driving me nuts over here.

"Hey Tinker!"
    She looks at me, her cute as hell blonde hair falling in her blue eyes. She looks just like Tinkerbelle.

"What's this shit supposed to mean?" Wiping her hands off on the dish towel on the counter, she sashays to me and bends over my leg to read the text. She smells like exotic flowers or some crap. All I know is it's doing my dick in.

Throwing my hair from my eyes, I lean back and eyeball her ass. I want to grab it, caress it, shove my dick up there so goddamn bad.

"Hey Tinker, wanna quickie?"
    My eyes dart upward to some fuck who I've never seen before on the other side of the counter. Crusty fat fucker.

"Hey fucker, want your teeth knocked out?" I snap, rising off the stool. He gives me a side-eye before walking away confused.

"Damn it Bishop, you can't do that shit! This is my home, and I have my duties just like you do," she huffs and stomps away.

I scoff. Only duty she has is tutoring me so I can get my cut, and into this club.

Then that bitch is mine.

Laughter forces me to bring my eyes from Tinker to smiling eyes of Machete.

"She's a club whore, brother. You're going to have to get a little more creative to lay your mark on that one."

"I'm up for the challenge." I jut my chin at him.

He slaps the counter, hackling like a jackal before walking away.

Coming Soon...

I hope you enjoyed Bloodlines. If you'd like to be contacted when the next Sin City Outlaws Book releases, please click here.

ACKNOWLEDGMENTS

I want to thank Brie and Heather. They did more than beta, they really helped shape this book into what it is, along with my other betas Natalie and Sarah.

Huge, thank you to Social Butterfly PR and Emily. They rocked helping me share my work. I highly recommend them.

I want to hug and kiss every blogger who has shared, liked, and read my work. I know there are tons of releases every week, and knowing you chose mine means more than I can ever express.

My street team, you Little Devils, you're always standing beside me. For that, I thank you.

You, the reader. Have I told you I fucking love you? Because of you... I get to do what I desire the most. Make up worlds I only wish I could be apart of.

NOTE FROM THE AUTHOR

This book was in the middle of being written during a crazy time in my life. Let me try and explain...

As I was literally writing the words of Mac calling simone Pocahontas, I got an email from a Ancestory website that I had a potential match that I was related to someone. It was something I set up a long time ago, not in the hopes of finding family but to figure out what I had in my blood. Who was I? Where did I come from? I spit in a tube, and weeks later I found out I was a Heinz 57. Just a lot of stuff running through these veins. But this email told me I had a close family member I never knew. I emailed them back, and they shared with me that I am a twelfth great granddaughter of Pocahontas, along with some other cool things. (This whole family tree thing was his hobby.) Anyway, you can image my surprise at this off the wall information, especially that I was a granddaughter of freaking pocahontis!

This story means more to me than any of them, as it shows the bounds of family. Not having common bloodlines, is something I know personally and maybe that's why biker stories touch me more than anything else. They go to show that we pick our family, not our blood.

Anyway, enough of my rambling. I hope you enjoyed the book, and little about myself!

Peace!

ALSO BY M.N. FORGY

Devils Dust MC series

What Doesn't Destroy Us Links (Devil's Dust Book 1)

The Scars That Define Us (Devil's Dust Book 2)

The Fear That Divides Us (Devil's Dust Book 3)

The Lies Between Us (Devil's Dust Book 4)

What Might Kill Us (Devil's Dust Book 5)

Sin City Outlaws MC Series

Reign (Sin City Outlaws MC 1)

Mercy (Sin City Outlaws MC 2)

Retaliate (Sin City Outlaws MC 3)

Illicit (Sin City Outlaws MC 4)

Stand alones

Relinquish

Love Tap

Plus One

Free Ride

STALK THE AUTHOR

Stalk her on Facebook
http://bit.ly/2u6GKHf

Stalk her on Instagram
https://www.instagram.com/m.n._forgy_author/

Sign up for her newsletter
http://mnforgy.com/newsletter/

www.mnforgy.com

Made in the USA
Columbia, SC
26 August 2018